PREPPED

PREPPED ⚠

BETHANY MANGLE

///////////////////////////

Margaret K. McElderry Books

New York   London   Toronto   Sydney   New Delhi

MARGARET K. McELDERRY BOOKS

An imprint of Simon & Schuster Children's Publishing Division

1230 Avenue of the Americas, New York, New York 10020

Text © 2021 by Bethany Taylor Mangle

Jacket illustrations © 2021 by Rebecca Syracuse

Jacket design by Rebecca Syracuse © 2021 by Simon & Schuster, Inc.

MARGARET K. McELDERRY BOOKS is a trademark of Simon & Schuster, Inc.

For information about special discounts for bulk purchases, please contact Simon & Schuster Special Sales at 1-866-506-1949 or business@simonandschuster.com.

The Simon & Schuster Speakers Bureau can bring authors to your live event. For more information or to book an event, contact the Simon & Schuster Speakers Bureau at 1-866-248-3049 or visit our website at www.simonspeakers.com.

Interior design by Irene Metaxatos

The text for this book was set in Minion Pro.

Manufactured in the United States of America

First Edition

10 9 8 7 6 5 4 3 2 1

Library of Congress Cataloging-in-Publication Data

Names: Mangle, Bethany, author.

Title: Prepped / Bethany Mangle.

Description: First edition. | New York : Margaret K. McElderry Books, [2021] | Audience: Ages 14 up. | Audience: Grades 10-12. | Summary: Raised among doomsday preppers, Becca Aldaine's life has centered on planning for the worst, but when her escape plan is jeopardized, she turns to the boy she is expected to marry and hopes for the best.

Identifiers: LCCN 2020031253 (print) | ISBN 9781534477506 (hardcover) | ISBN 9781534477520 (eBook)

Subjects: CYAC: Survivalism—Fiction. | Family life—Fiction. | High schools—Fiction. | Schools—Fiction. | Arranged marriage—Fiction.

Classification: LCC PZ7.1.M364675 Pre 2021 (print) | DDC [Fic]—dc23

LC record available at https://lccn.loc.gov/2020031253

TO MOM & DAD:
WHEN YOU SIGNED ME UP FOR A LIBRARY
CARD, YOU DIDN'T JUST GIVE ME THE WORLD—
YOU GAVE ME ALL OF THE WORLDS.

1

EVEN THE CHILDREN COME TO WATCH US DROWN. FOUR OF
us line the banks of the duck pond in insulated clothes, shivering through alternating spikes of adrenaline and fear. Rays of waning sunlight speckle the black surface of the water, punctuated by ripples of movement from the fish unfortunate enough to reside here.

Dad waits for the entire community to assemble before launching into his usual pre-training speech. He adjusts the collar of his fleece-lined jacket and clears his throat against the side of his fist. "Our focus today is cold-water survival. We don't know if we'll ever fall through ice or have to wade across a river to search for food."

"Right on!" someone shouts.

The cheer electrifies the rest of the group. They surge forward, as if eager to watch my misery up close. From the rear, a woman's voice calls out our unofficial motto: "Always be ready for the worst day of your life!"

Dad shoots a withering glare in the direction of the speakers. Our neighbors shrink away, chastened. "As I was saying, disaster can strike at any time, folks. That means winter. That means tougher hunting. That means walking farther and working harder to stay alive." He turns to us, gesturing at the colorful flotation devices piled by the bank. "During this scenario, your objective is to don a life preserver and conserve your body heat for ten minutes. The water is forty-one degrees."

I glance at my sister as she peeks out from around my mother's waist. When no one's looking, she mouths, *Always be ready*, complete with a dramatic eye-roll and a sassy wobble of her head. My jaw tenses with the effort of restraining a laugh. Katie's small mockeries make this tolerable.

As soon as Dad's finished grandstanding, she rushes over with my neon-orange life vest and presses a kiss against the collar. "For good luck!" she chirps as she tosses the vest into the water. After watching it partially submerge and then bob to the surface, she prods me with her elbow. "Why do we call this the duck pond if it's full of geese?"

I suck in a ragged breath as I untie my shoelaces and kick my boots into a nearby bush. Thick muck squelches between the toes of my athletic socks. "I'll tell you later," I mutter, distracted by the slow drift of unidentifiable brown goop across the pond.

"I was just wondering."

"Line up for your safety inspection," Dad barks.

I shuffle into position and pat my pockets to make sure they're empty. My watch is water-rated. The life preservers are already in the water. All set.

Dad pauses next to the boyfriend he chose for me, giving him a firm handshake and a smile that shows more teeth than affection. In my family, that's practically a French kiss.

"Really excited for training, sir," Roy says. "Been looking forward to it all week."

I resist the urge to smack my palm against my forehead. Not for the first time, I wonder what is so *moving* about my father that could make a teenage boy into such a programmed robot. Maybe Roy shouldn't go in the water after all. It might ruin his circuits.

Dad gives me a curt nod as he examines my clothing choices. Finding nothing else to comment on, he continues down to assess Heather and Candace. At thirteen, they're the only others old enough to participate in this particular task. Or young enough. The adults hold their cold-water survival in the river, having graduated from Doomsday Prepper 101 under the direction of my grandparents. By blood, I guess that makes me a third-generation misfit.

Dad nudges our shoulders as he returns to the far bank to observe. "Take off any extra layers or you're wearing them in the water. The scenario begins in thirty seconds."

I'm not sure if there's anything as embarrassing as having a parentally selected boyfriend, but stripping down to skintight leggings in front of all our neighbors has to come close. I avert my eyes as Roy peels off his jeans and folds them into a precise square. He tries to help me out of my sweatpants, but I hop away, glaring. "Don't even think about it."

At Dad's cue, the scream of a whistle pierces the quiet aura of anticipation hovering over us. Like swimmers launching from their starting blocks, Roy and the girls execute expert dives and plunge into the deepest part of the pond. I will my legs to move, but my muscles betray me.

It's only two months until I can run away to college and leave all of this behind. Somehow, knowing the wait is nearly over makes it harder to endure this nonsense, no matter how much I'm conditioned to expect it by now. At least I'll have a great conversation starter at freshman orientation. *Hi, I'm Becca. I occasionally hurl myself into duck ponds and eat grubs for dinner. Want to be roomies?*

Another few seconds pass and I still can't conjure the mental fortitude required to willingly leap into a cesspool. The longer I look at the water, the more disgusting it appears. I haven't even touched it and I'm already yearning for my custom-molded ear-plugs and anti-fog goggles.

"Becca's a chicken!" Katie shouts. She bends her arms into mock wings and prances in circles, pecking at the air. "Bawk! Bawk! Bawk!"

"I am not!" My sister always knows what to do, what to say, to make all of this into a silly game. There's no malice in her jokes, unlike the jeering and heckling that rises from the crowd. Dad is silent, probably considering how he'll punish me for my hesitation.

I set the timer on my watch and jump, refusing to give the onlookers the satisfaction of hearing me scream. My skin pulls taut over my body, the shock of the sudden cold worse than any chemical paralytic. The glowing face of my waterproof watch taunts me as I sink. It takes nine seconds for overwhelming panic to seize my heart at the sight of the black, lethal nothingness surrounding me.

Driven by pure instinct, I fight to the surface and scan for a splotch of orange somewhere in the mayhem. The weight of my clothes threatens to pull me under as I break into a sloppy, one-armed sidestroke. I consider stripping off my water-logged socks, but they're my only defense against the sticks and stones lining the bottom of the pond.

Candace and Heather float by in their life preservers, breathless and pale from the exertion of retrieving them. I clench my teeth in anger. Anyone tiny enough to wear extra-small safety equipment should not be subjected to this insanity, regardless of their age. They belong in floaties, with pool noodles and inflatable sharks, not forty-one-degree water deep enough to swallow them whole.

I flop toward my life preserver and lunge for the strap. It slips between my fingers, but I manage to keep a grip on the buckle. I hold it steady with my hand as I dip below the surface and emerge beneath it, stuffing my head and arms through the appropriate holes. I don't breathe again until the straps are secure.

Roy swims to my side, his hair plastered over his forehead like a sheepdog at bath time. He opens his mouth to speak, but he's cut off by the sound of Heather's sudden crying. Our heads whip around in unison to find her sinking in her life preserver, her thin torso slipping through the bottom of the too-large vest. She bites the fabric and pushes herself up by the armholes.

"Come on," I wheeze. "Let's help them."

Roy nods.

Together, we corral the girls and shove them onto a broken branch hanging diagonally into the water. Their skinny arms latch around the lifeline, their feet scrabbling for purchase against the soggy bark. After another moment of struggle, Candace sets her feet on Heather's shoulders and propels herself higher. Heather tumbles back into the water, shrieking.

"That's my girl!" Candace's father shouts from the bank. "She's a fighter!"

Once Heather clambers onto a lower segment of the branch, Roy slides his hands through my life preserver and crushes me to his chest, panting in rapid, shallow huffs. He breathes against my neck, which would normally repulse me, but the warm air is a salve on my freezing skin. "Can't be much longer," he gasps.

I cradle my knees to my chest and try to maintain a heat-conserving survival posture. My fingers slide and grapple against the slippery fabric of my leggings as the chill seeps all sensation from my body. "Until they let us out or until we die?"

"Not sure," he jokes.

"That's comforting."

Roy directs my torso upright as I roll sideways, both of us fighting to keep my airway clear. My throat closes with panic at the first taste of the brackish water. His palms clamp down on my shoulders, holding me steady. "Drowning in a life vest." He shakes his head, chuckling despite the fact that we're in a duck pond, dying. "Only you."

I squeeze my eyes shut and focus on my breathing, ignoring the pulses of pain beginning in my toes and radiating across my shins. It starts as pins and needles and evolves into a slow burn. "My toes are numb."

"Cold incapacitation already," Roy marvels, his words punctuated by breathless huffs. "Must be your low body-fat percentage. Fascinating."

I don't have a reply to that. My ability to speak, to think, diminishes by the second. The water that initially felt chilly is now an ice bath.

Oblivious to my decreasing tolerance for both the temperature and his brainwashing, Roy drones on, saying, "Really great training scenario. One of my favorites. Never know when we might have to survive in cold water."

I fidget out of his grip and paddle a few feet away, swiping at the dirty droplets smeared across my prescription safety glasses. Roy's frown is a hazy squiggle. I swat at his hand as he reaches for me again. "Just let me die in peace without having to listen to more doomsday-prepper bullshit, all right? I can't take it anymore."

He recoils, sucking in a sharp breath.

"No, no, I didn't mean it like that." My brain-to-mouth filter is malfunctioning. "You're right. It's an awesome training idea."

I can tell from Roy's dubious stare that he doesn't believe me, just like I don't believe in throwing children into half-frozen duck ponds to prepare for the imminent end of the world. Wincing with pain and frustration, I swim over to the bank and tuck my body into a hollow carved by higher waterlines. A pair of familiar brown work boots juts over the lip above my head.

"Dad," I plead, extending a hand within his grasp. "I think ten minutes is too long. It hurts. We're going to get hypothermia."

With horror, I realize that my fingers are brushing against a clump of reeds, but I feel nothing. "Mom?" She's a nurse. She should know better.

Dad leans forward, scowling at my mother before she can intervene. For a moment, I think he's going to rescue me, but he only places a foot against my shoulder and pushes me back into the pond. "You're embarrassing me. No one else is complaining."

"Quitters don't get dinners," Roy parrots as he catches my arm and hauls me into deeper water. His parents beam with pride.

I pivot onto my back and beg the clouds to reveal a sliver of sun. The chattering of Roy's teeth fades into the background, replaced by the dull throbbing of my sputtering heart. My breathing becomes slow and labored. I close my eyes.

The next sensation I feel is Roy's finger poking against my cheek. I don't have the energy to yell at him for touching me. "Becca."

"Go away. I'm tired."

He picks up my limp wrist and holds it in the air. "One minute."

I lift an eyelid in time to watch the stopwatch flick to fifty-eight seconds. Perhaps sensing my inability to move, Roy tows me closer to shore like a stunned turtle. The girls join us in the shallows, all of us pressing together for warmth.

At twenty seconds remaining, Dad brings the whistle to his lips and blows. Everyone else dashes for shore with the last of their strength, but I stay behind, knowing that I haven't done my full stint in the water. I keep my eyes glued to my watch until the alarm starts beeping. "Can I get out now?" I ask.

Dad glances at my mother for confirmation. She shrugs. "Yes."

I crawl onto the bank, hot tears steaming against my frozen cheeks. Katie offers me her arm, but I shake my head. She isn't big enough to support my weight. When I fall, it won't be a gentle surrender. It'll be a demolition.

Instead, she fetches my clothes and helps me change. It's funny how feeling on the verge of imminent death erases any qualms about stripping in public.

"Your muscles will start cramping if you don't keep moving," Mom says as she peers down at my pathetic form. "Come on. You can do it."

I wobble to my feet and limp after the rest of my family, steeling my bones for the arduous trek home. Katie turns to watch as I crumple to the ground and struggle to lock my knees enough to stand again. "Daddy, can Becca ride in the truck? We can both fit if I sit in her lap."

"No, she's filthy."

"George," Mom whispers, patting his shoulder. "She's exhausted. There's no valid reason to make her walk."

Dad points to my mud-soaked clothes. "She'll get the seats all wet. What if mold starts growing?"

"It's only for, like, two minutes." Katie folds her arms and stomps past Dad, pouting as she works her youngest-child wiles.

"Fine," he relents, smiling when she smiles. "She can ride in the truck."

"Really?" A slow blush bleeds across my cheeks. The resentful part of me wants to ignore this morsel of kindness, but in spite of myself, I savor it. "Thank you." The latter part is really for Katie and her seemingly preternatural ability to use Dad's doting for my benefit. It's not my fault that his love skipped a generation.

I reach for the passenger door of Mom's old pickup, desperate for the heater and shelter from the wind. The center of the bench seat has never looked so inviting, even if I'll have to contort my lower legs around the gear shift. Dad hits the lock and jerks his thumb over his shoulder. "No, the *back*."

"Sure. Right." I'm so grateful for the lift that I don't even mind occupying a space usually reserved for fertilizer and chicken feed. I bounce between the tailgate and the bumps of the wheel wells, the ridges of the bed liner scraping against my spine in a violent massage.

The truck shudders again as Mom hops the curb where the unpaved trail leading from the pond juts against the main road weaving through the neighborhood. I heave a half-hysterical sigh of relief when I spot yellow siding and black shutters in the distance.

When the truck rumbles into the driveway, I'm already dreaming of a hot shower and a hair dryer, not to mention clean underwear. I slide down the side of the pickup, using the tire as a foothold, and march toward the front door with single-minded purpose.

Dad has other ideas, though. He grabs the collar of my shirt and yanks me back. "You're grounded. And inventory while you're down there!" He hustles Mom and Katie into the house, cursing at the dog as she darts into the yard.

"No problem!" I stand there and seethe in secret as Belle approaches to investigate all of my interesting new smells. At least half of them are goose feces.

Once it's clear that Dad isn't going to change his mind, I maneuver around the side of the house to stand beneath Katie's window. Belle stomps her paws in the ever-increasing puddle forming at my feet. Just when I'm thinking about giving up, Katie sticks her head out from the second floor and smiles. "Grounded again?"

"Literally," I croak. "Help."

She holds up her index finger and vanishes. One minute. I count the seconds, feeling each like an eternity. She returns after *three* minutes with my backpack and dangles it past the sill. "Don't tell Dad. Or Mom. It's okay if the dog knows." She giggles.

"Did you pack my physics stuff?" I ask. I should be worried about the fact that I've almost stopped shivering, but the worksheets that are due tomorrow somehow seem more pressing than my growing risk of hypothermia. "It's the purple textbook and the purple notebook. And my pencil case."

Katie sighs and tosses the bag onto a patch of dead grass. It lands with a *thud* that might be the spine of my book disintegrating. A physics textbook ruined by gravity. Ironic. "I remembered," she says. "Geek."

"Don't be a smart-ass."

She raises her eyebrows. "You said a bad word."

"Your face is a bad word."

"Your face is a bad turd!"

I've been bested by a ten-year-old. "Good one. See you in the morning. Thanks."

I sling the pack over my shoulder and begin the slow hike into the woods, ignoring the stabs of pain that result from each step. The thorn bushes tug at my clothes as I stumble along the only clear route in a forest filled with concertina wire and anti-vehicle barrier systems. Belle follows, her whines drawing me back to reality as my vision blurs and the world spins.

Finally, I reach the inconspicuous clearing that houses the bunker. I crumple onto the ground and search through the undergrowth to find the boxy outline of the hatch. Belle sniffs at my cheek, her concern evident in the low swaying of her tail, her eyes that seem to ask, *If you die, who will feed me?*

"I'm not dying." Maybe. I think. I heave the hatch open and kick my way across the narrow chute until I feel the ladder beneath my feet. I lean back in midair, my hamstrings straining with the effort of clinging to the rungs with only my legs. "Don't freak out."

I push her snout clear as I close the hatch and secure the locking mechanisms on the underside. Belle shuffles around on the surface, her nails skittering as she settles in for an abbreviated vigil, at least until the damp and the cold drive her away.

I lean against the wall, feeling the pressure of the earth and steel surrounding my family's apocalyptic vacation home.

I'm buried alive.

Grounded.

2

WITH MY HEELS PUSHED FLUSH AGAINST THE LADDER, I walk six steps into the darkness, pivot to the right, and reach for the handle of the bicycle in the center of the room. I slide onto the seat and set my feet against the pedals, my aggrieved muscles spasming with every rotation of the wheels. The whirring of the drive belt fades to a faint hum as I let the handlebars support the bulk of my weight.

After an hour, I'm too exhausted to continue. Even with some ice remaining on the river, the hydroelectric generator has to be contributing some baseline power. I drag myself to the nearest control panel and hit a single switch on the side marked NON-ESSENTIALS. The light bulb above my head flickers to life. I heave a sigh of relief.

Once the lights are on, the bunker doesn't seem quite so desolate. The bathroom is off to the left, separated by a polka-dot shower curtain that's defenseless against Katie's noxious girl farts. Six bunk beds are stacked side by side in the far alcove, enough to accommodate all twelve of us assigned to Bunker One. The miniature nightstands positioned between them are labeled with stamped metal name tags.

So far, no one has bothered to tell me whether Roy is planning to relocate here after our supposed wedding or if I'll have to move my portion of the supplies across the street to Bunker Two. It doesn't matter. I'm not going to be another puppet in their inter-bunker marriage scheme, the world's creepiest method of ensuring we have a diverse gene pool for repopulating the planet. I still remember Dad's excitement—"Look, they're *Asian!*"—when Roy's family moved in across the street.

I turn sideways to shuffle through the narrow walkway formed by aluminum shelving and hulking stacks of waterproof, military-grade cases. Splotches of mud dot the floor behind me, but mopping would require breaking the tamper-evident tags on the water pump. Unfortunately, so would a bath.

I upend my backpack on the floor, spilling out miscellaneous school supplies and an empty lunchbox. A plastic bag remains lodged in the bottom. I tear apart the sides of the bag and almost stick my head inside in my eagerness to inspect its contents.

When a child gives you a care package for your overnight stay in a bunker, it apparently includes toothpaste, an unusable bar of soap, and a granola bar. Oh, and a dry washcloth. I'd have better luck cleaning myself with a paintbrush. "Did you seriously not pack me a bottle of water?" I yell in the direction of the house. "Come on!"

I eat the granola bar in calculated bites to make it seem more substantial. If my last task wasn't to inventory all of this use-less survival crap, I'd gorge myself on the packets of freeze-dried space food. It's almost worth risking my parents' wrath, but they know every item by heart, down to the last inch of rescue rope. For some reason, that doesn't spare me from having to count it all again.

I grab the clipboard with the supply lists and start unpack-ing pallets, ignoring the squishy sensation of my waterlogged palms rubbing raw against the plastic crates. If it were up to me, I'd throw out the potassium iodide tablets, Geiger counters, and hazmat suits and install a television instead. Unfortunately, that's too big to fit the five-by-five-inch size restriction on our two personal items.

One day Katie will be down here counting vacuum-sealed packages of beans and glass tubs of coconut oil like there's noth-ing else she should be doing on a Tuesday night. It won't take her long to realize there isn't any dog food down here. I've never had the heart to tell her that Belle isn't really a pet—she's a home security system.

It makes me wonder if there's anything that isn't supposed to be expendable, kept around for the sole purpose of surviving, which isn't the same thing as living. This bunker isn't a sanctu-ary; it's a tomb. If the apocalypse happens in my parents' life-time, will they recognize how pathetically futile this all was? The end of the world may come, the surface scorched beyond recog-nition, but we'll be underground in this metal coffin that might as well be a sand castle in a storm.

I finish the inventory and return the clipboard to its desig-nated hook. Binders full of manuals and procedures hang beside it. It's the closest thing we have to a library down here. Real books would be considered frivolous.

I pull down the red binder full of emergency guides and skim through the pages, initialing and dating next to the sign-off sheet clipped to the front cover. It should be comforting, knowing that there are instructions in place in case anyone dies or our generating system fails to function, but it's not. Even my tragedies are planned in advance.

Once my end-of-the-world responsibilities are fulfilled, I sit at the steel desk to complete my real-world physics homework. The stick-figure drawings relax me, reminding me that some things are constant for a reason, like gravity. As long as I don't think about anything except for the cold practicality of these word problems, life seems simpler somehow, like we're all just human-shaped masses being blown about in a tangle of invisible forces.

My eyelids start drooping halfway through the worksheet, but I persevere, smacking my cheeks with both hands for reinforcement. And there are field hockey players who complain that they're too tired from practice to finish their homework. "Try demonstrating Newton's Law of Cooling with your internal organs sometime," I grumble aloud. "Field hockey. Give me a break."

I grope my way to the wall and flick off the light in a half-hearted attempt at energy conservation. Between charging my cell phone and the fact that the battery bank along the south wall diverts all power to essential services, like the aboveground camera system, the lights are probably about to turn off anyway. It makes me feel better if I'm the one to do it.

Each bed is layered with two kinds of blankets. Personally, I prefer the scratchy woolen kind over the crinkly space blanket. As I collapse onto the bottom bunk, I can't help but envision a postapocalyptic life in this place, a permanent banishment underground where the only pastime is waiting to die.

I lie awake for hours, my body numb from feet to forehead. I wish that Belle were here to burrow into the covers beside me, tucking her wet nose against my cheek as she falls asleep in that instantaneous way only dogs can accomplish. In this crushing darkness, I miss the feel of her paws on my skin, rough and warm like asphalt shingles baked in the summer sun. I know that the bunker only has space for essentials, the physical things that we absolutely need to survive, but isn't there any room here left for love? Isn't there?

3

CRAWLING OUT OF THE BUNKER THE NEXT MORNING FEELS like being birthed again. I squeeze through the hatch, swinging my shoulders in angry arcs to free my backpack from a snag. The moment my feet settle onto frosted leaves and solid earth, I break into a sprint for the house.

As soon as I'm inside, Belle serpentines around my ankles, her eyes crusted in gunk from her solo hibernation in *my* bed last night. "Hey, pretty girl," I say, nudging her aside as I tiptoe to the kitchen. "I missed you."

I fill her bowl with kibble and clear the mess from Dad's break-fast, moving his milk-soaked dress shirt from the back of a chair to the laundry sink. He turns eating cereal into a contact sport on a fairly regular basis.

"Can you make eggs?" Katie asks from the doorway, her eyes crinkled from squinting against the light. Her Spider-Man slippers are a gentle patter against the tile as she moves to the refrigerator and peers inside. "Scrambled with ketchup?"

"I need to take a shower." My clothes are a mummified cast of polyester and filth. My hair hangs in muddy ropes. "Somebody forgot to give me a bottle of water with the soap and the washcloth, so I couldn't clean myself off in the bunker."

Her bottom lip quavers, but I suspect that it's more of a ploy to deflect my irritation than actual regret. "Sorry."

"It's okay." I extend a hand to pat her shoulder, then rethink the action once I realize how much bacteria must be vacationing beneath my nails. "Have some cereal for breakfast. Try not to drown in it like Dad."

"I'm bored of cereal."

"I won't have time to take a shower if I make breakfast," I explain. It's not often that I put Katie second, but I'm not waltzing into school looking like a papier-mâché project. "And before we leave, you need to brush your teeth."

I look even worse under the sour yellow light of the bathroom, my cheeks paunchy and jaundiced in the reflection of the mirrored door of the medicine cabinet. Inside, there are bandages and bottles of antiseptic, but none of those remedies can dull the pain of being stuck in this stagnant loop of school and scenarios, scrambled eggs and stained shirts.

As usual, the tub is bone-dry. I'm going to have to talk to Katie again about personal hygiene. She starts middle school next year, the place where nice kids get a crash course in cruelty, and smelling like a water buffalo isn't the same thing as taking a bath.

I turn on the shower and dip my foot into the stream like a pointe dancer, scrambling inside once it's hot enough to make

Satan have a heat stroke. The steam scorches my skin, boiling away the shame I feel at this subpar body, scratched and dented like an unloved rental car.

My arms bear latticework scars from running through thorn bushes during training, my feet the thick calluses of summers spent in work boots. When I graduate and escape to college, I'm going to be ordinary. That's a promise. I dig bits of dirt out of a scrape on my elbow to seal the oath in blood. I refuse to let this infernal town literally get under my skin.

I feel better once I've changed into fresh clothes that smell of lavender fabric softener instead of puddles and sweat. My phone chirps a reminder in my pocket as I head back into the kitchen and start making Katie's lunch. I have ten minutes until the bus is supposed to arrive and my hair is still soaking wet. Great.

"Can you sign my permission slip?" Katie asks, holding out the form. "We're going to the aquarium on Friday!"

I shove a cut-off piece of crust into my mouth to stall, the paper pinched between my fingers. Like any self-respecting teenager, I can easily forge my parents' signatures, but I'm not sure if I can get away with it this time. What if someone mentions the trip to my parents or they see a newsletter from the school? "We're out of preserves. You'll have to live with grape jelly."

I turn back to the cutting board and slather peanut butter across the bread. The permission slip sits on the counter a few inches away like an eviction notice for my younger sister: Time to leave the real world. Normal kids go on field trips, not us. There are too many people in such a public place, too many dangers, the insidious threats that haunted my bedtime stories as a child.

Katie tugs on my arm, insisting. "Sign it!"

"I can't," I reply, stuffing her sandwich into a plastic shopping bag with a juice box. "Mom and Dad will freak out."

"This is why the kids at school laugh at me and say we're weird." She crosses her arms into a makeshift shield across her chest. "I don't care about the dumb rules and I'm not going to get kidnapped. We're bringing chaperones. Caroline Garcia's mom is one of them. Isn't she your teacher?"

"I didn't know Ms. Garcia was going." While it's reassuring to know that my favorite teacher will be attending, I don't want to become a pushover. In order to survive this place, there's a time to rebel and a time to relent. "Let me think about it."

Her entire body wilts like I just sucked out her soul and punched a kitten. In that moment, she reminds me so much of myself at her age, pouting in the library while my classmates went to the zoo, that I sign the slip in my mother's looping, perfect script. "You know how Belle makes Sad Dog Face when she begs for food?"

Katie dips her chin in a slow nod, clearly not following along. "Yeah?"

"Your Sad Human Face is on point," I say, ushering her out the door the moment she finishes buttoning her coat. "Don't mention the trip to anyone else."

She clutches her Batman backpack against her chest, dancing between one foot and the other as she tries to conceal her excitement. "I won't."

I bend down and look her in the eyes to make sure she isn't lying. Little kids are squirrely like that. "For real, no one likes a snitch."

It's calming to realize that Katie is okay with these small acts of defiance, that she recognizes there's something strange about our daily routine, even if it doesn't add up completely in her fourth grader's brain.

Part of me recognizes that she should enjoy these experiences while she can. It's only a matter of time before our parents put an end to her eccentricities. They'll confiscate her superhero posters and action figures the same way they threw my stuffed animal collection in the garbage on my fifth birthday. I don't think it will change her, though. Mom and Dad made the critical mistake of letting her become a person first.

"Don't make Mrs. Hepworth's hair fall out," I say as I follow her outside. "Be good."

"I think she wears a wig," Katie replies, giggling. She hugs me around the waist and scampers across the lawn to the neighbor's house. Mrs. Hepworth deserves some kind of international babysitting prize for watching Katie every day before it's time for her to go to school. Like Dad, that girl can make a mess out of anything. She could light a lake on fire.

I take my time as I meander down the street, my damp hair pulled into a messy bun and stuffed inside one of Dad's knit beanie caps. Some of our neighbors pause to wave as they get the mail or climb into their cars to leave for work. Others give me a quick nod, an adult acknowledgment now that I'm older and capable of fighting alongside them against the vague, omnipresent threat of the outside world.

I swear that I breathe clearer as I approach the corner, crossing the street that serves as an unofficial divide between our community and reality. It's strange to think that Heather and

Candace would be here if their mothers didn't insist on home-schooling them for safety reasons. I shake my head, laughing at the thought that Mom and Dad are actually considered moderate leaders, juggling a die-hard faction of isolationists against the practical need to be a part of society.

When I arrive at the bus stop, the kids from the adjoining neighborhood are already waiting, their feet stamping on frosted grass, hands slapping together. I stand apart from them and lean against the pole of the stop sign. The cold metal presses against my spine as I breathe clouds into the chill morning air. It's already April, but winter doesn't go down without a fight, not here in this Ohioan wasteland where even the sun shines gray.

"I hate this shit," someone mutters. "It feels like it's going to snow any minute."

"Why couldn't I have been born in Florida?"

"I'm going to die soon."

"It's supposed to warm up next week," I interject. "Fifty degrees on Monday."

The group falls silent, their mouths contorted into matching grimaces, except for a sandy-haired girl in all black, who offers a timid smile. I've broken the unspoken truce, the understanding that nothing of mine crosses beyond the stop sign into their neighborhood, including my words. They are oblivious and coddled, happily basking in the finality of our senior year, returning to homes full of laughter where talk of murder statistics and the benefits of hydroelectric generators have no place. I want to escape into their ignorance.

I'm so far out of orbit of the standard social circles—Nerd, Jock, Goth, Hot Girl, Skater—that I'm more of a third moon, not a planet. Actually, I'm just like Pluto, the planet that suddenly wasn't a planet anymore, demoted and excluded once my classmates were old enough to understand that *my parents are doomsday freaks*. For most people, being the center of the universe is a sign of conceit, but since I'm the only thing in my high school universe, I should at least be the center of it.

"Hey, Becca." I turn toward the voice and see Roy striding in our direction, his backpack strapped high on his shoulders, the shoelaces of his work boots double-knotted and tucked in to avoid posing a trip hazard. "Want my coat?"

"I'm fine," I insist, zipping my thick water-repellent jacket higher around my throat. "But thanks." It seems unfair that Roy, with his thoughtfulness and steadfast commitment to the cause, should be saddled with sour, resentful old me.

Without warning, he grabs my face and kisses me. His mother cruises by in her Buick and honks her horn in greeting. I take a step back as he leans in to deepen the kiss, coughing into the crook of my elbow as an excuse to put some distance between us. I don't think he buys it.

"Sorry," Roy says. "Have to kiss you or she'll think we're fighting and call your parents to talk about it."

"Sounds like a bad *Dr. Phil* episode." Including Roy, I guess my universe has a population of two. If my classmates are planets, then Roy is an asteroid belt, a strip of cosmic debris with the personality of a paper bag and the emotional depth of an ingrown hair.

"Loved the scenario yesterday," he says. The worst part about having to date another doomsday kid is that we have nothing else in common. My parents called it "setting us up," and it sure feels like I've been set up. They expect me to marry Roy for no other reason than it was decreed to be so.

I hate to break it to them, but even if Roy helps me in training, and sits with me at lunch, and is reasonably handsome, it's still not enough. You can't just throw flour and eggs at the wall and call it a cake.

My lips crack and bleed as I force them into a smile. The stinging pain helps filter the sarcasm from my voice. "Yeah, water survival is my favorite."

"Always learn more in group training than individual scenarios. Wonder what we're doing next time."

Roy's satisfied expression twists my guts into Twizzlers. He's a sellout, a *believer*. "The new schedule is posted in the meeting house."

"Been a little distracted lately. Can't stop thinking about your birthday present." The shadow of a blush creeps into his cheeks. "Hope you like it. Picked it out myself."

Oh, golly, Roy, I'm dying of anticipation. What could it be? A pocket knife with a can opener and a miniature pair of tweezers? A bottle of water-purification tablets? I hope it's another packet of dehydrated ice cream. "I can't wait."

No, really, I can't wait to have a birthday party full of my crackpot neighbors on Saturday. For activities, we can make tinfoil hats and search for coded messages on the backs of shampoo bottles. We can paint each other's nails and talk about the best way to collect rainwater.

"I'm so happy to be turning eighteen," I say, the first truth I've spoken to him in a long time. Well, besides last night, when I blurted out that I think our entire lives are founded on bullshit and paranoia. He doesn't mention it, though.

The bus wheezes to a stop and we file down the aisle like cows in a cattle chute. I slide into one of the two-seaters and plop my backpack next to me in a futile attempt to make Roy find another place to sit. He shoves it under the seat, placing his foot through one of the straps to keep it from sliding to the back of the bus.

The girls sitting across the aisle exchange matching scowls. My habit of selecting a new seat each day upsets their bovine affinity for routine, as if their heads are going to explode because something has changed on this morning that is exactly the same as every other morning.

Behind them, an underclassman I don't recognize snuggles with her boyfriend, their hands clasped around a cell phone as they watch a video together. She muffles her laugh against the collar of his coat, planting a kiss on his cheek before turning back to watch.

I glance at Roy in my peripheral vision. For a moment, I envision us meeting in another time, as other people. Lab partners. Gym class teammates. It makes me wonder.

"Help me with this?" Roy says, gesturing to the English worksheet in his lap. "No idea what half of these vocab words even mean."

I shrug. "You'll have to ask someone else. I don't English."

"Still better than what I can do," he says. "Math?"

"Why don't you ask your dad? He's a teacher."

"A *gym* teacher," Roy points out.

"Fine." I flip to the orange tab in his color-coded, multi-subject homework binder. There are three blank worksheets inside. "I can math, but I can't math all this math in a twenty-minute bus ride. Why didn't you do any of this last night? Training was over at seven o'clock."

He picks at a tear in the seat in front of us, the fake leather perforated by pencil stabs and adorned with marker drawings. "Busy. Was reading about radiation poisoning."

"What's there to know about it? You get radiation poisoning and then you die."

He hands me his calculator and pulls up an article about Fukushima on his phone. His eyes glaze over as he scrolls down the page, either from fatigue or because he's in the middle of a dopamine dump from getting his daily end-of-the-world news fix. "Not always. Just causes gastrointestinal distress sometimes."

"Gives new meaning to the phrase 'shit yourself and die,' huh?"

Roy reads through the rest of the article while I try to make sure that he doesn't flunk twelfth grade. The jerking and jolting of the bus helps my handwriting blend in with his shaky scrawl. I don't make a habit of assisting other students, but Roy isn't competing with me for my coveted position as salutatorian. I'm surprised he's potty-trained.

Plus, I do owe him for making sure I didn't drown. A few algebra problems seem like a small favor by comparison.

"Ever think about the future?" he asks as we pull into the school parking lot and join the procession of buses. "After graduation?"

It's a very un-Roy-like question, one that intrigues me enough to lift my eyes from his homework. Maybe his mother's been badgering him. "What about it?"

"Like"—he pauses and examines the dirt crusted underneath his fingernails—"what we're gonna do. Together."

"Roy." I sigh. "Do we have to talk about this right now?" I can't break up with someone who I never wanted to date in the first place. It's like trying to break up with a bad cold or a stubbed toe. Still, I'm not cruel enough to get his hopes up by promising him a doomsday fantasy wedding where we frolic around in chemical suits and pick out our husband-and-wife bunker bunk-bed unit.

The minute I have my diploma in my hand, I'm out of here. Roy will end up with Candace or Heather instead. I know that he cares about me in his own dutiful way, but he'll get over it. Like everything else that's been forced upon us, because he has to. "I'm sure our parents have had it all planned out for years."

"Doesn't mean we can't change the plan," Roy says with an almost endearing naivete.

As if challenging the status quo has ever been an option. There's no way to make him understand without incriminating myself, so I say nothing at all, letting the silence drift into uncomfortableness.

"Got it." Roy chews on a piece of hard skin dangling from his lower lip. "Dropping the subject."

The doors of the buses fly open in unison and we merge into the flood of students surging across the horseshoe driveway in front of the school. With its weathered brick facade, crumbling sidewalks, and dying grass, this glorious institution of secondary education all but screams of budget cuts and small-town decay.

Half of the letters are missing from the sign out front, leaving a once-regal Tinker Peaks High School with a name that sounds like a vegetarian heavy-metal band: Tin Peas. As an unofficial school tradition, the seniors pry the letters off any time they're replaced. An ambitious prankster even scratched off the corresponding letters on the highway signs leading into town.

"See you at lunch," Roy says in parting. "Pizza day."

"Yes!" I fist-pump on my way to my locker. I've learned to revel in simple joys, figuring that enough of them can counterbalance the cesspool of suck that is my life.

I snap open the door of my locker, half expecting it to start glowing in golden light. This five-foot metal box is the only place that is completely mine, my bunker of secrets. The interior is festooned with recruiting propaganda for Carnegie Mellon's physics department and colorful maps of campus. I keep the posters and pamphlets for the same reason that prisoners keep pictures. It's a glimpse of somewhere else, anywhere else, a daydream that strengthens my teeth for gritting and my fists for clenching.

The admissions packets from other schools are piled under old worksheets. I took one glance at their mediocre scholarship awards and tossed them aside. They litter the bottom of my locker like sacrifices at a shrine. I need a full ride, or close. I need a miracle.

My stomach roils with butterflies as my gaze falls on the Carnegie Mellon application taped to the center of the collage. Their decision should arrive any day now. As usual, I'll have to intercept the mailman before Mom or Dad can see it, but even if they do, I'm almost eighteen.

I just know that Carnegie Mellon is my ticket out of this town.

By the afternoon, the words are sounding in my head like a

siren, fighting back my senioritis with reminders that final transcripts do matter. I take my seat in the front row and flip through my AP Physics notebook. Like yesterday and the day before and the day before that, Ms. Garcia rushes over to my desk and asks, "Did you hear anything?"

"Not yet," I reply, sighing. I wonder if she realizes that I'm nothing more than a copycat, chasing her alma mater, her knowledge, her joy. "Do colleges always take forever to respond?"

"It's only April. You'll hear back soon. After the recommendation letter I wrote for you, they can't say no."

"How long did you wait after you applied?"

"I filled out my application on a typewriter," she says. "I'm sure their admissions process has changed since the Reagan administration."

The bell rings and Ms. Garcia springs into action. She collects our homework and passes back our quizzes from two weeks ago. An F stares back at me in red marker, circled three times for emphasis. In microprint underneath, it says, *April Fools!* Not funny. I waggle my tongue in her direction, giving no outward indication that my heart is banging around my rib cage like a misguided torpedo.

She giggles under her breath as she flits by writing on the board with a piece of chalk in either hand. It's hard work keeping up with an ambidextrous, multitasking physicist. Ms. Garcia reminds me of a toy soldier, if toy soldiers had graying pixie cuts and leopard-print eyeglasses. She's a machine that runs on coffee and surreptitious sips of the energy drink that she hides behind her desk. Her last full night's sleep was probably in the womb.

In the middle of her lecture on kinematics, she pauses to examine the enormous aquarium that dominates the majority of the space on the wraparound lab counter. Her gold angelfish bobs on the surface of the water, its eye transfixed on the antiquated green chalkboard. Ms. Garcia paces the length of the tank, her fingers tapping a funeral hymn along the glass. "Oh, this is awful. Rest in peace, Faraday," she intones. "You were a splendid fish."

She plucks him from the water with a net that looks like a miniature pool skimmer. In front of her, Brian Wendland continues snoring, oblivious to the passing of Ms. Garcia's cherished pet. She arranges the fish's body in front of his folded hands, poking it one last time to ensure it's not playing dead, if fish can even do that.

With a sigh of disappointment and a grumble about life expectancies, she returns to the board and writes a message in bubble letters: *Brian's grade is sleeping with the fishes.*

"Don't wake him up," Ms. Garcia says. "I want to see how many of my classes he can sleep through. Maybe he'll still be here tomorrow. At least he'll be on time."

Aiden Pilecki leans over and flicks his fingers over Brian's head. "Here's a little valedictorian dust for you, buddy. You're going to need it."

I roll my eyes. "Yes, Aiden, we all remember that you're valedictorian."

"Jealous much?" he coos.

I live in a perpetual state of jealousy, but I'm not telling Aiden that. "You wouldn't last three seconds in the duck pond."

"Huh?"

I don't answer, savoring his confusion at my secret jab.

At the end of the period, Brian is still fast asleep. A few of the students hesitate to leave him behind, but most of us have no qualms about it. There's a certain solidarity in Advanced Placement courses, an unspoken understanding that the nerd club doesn't tolerate slackers, especially if the syllabus includes group work.

I wonder what a dead fish smells like after a few hours.

Ms. Garcia intercepts me at the door and blocks my path. "Do you have a minute?"

We sit on either side of her desk, my neck straining with the effort of seeing over the tottering stacks of papers strewn across it. "Have you thought about your science fair project yet?" she asks. "Proposals are due soon."

"I'm not going to enter this year," I reply, crossing my arms as a makeshift shield against her inevitable objections. "Last year was humiliating."

"You got second place. There's nothing wrong with that."

"I lost to a project about whether McDonald's cheeseburgers taste better than Burger King cheeseburgers in a blind taste test." I sigh. "I obviously can't compete with that kind of brilliance."

Ms. Garcia points at me with the back of her pen. "Don't be so self-deprecating. You're still my prize pony."

I just love being compared to farm animals. "I haven't even thought about a topic."

"So you'll do it?" She rubs her eye to displace the tear forming at its edge. "If you won't do it for me, do it for Faraday."

"Speaking of fish, is it true that you're chaperoning my little sister's field trip to the aquarium?"

Ms. Garcia groans and rubs her temples. "Don't remind me. There's a reason I don't teach elementary school."

"I'll do the project if you promise to keep an eye on my sister. She can be a handful."

"We have a deal," she replies. "But if you don't win this year, I'm sending you to the glue factory, prize pony or not."

4

EVERY FEW WEEKS, KATIE DECIDES SHE'S AN ADULT AND tries to move her place setting from the kitchen table to the dining room. Dad humors her while we divvy up the pot roast and pass sides from one end of the table to the other. At some point, he decides it's time to discuss doomsday matters and unfolds a piece of paper from his pocket. "Katie, you have to go back to the kitchen now."

"I don't want to," she chirps, bouncing against the seat. If my sister was a wind-up doll, that would be her catchphrase when you pulled the string.

Mom taps Dad's arm with the back of her hand. "Come on, George. Let her stay. It'll be nice to have a family dinner all together for once."

I stab my finger at the kitchen and nudge Katie's shin under the table while our parents are distracted. She scrapes her chair back with a huff and stomps away without bothering to take her plate. Ten seconds later, she changes her mind and comes back for it like I knew she would.

"If you start them too young, they get scared of everything and start acting stupid." Dad spears another carrot with his fork and points the end of it in my direction. "We learned that with Becca. Remember when she was developing claustrophobia? I'm not risking that with Katie."

I glower at him over the rim of my cup as I take a long, long drink of water. I wouldn't have been claustrophobic if they didn't lock me in the crawl space as an introduction to underground living. Normal girls are worried about training wheels or training bras. I got a training bunker.

Mom drums her fingers on the table. "I guess you're right. If we make concessions on the small things, we'll be back to debating the minimum training age again. Tamara and Ronald just don't understand that ten is too young for us to guarantee their safety. Even thirteen is pushing it."

"Yeah," I blurt before I can stop myself, eager to advocate for any policy that keeps Katie on the sidelines. "Katie and the other young kids aren't big enough to fit in half of the protective equipment they'd need to use, anyway."

Dad nods, his face reddening. "Though if I were you, I'd be more worried about my own performance. Katie is already curious and engaged. You, on the other hand, have just been going through the motions."

"Of course she's curious. She's a little kid. She asked me the other day how light bulbs work and why multiple moose aren't called 'meese.'"

"Anyway, back to what I was originally talking about," Dad says, holding the scrap of paper closer to the light. "We're practicing firefighting tonight and I wanted to make sure that you remember the basics."

I mask my sigh in an ordinary exhale. Firefighting. It couldn't have been something easy like making fly-fishing hooks or picking locks.

"How much time will a full air cylinder give you to work before it runs out?"

Depending on how much I'm convinced of my imminent death, I could probably suck all of the air down in fifteen. Panicking causes me to consume more air, which is more reason to panic. "Like thirty minutes at the most."

"What should you do if you get lost?"

"Follow the hose because it will eventually lead outside."

"What does our procedure say about circumstances where there is less than a fifty-percent probability of survival for rescuers?"

"It says that the reward has to be greater than the amount risked. If risking two people can save three others, then yes. If risking two people can only save one, then no." It's incredible to me that such complicated situations can be summed up by an elementary math problem. The worst part is that I know Mom and Dad would follow that principle. They'd let me burn.

I can't help but wonder whether Roy would do the same. He certainly saves me enough in training. Even when it would be easier for him to leave me behind, he doesn't.

"Why do we need to know how to fight fires?" Mom interjects, earning a smile from Dad. Given the choice, I'd rather have these quizzes with her. She makes everything sound so rational with her quiet speaking voice, so different from Dad's militant, brash manner.

I stuff a piece of cornbread into my mouth while I try to remember what I said last time. I should start keeping a dooms-day diary of all the correct responses. "It's a competency that not a lot of people have because we're conditioned to rely on the government to protect us in an emergency." I realize that I'm droning on in monotone and pitch my voice higher. "But when a huge emergency happens, there won't be enough trained people to worry about our little corner of Ohio."

"You don't sound excited," Dad remarks. "We've invested a lot of money into fire safety. Everyone else seems to appreciate it except for you."

"I do appreciate it! That's why I asked for an escape ladder for my bedroom in case the stairs are blocked." Or in case I can't make it to the front door when it's time to run away. I can shimmy down the side of the house in the dark and vanish.

"I want to see a lot more effort from you tonight."

I trudge out to the garage with Dad and help him load the bags of equipment and gear into the back of the truck. I can almost feel the frustration radiating off of him. I didn't think, from a biological perspective, that it was possible for creatures to dislike their offspring this much.

"Are you mad at me?" I ask, wondering why I still care. If the only times he seems to enjoy my company are when I'm faking my entire personality, then I should just accept that we're never going to have a relationship. I wish I could be more like Katie. She's a better actress than I am.

Dad is quiet as he shuts the tailgate and leans against the lip of the bumper. "I'm aggravated because you're not setting an example for the other kids. I don't know what's gotten into you lately."

I mumble an apology to my shoes. I hate the look of disappointment on his face, as though the first catastrophe to catch him by surprise was having such a loser for a daughter. It'll only get worse after I run away, if he'll even talk to me at all.

My parents and Katie climb into the cab to head over to the training facility. I wedge myself between two bags of gear in the back, counting the streetlights flicking by overhead.

Roy is so giddy with excitement that he jumps into the truck bed to help unload as soon as Mom sets the parking brake. "Need a hand?" he asks, extending his free arm.

I let him pull me to my feet. "Thanks." He's so nice to me that I feel guilty about ignoring his existence most of the time.

Tamara arrives a moment later with a series of cheery honks from our secondhand fire engine, its paint brighter where the department decals used to be. Katie scurries up to Dad with a pout already forming. "Can I sit in the fire truck?"

"It's not a toy."

"I promise I won't touch anything. Please?"

The corners of his mouth blip into a brief smile. "I guess it's all right. Just stay away from the compartments and tools."

Katie squeals and chases after the engine. I don't blame her for that; normal kids like fire engines too.

"The first part of the exercise is going to be donning the equipment," Dad calls over his shoulder as he ducks into the shipping container that we use as a practice burn building. Roy's parents follow behind, one toting a mannequin and the other carrying several wooden pallets.

Candace hovers off to the side, sorting through the various pieces of equipment with a confused expression. Heather trails behind her and whispers instructions in her ear as we arrange our gear in the right order. "Don't forget to check for holes, or you'll get burned."

I place all of the clothing in front of me, my helmet and other miscellaneous items to my left where I won't step on them. I smile at the girls. "Roy and I will go in first with the hose since we're bigger." Honestly, Candace and Heather are too small to do much more than try not to get crushed under the weight of their breathing air cylinders. "When we find the dummy victim, you can help us pull it outside."

"I'll stay in the doorway and help drag the hose," Candace offers.

Heather throws her hands up in the air. "You always take that job! It's my turn!"

"We shouldn't change our roles. We've never had a problem doing it that way before."

"You're just afraid of the dark!"

Candace opens her mouth to retort, but closes it when she sees the stare I'm giving them. "Rock-Paper-Scissors. *Now.* I'm not crawling into a burning building when you two want to kill each other."

They stick out their fists and chant aloud. Heather wins just as Tamara and Dad appear in front of us. Tamara points to the organized lines of gear. "You have four minutes to get dressed." She consults the stopwatch dangling around her neck. "In three . . . two . . . one . . . GO."

I kick off my shoes and pull the protective hood over my head as I stuff my feet into the thick firefighting boots. I jump to seat my heels and pull the pants around my waist. Halfway through securing the front of the coat, I realize that I didn't put on my suspenders. I lose twenty seconds there, then another forty struggling to get the cylinder on my back.

"Time's up," Tamara says, clucking her tongue in disapproval. "Three failures and one pass. That's terrible. Do it again." She rubs absently at the taut skin of the scar peeking out from her sleeve, a souvenir of her narrow escape from a California wildfire.

While we reset the exercise, Tamara and Dad huddle together, occasionally pointing at one piece of gear or another. Dad mimics pulling on the mask straps and glances at Candace. "This exercise is a good example of why I don't want the younger kids in training," Dad whispers. "If they get spooked and don't understand what's happening, it's going to be that much harder to convince them to do the next activity."

Tamara ignores him and takes a few steps closer. "Becca, you're having trouble with your breathing apparatus. Think about using a different technique. Candace, you need to pull those straps tight. We can hear the air leaking out of your mask."

"What about me?" Heather asks.

"You just take too long in general," Dad replies. "You need to speed up without getting sloppy."

After our fifth failure, I'm ready to use one of the hoses to blast Roy into the neighboring county. Even though he's passed every single time, he keeps doing the exercise for extra practice. He sidles over to my area and points at each item. "Saying them out loud helps. Keeps you from panicking and making a mistake."

"Panicking and making a mistake is kind of my forte," I admit.

Roy shrugs, but I think I see the beginning of a grin. "Like shooting an arrow through the greenhouse?"

I smack his chest with the back of my hand, laughing. "That was an accident!"

The next time Tamara starts the clock, I chant the steps aloud as I complete them. Hood. Boots. Pants. Suspenders. Coat. Putting on the coat and pants isn't the hard part. It's the breathing apparatus that makes this impossible.

Following so many failed attempts to swing an upside-down air cylinder onto my back without decapitating myself, I resort to using the easier—but more time-consuming—method of donning it laterally like an oversize backpack. Roy gives me a wide berth as I stoop forward and let the momentum carry the cylinder over my shoulder. I straighten as soon as I feel the frame settle in its proper place.

"Fifty-eight seconds," Tamara announces.

I struggle to manipulate the waist belt even though the connectors are the same design as a seat belt. With less than a minute remaining, the time pressure is overwhelming. Finally, I'm able to cinch down the straps and focus on the final steps.

"Forty seconds."

I palm my facepiece and mash it against my skull with enough force to bruise my jawbone. With my free hand, I tighten the straps behind my head and pull the fire-resistant hood flush against the frame of the mask.

I stare down at my feet, scanning through the dirty shield to find my helmet. I plop it on my head, buckle the chin strap, and snap the mouthpiece into the corresponding hole of the mask. "Done!" I shout over the hiss of incoming air. "Ha!"

"You have eleven seconds left to finish the exercise."

"What? I'm done."

"Are you?" Dad asks, sounding annoyed.

I quickly pat the various pieces of my ensemble. My boots are on properly. The air cylinder is turned on. It isn't until I run my fingers over the smooth shell of my helmet that I realize I've forgotten my gloves. I slip my thumbs through the loops that keep my sleeves from riding up and stuff my hands into the fireproof mitts.

Tamara stops the clock with one second left on the display. I exhale a slow breath as she inspects the arrangement of my gear. "I guess that's a successful completion of the exercise." She tugs on my pants to check that my suspenders are on.

"But it shouldn't take you that many tries to get it right," Dad adds.

Roy passes me an ax. "Good job."

"Thanks for your help."

We line up in front of the shipping container and wait to start the second half of training. I keep my left hand wrapped around the hose, my right around the ax. Mom lingers off to the side, offering a slight wave of encouragement when she catches me watching.

"One person is trapped inside!" Dad yells beside us. "Go!"

I almost point out that our procedure wouldn't support sending four people to rescue one, but that would just get me in trouble.

I reach up and crank open the door, reflexively recoiling from the thick smoke wafting down the length of the container. We grab on to each other's boots to form a long chain and crawl inside. Heather and Candace both call out when they reach their positions and stop.

Roy and I continue forward into the darkness. "I know there's a trap up here somewhere," I mumble, groping at the walls and pushing the ax ahead of me. It hits against a bouncy material, then gets stuck. I pull it with all my might, almost bashing Roy in the face with the handle as it springs free.

"Here's the chicken wire," I yell back to Roy. You only have to get stuck in chicken wire once before you memorize exactly where it is. "Help me find an opening."

He slides up next to me on his stomach and runs his fingers along the bottom while I search with the flashlight dangling from the front of my coat. Roy and I spot the seam at the same time. He pries the two sections of wire apart far enough for us to make it through.

Even though I resent being forced into dating, I have to admit that it's nice to have a built-in training partner. After this many years together, our actions are automatic and rehearsed. When I grab Roy's hand and press it against the slope of the floor, I know he understands that I'm warning him about the change in elevation.

We climb up the large metal ramp and shimmy between two overturned cabinets before I spot the glow of the fire in the corner. It's really more of a smoldering pile of wood and straw than a full fire, but I douse it with water just in case anyone checks.

"Found the victim!" Roy shouts, grabbing my arm and directing it toward the opposite corner.

I move a few feet forward until I feel the hard plastic of a limb. It's not a fair simulation of a body because the mannequin's arms like to fall off. With great care, I fold myself around the torso and drag it behind Roy, who pauses every now and again until I tap his boot to let him know I'm still there.

Halfway out, my spine starts to protest the weight of the cylinder, sending jolts of pain through my lower back. I grit my teeth and turn sideways for a moment to spare myself the weight. I can't remember when I'm supposed to run a mile for gym class, but I hope it's not tomorrow. I'll die.

"Becca?"

"Just need a minute."

"Come on," Roy calls. "Can't rest in a burning building."

Watch me. I hate to break it to everyone, but if the house catches on fire, they can find me hiding in the duck pond.

At my urging, Heather takes the dummy and hauls it the remaining distance to the door. I stand and walk the rest of the way, dropping my equipment the moment my foot crosses the threshold. I rub at my aching muscles, wincing as Mom steps forward with a bottle of water. "Don't forget to hydrate," she says, twisting off the cap and pressing it into my gloved hand.

"One more time?" Roy asks, searching the faces of the crowd.

Dad shrugs and claps him on the back. "Sure. Why not?"

5

AFTER TRAINING, I'M TOO EXHAUSTED FOR INDEPENDENT
thought, so I snuggle up on the couch with my laptop to
research other students' science fair projects. There's a finite
number of physics-related topics, and it's not cheating to borrow just the idea, right? My computer disagrees, failing to load
even the simplest of websites, though maybe that's because it's
from the Proterozoic Era and not because it's taking a stand
against my questionable academic morals.

Eventually, I locate a few interesting prospects, though some,
like creating my own radioactive cloud chamber, are beyond
both my capabilities and my budget. Others are too juvenile,
the physics equivalent of turning in a baking soda volcano as
an AP Chemistry project. Ms. Garcia is going to expect rock-
solid calculations, glammed-up presentation models, and an
explanatory speech worthy of a world-class orator. I'm already

so stressed about this that she should be happy if I show up to the science fair wearing pants.

"What are you doing?" Katie asks, dangling her head upside down over the screen. "Why do you always have so much homework?"

The clock in the corner of the screen has to be set to the wrong time zone. I glance at the living room wall and the other clock concurs. "Hey, you're supposed to be asleep by now."

"You could let me stay up."

"I could also rob a bank while riding a unicycle. What I can do isn't relevant."

She sits down on the couch and lifts Belle onto her lap as if the dog is going to defend her from bedtime. "What's 'relevant' mean?"

"Did you brush your teeth?"

Katie nods without meeting my eyes. I pinch her chin. "Prove it." She blows a cloud of putrid stank breath into my face, making me long for the stale air of the respirator. I gag and lick the sleeve of my shirt to get the taste out of my mouth. "Brush your teeth! *Now.*"

She tries to avoid using more than the tiniest drop of toothpaste. I snatch the tube, cover the bristles in "Berry Blast" paste, and shove the brush through the gap formed by her overbite. She whines and shuffles her feet, enormous gobs of tears rolling down her cheeks.

"Katie!" I grab the collar of her shirt like a cat carrying an insubordinate kitten by its scruff. "Are you seriously crying because I'm making you brush your teeth?"

"You're not the boss of me," she garbles, blue foam spilling over the edge of her lip.

"Fine." I rip the brush out of her mouth and throw it in the trash can. "When your teeth rot out and you're wearing wooden dentures like George Washington, don't come crying to me about it."

She wipes her mouth with the back of her hand and flicks toothpaste in my face. "You sound just like Dad. My teeth are going to fall out because I didn't brush them. Someone might murder me at a sleepover. A car will run me over if I play in the street. God!"

"ORAL HYGIENE IS SCIENCE!" I shriek, bodily hauling her over the threshold of her bedroom and plopping her onto her bed. I lower my voice to a gritty rasp, knowing that sound travels easily between the thin walls. "Being paranoid is not science. The end of the world is not science. The earth is pretty old. It's probably not going to end right this second. Just saying."

She launches to her feet and grabs her backpack, barely slowing her momentum as she lurches for the dresser. A moment later, with sleeves falling out of unzipped compartments and pairs of underwear stuffed beneath her armpits, she tries to storm past me.

I catch her around the waist and lift her in the air again. "Taking a vacation?"

"I'm running away!" she screams. "I hate living here! The kids at school are right! We're all freaks!"

We both freeze at the sudden groan emitting from our parents' room. "Look what you did," I snap. "If Dad wakes up and hears you talking like that, it will make the end of the world seem like a tea party. Now stop being ridiculous and go to sleep. It's late and we're both cranky."

"Fine." She throws her stowaway's bag into the closet. "But get out of my room."

I wait for her door to close before I stalk to the living room and pummel the pillows on the couch into deformed lumps. I take a seat and slow my breathing, leaning my forehead against the surface of the coffee table as the waves of frustration fade away. My laptop purrs beside me, reminding me of the science fair, but this strange position is somehow comfortable and I don't want to move.

Meanwhile, something itchy keeps falling across my face. I paw at it and feel the lacy skirt on the bottom of the couch. My eyes flash open and I realize that I'm lying on the floor, one leg propped on a cushion, the other crumpled beneath me. My laptop is cold and dead, the lens of its webcam gleaming like a single judging eye.

I crawl out of the crevasse between the furniture and stand with the assistance of the window sill, careful not to bump against the massive rifle rack bolted to the wall. Outside, the sky is a light orange, enough that I know I've overslept. And if I've overslept without anyone else noticing, so has Dad.

The next few minutes are a blur of waking him up, waking up Katie, and throwing on clothes that I tossed in the hamper at some point last week. I leave my lunch money on the kitchen counter for Katie, figuring that I can guilt the lunch lady into fronting me a meal.

"I left you cash for lunch," I call into the dining room when I sense someone approaching.

Instead of Katie, Dad stumbles into the kitchen wearing nothing but his boxers. He shoves a handful of cereal into his mouth and washes it down with milk straight from the jug. "The only thing you have to do is wake me up on time when your mother's on day shift," he grunts, dribbling milk onto his bare chest and stabbing a finger at the calendar. "And you can't even do that right."

"You could reset your alarm after Mom leaves," I suggest when he's out of earshot. "Like a normal person." Plus, he's a welder. It's not like running a few minutes late is going to delay a rocket ship launch.

With Dad home, I don't have to worry about waiting for Katie to get ready. She's probably still pissed at me anyway. I leave my shoes unlaced as I bolt out the door with my backpack half zipped and my brain half fried.

"Running late," Roy says as soon as he sees me. It's a statement, not a question. He points at my feet. "Shoes are untied."

"Yeah, I know." It's like talking to a movie narrator. I bend down and tie them. "You could have called when you noticed I wasn't here."

He grimaces and exhales a sigh through his nose. "Thought maybe you were sick."

As if I haven't dragged my sorry ass into school when I had laryngitis, food poisoning, and that awful case of pink eye that I suspect I contracted from the dog compulsively rubbing her butt on all of my worldly possessions. Scholarships are the only way that I can afford to go to college. Free money is worth a few days of drinking Dayquil for lunch. "I've had perfect attendance for five years. You know that."

Roy's head whips to the side as the sound of screeching tires breaks our awkward silence. A truck blurs by in a flash of mismatched body panels and faded bumper stickers, the smell of burning rubber permeating the air. Thick clouds chug from its exhaust, sending out smoke signals that something is wrong behind the wheel. At first, I assume it's a texting teenager, some irresponsible classmate of mine who will right the vehicle after his message is sent.

Farther up the road, a familiar blue car backs out of our driveway, its rear lights glowing like cats' eyes beneath the horizon. The truck weaves closer, its bald tires skipping and skidding, playing hopscotch with the double yellow line. It hurtles forward even faster, accelerating at a rate that makes a last-minute correction all but impossible. Paralyzing dread ices over legs that should be running toward my father's car, lungs that should be calling out warnings.

Roy shoves past me and starts waving his hands, shouting, "Mr. Aldaine! Watch out!"

In the millisecond before impact, I am trapped in that moment of helpless waiting, the feeling of limbo between a trip and a fall. I don't know if I close my eyes or if they're simply unseeing as the cars slam together with an unearthly roar, the scream of steel monsters going to war in the streets.

I charge toward the scene, my backpack falling from my shoulders as I stumble over potholes and evade scattered pieces of debris. My father is a crash dummy, his body splayed out across the steering wheel like a marionette with broken strings. Blood pools against the lenses of his thick-rimmed glasses, trickling down his cheeks in rivers of red.

I put all of my weight against the door handle and pull. It doesn't budge. The side-view mirror dangles uselessly from its wire like a fish waiting to be unhooked. I knock quietly against the window, the same way I knock when it's time to wake him up from an afternoon nap. "Dad?"

"Calling 911," Roy says to me as he rips his gloves off with his teeth and dials the number. "He awake?"

"Dad?" I repeat. He doesn't answer. My gentle knocks turn into palms smacking against the window, then fists. "Dad? Daddy?"

No. No. No. No. No.

I sprint around to the front of the car and clamber onto the hood. It sags beneath me, the metal torn and jagged from the force of the impact. If the collision could do this to something as strong as steel, how could my father's bones possibly endure?

One of the other students grabs my shirt and tries to pull me back. "Just wait for the paramedics," she insists. She's an outsider, one of the kids from the neighborhood adjoining ours. "You're going to get hurt."

"I have to know if he's alive!" I blindly swing my arm behind me until my elbow connects with something solid. The grabbing hands fall away. There are shouts in the distance and the sound of pounding feet as adults start to arrive. More outsiders.

I knock against the shattered windshield. "Dad? Can you hear me?"

Nothing. His eyes are still open, his glasses hanging across the bridge of his broken nose.

I scan my father's body as carefully as I can. There's a lump on his leg where the bone is sticking through. I want to help, but I don't know what to do. All of those nights studying trauma medicine with Mom have got to be worth something. I can't go home and tell Katie that I let him die here. She will never forgive me.

A woman runs up beside me and grabs my shoulder. "Are you okay?"

"I wasn't in the accident," I mumble, blindly waving at her to go away. She keeps talking, so I press my ear closer to a hole in the glass. Faintly, I can hear Dad's haggard breathing, the sound like water getting sucked through a pool filter. His torso rocks with the effort of it.

I beat my fists against the hood. "Don't die," I whisper, thinking of all of the times I wished he would disappear for good. "I didn't mean it. I'm sorry that I didn't wake you up on time. This is all my fault. I'm sorry. I love you."

All around us, fragments of glass sparkle in the light from the approaching ambulance. "Is he dying?" I ask Roy, soaking up my tears with the edge of my sleeve.

"I don't know," Roy replies, tugging on my arm. "Come on."

I crawl back to the windshield and lean my forehead against it, the pane of glass between us like a curtain between worlds. "This is not goodbye. Do you hear me? This is *not* goodbye."

Roy pulls me off the car and carries me away in the style of a newly married bride, setting me down on the lawn across the street from my house. He takes a step back to put some distance between us, but I lurch forward, dragging him to me by the fabric of his shirt. I bury my face in it, wanting someone, anyone, an anchor. "He wouldn't have been here if I didn't wake him up late. He would have been at work by now." I choke and sputter on my tears. "It's all my fault."

Roy cradles me to his chest, swaying and rubbing my back. "It's not your fault, Becca. It's not your fault."

"It is my fault. All I had to do was wake him up on time." Now

I can't. The last thing he ever said to me is true—I can't do anything right. "I'm worthless."

"No." Roy drags his fingernails across his scalp, brushing hair from his eyes where it hangs low in the front. "It was the other driver's fault. Not you. Not your fault."

"What was wrong with her?"

"Drunk," he replies, indicating a hunched figure in the distance. "Super drunk."

"I'm going to kill her," I say as anger transfuses my sadness, diluting it to a more manageable ache. As Dad would want, I'll assess the threat first, cry later.

Roy blocks my passage with his arm. "Don't make a scene."

"It's already a scene! A *crime scene!*" I hiss. "She could have hit my sister on the way to the bus stop."

He drops his arm.

The pickup is parked with its nose against an oak tree, the wheels cocked inward in a hug around the trunk. A party plate, the yellow plate with red letters that Ohio assigns to drunk-driving offenders, hangs sideways from the truck's rear bracket. I step onto the running board and peer through the window. Beer bottles fill the passenger side foot well. A greasy paper bag stuffed in the cup holder serves as an ashtray. Cigarette butts poke out in every direction like a deep-fried blooming onion.

I stalk over to where the driver is sitting on the curb, taking in her chagrined smile, the way her chewed, bloody fingernails scrape at the label of the water bottle in her hands. A vitriolic disgust rises inside of me. "How many?" I ask her. "How many times?"

She blinks in slow motion, her eyelids heavy with yesterday's mascara. "Huh?"

"How many times have you been arrested for drunk driving?"

She looks down at her fingers like she can't count to ten without them. She flicks up both of her index fingers and holds them in the air. "Two times, but I'm not drunk now. I saw a deer."

She'd be better off saying she saw a unicorn tap-dancing in the middle of the road. I arrange my hood around my face and crouch beside her before the police officers hovering nearby can realize who I am. I take the bottle of water from her and hold up the label. "There's a little over one pint of water in this bottle," I tell her.

"So what?" She joggles her head in confusion, a mop of unkempt blond hair cascading across her face. She might have been beautiful once, back when her Cleveland State sweatshirt wasn't quite as faded and her ailing truck was fresh off the lot.

"There are eight pints of blood in the human body," I explain, shaking the bottle for comparison. "If you ever come through this neighborhood again, I'll pour all eight of your pints straight into the fucking gutter."

"You're sick," the woman snaps, teetering on the edge of the curb as she tries to shove me away. Tears of self-pity flood her eyes, her ruined makeup transforming her cheeks into a watercolor painting. "I'm going to sue you for threatening me!"

One of the police officers steps in between us. He looks too young to have so many stripes on his sleeve and such a serious buzz cut over the stern ridge of his brow. This accident is probably the most exciting thing he's seen all year. Tin Peas isn't exactly a criminal hotbed. "All right, let's just calm down," he says to the driver. "You're not really in a position to be suing anyone, Jackie."

"She threatened me!"

I summon the grief that I was holding back before, allowing it to burn across my eyes and settle into the quivering muscles of my chin. In a blink, I've gone from predator to frightened child. My capacity for violence is like a shadow, a specter hidden at will behind an innocent, rehearsed smile. "I just told her that she needs to get help," I lie. "And if she wouldn't, then someone should make her go to rehab. Is my daddy okay?"

"That's your dad?" He steps in front of me and blocks my line of sight to the other car. "Jesus."

"He wouldn't wake up," I say, pleased to hear the crack in my voice. "Then this lady was yelling at me. I didn't threaten her."

"Uh, we should call your mom. You live around here?" Buzz Cut wraps his arm across my shoulders and escorts me farther away. I turn into his chest and cry against the baby-blue shirt that smells of cigarette smoke and starch. Behind his back, I flip Jackie the middle finger.

Buzz Cut confers with a paramedic in low voices. "They're calling an airlift to transport your dad. Is your mom home?"

I shake my head, too busy chewing off the lining of my cheek to form a response. "She's already at the hospital. She's a nurse."

"I can give you a ride."

"Coming too," Roy says as he overhears our conversation. He jerks his chin in my direction. "Right, sis?"

I nod, not wanting to be alone long enough to think about the severity of Dad's condition.

Buzz Cut tolerates the fib and unlocks his back door. We

slide inside behind the metal partition, wiggling to get comfortable against the molded seats with cutouts for handcuffs. "Don't worry," Roy soothes. "There are good doctors at Tin Peas Trauma."

"This is a little worse than the time you dislocated your knee."

We pop a K-turn behind the fire engine and drive past the scene on our way into town. I crane my neck to catch one last glimpse of Dad's sedan. Underneath the hood, the battery case is cracked cleanly in half. Oil drips into a puddle like a tincture. The car rattles and shakes, groaning its death throes as rescuers slice through the frame. It spits acid and rainbows into the stillness of dawn.

6

BUZZ CUT LETS US OUT IN FRONT OF THE MAIN ENTRANCE TO
the hospital, his eyes tilted skyward as a helicopter passes overhead. "I hope your dad has a speedy recovery."

"Thanks," I mumble. "I hope Jackie has a speedy conviction."

Roy and I check in at the main desk in front of the revolv-
ing door. The receptionist is clearly oblivious to the fact that my
father just arrived on the helipad. He isn't wearing his trademark
expression, a combination of pity and sympathy that makes him
look like a dejected bloodhound. "Your mom lock herself out of
her car again?"

"Yeah," I reply, slapping a visitor sticker across my chest. "I
know the way. Thanks."

At the elevator, I turn to ask Roy for some privacy, but he's
already vanished.

I find Mom on her regular floor working on charts at the

nursing station. She glances up in surprise and for a moment I think she doesn't know about the accident. "What are you doing here?" she asks as I dart past the counter and crush her in a hug.

"I came to see Dad," I mumble against her employee lanyard.

"You do know what happened, right?"

"Yeah. He's going into surgery." A coworker passes by and makes the bloodhound face at us. Mom, usually so focused, can't stop moving. She taps her pen against a clipboard, pulls down her undershirt, tightens her ponytail. "I should have come home to be with you, but I couldn't leave him." Her voice breaks when she tries to speak again, so she remains silent, biting her lip. "I should work on these charts."

"I'll just wait for some news, then," I say, unsure how to process her erratic behavior, the unreciprocated hug.

I wander into one of the less-traveled branches off the main wing, where rows of stiff-backed chairs are arranged in threes, each seat perched on a shared metal beam. I sit in the closest one, the soles of my shoes hovering above the freshly mopped floors. I've been here often enough that these hallways are familiar scenery, but the purpose of my visit is no longer leisure, and the place feels harsh with clinical austerity.

Mom joins me long after I've memorized the chips of paint on the opposing door, the hairline cracks forming around the wooden bannisters screwed into the wall at waist height. She rubs her elbow against mine in greeting, her hands occupied with two cups of vending-machine coffee.

Desperate times call for desperate beverages. I stare at the dark surface of the liquid and pretend that it's the window of a Magic 8-Ball preparing to reveal my father's fate. "Do you think he's going to die?" I ask, banging the back of my skull against the wall. "It was so horrible. I didn't know what to do."

"I don't know," she says. "His injuries are extensive, but he's receiving the best possible care from our top doctors."

Her voice is soft and soothing, a glimpse of the bedside manner that she uses with other people's families. There's no indication that she's talking about her husband, the man who has snored and farted next to her every night for two entire decades. I wonder if she's in shock. "Are you okay?"

Mom sips at her coffee, hissing as it burns her tongue. She squeezes the cup hard enough that the plastic lid pops off and tumbles to the floor. "I don't know. I don't know how this happened. A drunk driver. We never thought about a drunk driver. It seems so silly now. Such an oversight." She shakes her head. "Such an oversight."

"I'm sad," I say, scrubbing at my reddened eyes, my vocabulary reduced to that of a child. "Aren't you sad?"

"Of course I'm sad." Mom's voice is strangely flat, almost robotic. "This was preventable. We should have seen this coming. We have to protect ourselves. None of us are safe." It's like in the absence of an ability to think clearly, she's just spewing one doomsday slogan after another.

I shake her shoulder with little effect. "This wasn't anyone's fault except for the driver's, Mom. She was wasted." Her aloofness kindles a mixture of rage and anguish that gnaws against my resolve to be strong. Tears zigzag down my cheeks in a slalom course. "We can't defend against every possibility."

"Rebecca," Mom chastises, gripping my arm above the elbow until my pulse throbs against her fingers. I recoil, unused to such a bold touch. She leans in closer. "When do we cry?"

The sudden question catches me off guard. It's the kind of thing Dad would snap at me over dinner. I scramble to find an acceptable answer. "When we're safe."

"And when are we safe?"

I glance up at the ceiling to stem my tears, letting the white light of the fixtures burn away the memories of Dad's crumpled body, the crown of matted, bloody hair ringing his head. "Never. We're never safe."

"Terrible things happen every day," Mom says. Her eyes glow with a fanatical intensity that I don't recognize in her. "This is why you have to be ready. You have to be ready."

"I know," I reply. I think of all the lectures and horror stories that I've heard over the years, the thousands of news articles my parents have read aloud at the dinner table like a prayer. Murder. Rape. Genocide. Drug addicts who rob their own families. Terrible accidents that ruin the lives of ordinary people. Who knew that any of these misfortunes could touch us in our fortress of preparedness, penetrating our shield of expecting the worst at any time, every day, always?

Mom presses a crumpled wad of cash into my hand. "I'm going to go check on him. Why don't you get something to eat?" She phrases it as a question, but I know it's an order. Never miss a meal.

The elevator shudders on the way to the ground floor. For a moment, I imagine what it would be like to free-fall those five stories, my lifeline snipped in a spectacular finale of probabilities and smoke. A car accident, on the other hand, is so mundane. My father can't die that way. He deserves to be eulogized in headlines, a death befitting of someone who has wasted his entire life contemplating its end.

The doors open and I emerge unscathed into the brightly lit lobby. A long-haired valet balances on one elbow against the edge of the coffee cart as he flirts with the girl standing behind it. I can't hear her laugh, but I can see the interest in her face, the shy drop of her eyes and the slight pull of her lips at the corners. Nearby, sitting on one of the hard couches in the waiting area, an old man wrings a magazine between his hands, a pile of crumpled tissues arranged around the sides of his legs. For the first time, I get a sense of how strange it must be to work in a hospital, to have the happy feeling of a good shift intersect so naturally with another person's tragedy.

The cafeteria is empty except for a mother-daughter duo in the corner and a few clumps of exhausted night-shift doctors sipping at coffees and poking at their bagels like lab specimens. The kitchen is closed, so I settle for a premade tuna sandwich and a bottle of water, charging it to Mom's employee account and pocketing the ten bucks she gave me.

I choose a table by the woman and the girl to avoid potentially overhearing the details of a patient who came in by helicopter, his pockets stuffed with the multitools and safety gadgets that couldn't save him.

The woman dissects a brownie into even portions with mathematical precision while her daughter stacks single-serving coffee creamers into a pyramid. In between bites of dessert, they exchange a half-hearted laugh, though the spirit of it doesn't erase the wrinkles of worry that ripple across their foreheads like tidelines. They push the last piece back and forth across the plate, leaning back in their chairs and averting their eyes from it. Envy smolders in the pit of my stomach. I could gorge myself on that kind of love.

I force myself to eat a few bites of food, stopping when Roy's hands appear on the back of the chair across from me. "Mind if I sit?" he asks.

I shrug. "Be my guest."

He perches on the edge of the seat, one leg hanging off the side. "Status update?"

"My mom went to check on him a few minutes ago," I say, glancing at my phone. No new calls. Only a text message that says katie didnt go to school. still at mrs hepworths house.

Roy nods. "Okay."

"My sister stayed home today. Am I supposed to tell her about the accident?" A swell of anxiety rises within me. I hate talking to Katie like she's a child, but she *is* a child, and I don't expect a ten-year-old to be able to comprehend the extent of Dad's injuries.

"Dunno."

"Would you just speak actual fucking words?" I slam both of my fists against the table. The scabs on my knuckles tear open again, my souvenirs from martial-arts practice last week. "I'm so sick of you grunting things like you're Frankenstein."

"Sorry." He clears his throat. "I don't know what to say."

"Just please don't tell me how this was preventable," I mutter, hanging my head. "I can't think like that right now."

"I would never say that," he blurts, his hand darting out toward mine. For once, his voice is clear and strong with a hint of emotion tinging his tone.

But when I look up, his expression is blank, the same slack-muscled look that he wore as he conversed with the 911 dispatcher this morning. I almost laugh. Roy is the flatline to a heartbeat, a statue in a flash mob. Being mean to him is like taunting a beetle stuck upside down, legs flailing. "I'm sorry for yelling at you. This is just a lot to deal with."

"No problem."

"I didn't mean to hurt your feelings." As if that's possible. I could stab him in the back and he'd compliment the sharpness of the knife.

"Only have one of those left," he jokes. "Saving it for a special occasion."

I put half of my sandwich onto a napkin and slide it across the table as a peace offering. "Why did you want to come with me?"

"For support," he answers without hesitation, almost like we're a real couple. For a split second, I think I see something flash in his eyes, an emotional vulnerability that was never there before. Doesn't he realize that this, like everything else, is just pretend?

"Thanks," I say. "Don't get too excited about the sandwich. Tuna was the only kind left."

"Hospital tuna," Roy adds. He takes a bite, grinds the food between his teeth, and winces. "Yup. Awful. Crunchy and awful."

"This is probably what they serve when they need more beds," I say, smearing on some mustard in an attempt to make it edible. "I'd rather die than eat this stuff every day."

Roy lowers his head at the word "die," the last verb that anyone ever needs to know. "You all right?"

"No." I rip off another piece of my sandwich. It tastes even worse with condiments.

All my life, I wanted my father to be like other fathers, the ones I saw on television or watched in the grocery store. Just for a moment, I wanted him to be the father he is with Katie. I wanted to be his little girl. That will never happen now. It can't. He's going to die.

My throat constricts as the chunks of tuna whip my stomach into rebellion. Pressure builds in my chest until I lean over, spraying a yellow-green seafood special onto the floor. A chunk of onion lodges in my nostril.

"Oh, God, I'm so sorry," I splutter. There aren't enough napkins to wipe off Roy's shoes. The smell alone is enough to make me gag again. The mother and daughter cover their mouths and scurry off to the back recesses of the room, clutching their trays and drinks. A cafeteria worker rolls out a yellow bucket with a mop handle sticking out, her eyes pointed up toward the ceiling.

"'S'okay," Roy replies as he scrapes one boot clean with the edge of the other. "Didn't like these shoes anyway."

▲▲▲

One of Mom's coworkers agrees to drive us home, the windows of her SUV cracked to keep the smell of barf at bay. "I'm so sorry," I say from the back seat.

She meets my eyes in the rearview mirror and smiles. "Hon, I'm a nurse. You couldn't gross me out if you tried."

"Thanks."

On the way to our neighborhood, I send Mrs. Hepworth a text. Katie can come home now. I'll be there in a minute.

Glass and red plastic line the shoulders of the road in front of my house. Dad's car is gone, the tow company summoned by a well-meaning rescuer, maybe Buzz Cut. Jackie's truck is missing, too, leaving few signs of a struggle, like the accident was a deleted scene and the props are put away in a box backstage.

Roy insists on escorting me inside, his arm laced through mine as we march to the door. My backpack is sitting on the single front step. I'll have to check the camera footage and see who returned it.

Katie is in her bedroom reading a comic book. She sees Roy and freezes, hurriedly stuffing it behind her back. He pretends not to notice. He'll probably go home and rat on her later, telling his parents that George Aldaine's youngest daughter is still allowed to have childish things.

"Roy won't tell anyone about your comic books. Right, Roy?" I fix him with a stare that lets him know I mean business. It unnerves me that parents are introducing their kids to this lifestyle earlier and earlier. My six-year-old neighbor wailed for days after his mother banned *SpongeBob* from their house. I could hear his screaming through the walls of my bedroom. "Everyone has secrets. Isn't that true, Roy?"

"Yeah," he agrees, even though he hero-worships Bear Grylls and probably thinks that drinking your own pee is an acceptable solution to ordinary problems. "Won't tell anyone. Cross my heart."

I collapse onto the edge of Katie's bed while Roy paces around the tiny bedroom searching for another place to sit. He settles on the floor in the corner. "How was your day?" I ask.

"It sucked," Katie says, pouting. "Mrs. Hepworth told me that she thought I was sick, but I wasn't sick, and she wouldn't let me go to school even though Julissa's mom bought cupcakes today."

"Brought," I correct.

She folds her arms. "If they came from the store, she bought them, too."

"Valid point."

"Why is Roy here?" She peeks at him in her peripheral vision. "He's a boy and Dad isn't home yet."

"We have to tell you something."

"Are you going to have a baby?" she asks, her spine snapping to attention as she shuffles back against the wall. "Can I name it?"

Roy chokes on his next breath and has to bang his fist against his chest to recover. Red splotches blossom across his cheeks. "No baby."

"There was an accident this morning," I deadpan, needing to force out the words while I still have the courage.

"Yeah," Katie says. "It was really loud. I heard it over the TV."

"Did Mrs. Hepworth tell you anything about it?"

"No." She shakes her head. "Mr. Hepworth looked out the window and said bad words."

I wish that I could start off with a placation, some positive detail that could provide her with a little hope. There aren't any, though, not when Dad's condition is unchanged and Mom's coworkers are acting like I'm a depressed puppy in a Sarah McLachlan ASPCA commercial. "Dad was in that accident. He's in the hospital."

Katie's bottom lip slides forward, her eyebrows mashing together in concern. "Is he okay?"

I look to Roy for help. By the time I bring my gaze back to Katie, she's taken my silence for an answer. She hurls herself across my body and bolts for the door, throwing it open as far as it will go with Roy sitting behind it. I chase her as far as the living room, but she's too nimble to catch. She disappears into the backyard, Belle howling after her from a lookout post on top of the couch.

PHYSICS PROBLEM: Will a distraught ten-year-old in motion at a constant velocity remain in motion unless acted upon by an outside force?

"Might want to leave her alone," Roy whispers, as if reading my mind.

Alone. That's what she'll be when I creep to the bus depot with a one-way ticket to Pittsburgh in my pocket, abandoning her to the care of substitute mothers like Mrs. Hepworth, the house quiet with Mom's absence as she works to support a shrinking family.

"Today is the worst day of my life," I say, weaving my fingers together like a dreamcatcher to capture my future as it slips from my grasp. "This changes everything."

Outside, Katie falls to her knees in the rain-slicked grass, pounding her fists against the ground like the noisy upstairs neighbor of the Underworld itself.

7

THE REST OF THAT EVENING AND WELL INTO THE NEXT
morning, Katie refuses to leave her room. I slept in the hallway, my fingers stuffed between the bottom of her door and the
seam of the carpet, but she didn't come out once, not even to
use the bathroom. At some point, Mom must have snuck in,
stepped over my body, and gone to bed. Her coat dangles from
the handlebar of the exercise bike in the living room, her purse
and coat dropped in a heap in the entryway.

I make scrambled eggs to lure Katie, but I only succeed in
attracting the attention of the dog. Roy is knocked out on the
couch with his bare feet on the armrest and his torso wrapped
in his upturned jacket. I drop a few clumps of eggs into Belle's
bowl and bring the rest to Roy. My stomach is still too upset to
eat anything.

"Breakfast in bed," he mumbles. "Spoiling me."

"It's breakfast in couch."

I sit cross-legged on the coffee table while he inhales his breakfast like it's made with ambrosia. It's so weird to have Roy in my house overnight. He looks softer with his hair tousled from sleep, his face open and unguarded. "Delicious. Thanks."

As I shift my weight, a piece of paper crinkles under my butt cheek. I reach down and unstick the note. It's from Mom, the hospital logo emblazoned on the top, along with the phone number to the Sunshine Club. "'Medically induced coma,'" I read aloud. "'Bought lunchmeat. No visitors allowed. Bring in the trash cans.'" I don't read Roy the last part, which says, *Do you need birth control?*

"I think my mom is having a breakdown," I tell Roy, though I can't explain the full extent of my worries. It's more of a feeling, the vertigo of standing too close to the edge. "She's all over the place."

"In what way?" he asks, chasing a smudge of egg around the bottom of the bowl.

"She's just acting different. Jumpier. I'm worried about her."

I retrieve a pen and scribble a bare-bones response: *Prognosis? Will handle trash cans. My birth is already under control.* I return the note to the coffee table, which doubles as a family message board, even though all of us have these handy pocket-size computers called cell phones.

"I need to deal with Katie," I tell Roy, sighing. It's difficult to stuff down my grief at the thought of losing Dad, but I can't mourn right now, not when Katie needs stability and support. I have to put her first. "Don't miss school because of me. I'll figure out a way to get there."

He eases back onto Mom's collection of embroidered pillows, grinning as he sees the one that reads FRIDAY DOESN'T APPLY TO NURSES. "Bus already left. Could skip and have a mental health day."

"Stop being a bad influence," I chastise. "I have an English test. And speaking of English, you're still doing the Frankenstein thing."

He clears his throat. "I didn't know it bothered you that much. Sorry."

I never cared enough to mention it before. Commenting on Roy's constant mumbling would have implied that I wanted to talk to him in the first place. But I'm no longer itching for earplugs the moment Roy opens his mouth. That's as good as wedding bells, right? "Can you help me with Katie? She's killing me here."

Roy coaxes her out by shoving a twenty-dollar bill under the door. His negotiating tactics are admirable, if not expensive. Katie emerges fully dressed, her hair knotted into a lopsided braid. "Do I have to go to school?" she asks.

"Part of the deal," he replies.

"I want to see my dad. Do you know anything about my dad?"

Roy drops into a crouch and speaks to her eye to eye. "Nothing certain yet."

"Is he going to die?" she mumbles against his shirtsleeve as she gives him a sideways hug. "I want him to come home."

When I watch Roy's easy nature with her, I almost don't hate his guts. I mouth my thanks over Katie's shoulder as I bundle her in a coat and march her out the door.

"What about my lunch?" she asks. "Who's taking care of Dad?"

"You have twenty bucks for lunch."

She stomps the rest of the way to the corner. "Roy didn't say it was twenty bucks minus lunch money. We have to take bagged lunches today because we're going to the aquarium. It's probably just a lousy cheese sandwich."

"I love you," I say. "I know this is hard."

"If you loved me, you wouldn't make me eat a lousy cheese sandwich."

"Katie!" I squeeze her name between gritted teeth, my eyes widening in exasperation. "I don't have time to make you a sandwich with two-thirds peanut butter and one-third pre-serves and cut off the crusts and measure the sides to check that they're symmetrical."

We reach the bus stop in unison with the bus itself. Katie waits for the outsider kids to board, rubbing her palms on the sides of her jeans.

"Come on," the bus driver says. "Are you okay?"

Katie regards the open door of the bus like they're the jaws of a gigantic yellow demon. "I'm not going." She anchors herself against my body, her arms latched around my waist in a vise grip. "It's not safe."

I lift her into the air and physically plant her on the steps. "You're going to be fine. You've ridden the bus loads of times and nothing bad has happened."

"Dad drove his car every day," she reasons, "and nothing bad happened to him until yesterday."

I hate when she uses logic to justify whatever behaviors are pissing me off. She can't just throw a fit like a normal child. Part of me wonders whether this is how the brainwashing gets passed down through the generations. Every time someone gets hurt or dies, the world gets a little scarier. I think of my grandfather catching a fatal case of pneumonia after attempting a winter survival course. My grandmother, who keeled over in a tree stand at seventy years old and fell to her death. It never ends.

"What about the aquarium?" I ask. "Think about how much fun that's going to be."

"I don't care. I want to see Dad."

The bus driver taps the steering wheel and rolls her head around to glower at us. I stab my finger in her direction and she swallows whatever protest she was going to make. "You can't visit right now. It could hurt him even more, because we have germs and he's recovering."

"I'm not going to school!" Katie cries, enunciating each word with a punch to my chest. "I'm not going! I'm not going!"

I grab her hands and hold them away from me, my sternum throbbing alternately with the throbbing in my head. "When you're a grown-up, you'll understand how much it hurts to have someone punch you in the boob. If you don't go to school, I'm going to take away all of your action figures."

She recoils, her lips pulled back into a snarl. "If you touch my Iron Man action figure, I'm going to punch you again."

"I'll throw him in the trash with the dog poop and you'll never find him." It's a perfectly legitimate threat. Belle might be small, but she's a champion pooper.

"Iron Man would kick your butt," Katie snarls. "He'd blast you into a million pieces!"

"Iron Man wouldn't be afraid of riding the bus!"

That argument seems to do it, at least. She visibly settles as she chews on the idea, the tension dissipating from everywhere except the tiny creases in her forehead. "You're right. Iron Man wouldn't be afraid of the bus."

"Go look at fish," I say, sighing. "Please?"

The bus driver fiddles with the handle that controls the door and it jerks against my shoulder. "Can you not?" I shout at her, filtering out profanity for the sake of the kids on board. "My dad is dying and my sister is having a freak-out, so feel free to stop being a buck-toothed, turd-faced jerk anytime now."

"He's dying?" Katie asks as I step back and the doors close in front of her. She presses her palms against the glass, tears raining from the skies of her pale blue eyes. "Becca! Wait! Please!"

I don't know what else to do, so I leave as fast as I can, listening to the sound of the bus rumbling down the road. Roy waits by the curb, his hands resting on the handles of the trash cans. I grab the recycling bin and we deposit them next to the porch where there are three square depressions in the mulch. It would be nice if everything were so simple, if somewhere in the world there were a Becca-size hole that I fit into.

"So," I begin, "how do you feel about hitchhiking to school?" One of the benefits—okay, the only benefit—of living in this crap heap of a town is that everyone knows everyone. I could flag down a passing vehicle and discover Belle's veterinarian sitting behind the wheel. "We probably won't get murdered. I think."

"Dirt bike?" Roy suggests. "Have a—I have a license for it."

His idea sounds slightly less shady than hitchhiking. "I find it hard to believe that your parents let you have a dirt bike."

"It's good for weaving through cars on clogged highways,"

Roy explains. "Might need it for scavenging someday."

Ah, of course it's for doomsday reasons. If the shit hits the fan, people will try to escape in their cars and bottleneck at the bridges crossing the Grand River. A dirt bike might make it through, though. It's a good idea, if only because it helps me get to school.

Roy's property is speckled with outbuildings presided over by a dilapidated barn that functions as our community meeting building. He leads me to the smallest of the structures and opens the double doors at the top of a wooden ramp. A purple couch with fade lines from the sunlight is tucked against the wall beside an ancient tube TV and a circular table. Papers and notebooks litter every surface along with food wrappers and discarded water bottles.

"Is this your man cave?" I ask, astounded by the messiness. Roy's room in the main house is sterile enough to serve as a surgical suite.

He stretches his arms out and touches both walls. "More like a matchbox."

Roy's dirt bike is less impressive in person, the tires almost as small as a bicycle's. It's cornered in the rear of the shed, penned in by cardboard boxes stacked to the ceiling. The pictures on the front range from a coffee maker to a hammock stand. "Looks like your man matchbox is becoming a storage unit."

"They're empty," Roy says, kicking one and toppling the rest onto the couch in a cardboard avalanche. He raises his eyes to mine. "Could come in handy. Wrapping presents. Picking up supplies. Moving."

"In that case, I think you need a hoarding intervention. And a maid service."

"Maybe," he agrees, retrieving two helmets from their pegs and offering me one. "You don't have to wear it if you don't want to."

"Riding a dirt bike without a helmet sounds like a great way to test the theory that a severed head can still see for a few seconds," I reply.

He passes over a neon-orange helmet covered in reflective tape, pausing to scrub the white sweat marks from the pads with the side of his sleeve. "Might mess up your hair."

I cram my head inside and fasten the D-ring strap under my chin. The pads are tight against the lower half of my face, mashing my cheeks together like a push-up bra. "My dad is in critical condition and my little sister is bawling on the school bus. Do you really think I'm worried about *my hair* right now?"

Roy starts the bike and throws a leg over the seat. "Not answering that."

I climb onto the back, my sneakers sliding against the grooves of the passenger pegs. "Is it even legal to ride a dirt bike on the street?" I shout into his ear. "It doesn't have a license plate."

"Also not answering that," he replies, arranging my arms around his waist and easing the bike down the ramp.

Once I grow accustomed to the tugging sensation as we accelerate and slow, riding through the open air is actually liberating. I keep my head turned sideways against Roy's shoulder blade to prevent the beak-like visor from pecking into the back of his neck every time the bike rocks through a gear change. The world around us melts into a panoramic of lights and flashes, pockets of color that burst in my vision only to disappear as we fly past.

Before long, I'm laughing as a heady mixture of exhilaration and uncertainty crackles across my body like a shockwave. I'm too alive to feel the coldness of the wind, to feel anything except happy-sad and terrified and free. Roy is the conductor of this mad dash. I cling to him for comfort, inhaling the scent of earth and aftershave from his skin, reveling in this brief reprieve from the maelstrom of shit that is my life.

We arrive in record time compared to the stop-and-go crawl of the bus. Roy's hand lingers on mine as I detach my arms from his body like a reluctant barnacle. "Have fun?" he asks.

"Yeah. Thanks." I hang my helmet on the foot peg, unnerved by the closeness we shared only moments ago. Roy is supposed to be synonymous with annoying, not comforting, not safe.

We barely cross the threshold of the school before the secretary accosts us from behind the sliding glass window at the front of the administrative offices. "Do you have notes from your parents? You're both extremely late."

"We're late?" I drawl, my hands flying to my face in mock surprise. "I thought school started at nine o'clock."

I roll my eyes hard enough to detach my optic nerves as we sign in on the tardy list. I should have lollygagged longer in the parking lot. I could have missed another enthralling lecture from Monsieur Wheeler.

The secretary clicks her tongue, consulting a sheet pinned on the bulletin board beside her. "Mr. Kang, you should go to your second-period class. Ms. Aldaine, you have a pass to the guidance office."

I take it back; I'd rather go to French. "Why do I have to go to guidance?"

"I don't know," she replies. "Attitude?"

The guidance office is literally a closet, repurposed after budget cuts and overcrowding forced Tin Peas High into subsistence mode. The school's lone counselor is a droopy-eyed lump with a receding hairline and a wardrobe from 1912. I enter his office without knocking, plopping into the metal folding chair in front of his desk. "What do you want?"

He scribbles something in my file that starts with the letter *B*. Becca? Belligerent? Bitch?

Becca the Belligerent Bitch has a nice ring to it.

"I'm very sorry to hear about your father's accident," he says. I should have known it would be gossip by now, the news traveling like an earthquake with my family at the epicenter. It's only a matter of time before the secretary and the rest of the school find out. "An injury to a parent can be a traumatic experience for students."

I nod at the appropriate intervals in the hopes that it will speed along the conversation. It doesn't. For over half an hour, he drones on in a bored monologue like one of those white noise machines that sounds like dolphins.

"You live on the east side of town, right?" he asks. It's such a careful, precise question. Between the school's laughably small student body and the fact that he has my file sitting on his desk, it's kind of ridiculous for him to pretend that he doesn't know I'm a doomsday kid.

"Yes," I reply, pulling my lip up to the side in what I hope comes across as a smug little smirk. "I live on the east side with the other crazy people."

"That's not what I meant."

"That's exactly what you meant," I snap. "Don't bullshit me."

He appraises me for a moment, the top of his pen pinned between his teeth. "That's fair."

"Are we done?" I don't want to sit here while he gapes at me like I'm some kind of sideshow curiosity. "It's time for lunch."

He gives me a folder of crisis counseling materials, complete with a business card for the district's rotating social worker and a schedule of when she'll visit Tin Peas High again. "Melissa Teague," I read aloud, chuckling. "We're old friends. That's what happens when everyone in town thinks your family tries to commune with aliens. We don't, for the record."

I keep laughing as I peruse the "Healthy Home Life Checklist" that asks if my parents are emotionally unavailable. Yes, my parents' emotions are currently out of the office, but I'd be happy to take a message. "Can I go now? If I feel a burning desire to talk about my feelings, I'll go see Ms. Garcia."

"Actually, she took a personal day," the counselor says as I turn to leave. "But I'm here for you if you need anything."

"Oh, good," I mumble to myself, slamming the door hard enough that his name plate falls off. "I was so worried."

I know that I should stop at my locker to swap out my textbooks for the second half of the day, but I can't handle seeing my collage, the shrine to Carnegie Mellon that lurks behind the gray metal door of locker number fifty-seven. It's selfish to blame my father for almost dying, but if the accident had never happened, my future wouldn't feel so uncertain.

Selfishness wins out as I consider spending my twenties making symmetrical sandwiches and washing Katie's socks while my classmates are doing keg stands. There has to be a way out, some unseen loophole that I can leap through. This can't be the rest of my life. I won't survive it.

To further improve my mood, the lunch menu consists of dry chicken patties with powdered mashed potatoes and yellowing carrots. I follow the person in front of me, pausing at each station to get my premeasured slop and a carton of chocolate milk. The meal puts my account further into the negative.

"I'm going to have to place you on the alternative lunch program if you don't settle this balance," the lunch lady warns at the register. "Peanut butter and jelly with water."

"Will the sandwiches be symmetrical?" I sigh. Mom gets paid this Friday, but she'll probably earmark most of it for the automated external defibrillator she's been threatening to buy for months. "I'll find the money."

I join Roy at our usual table. He's already finished with his lunch, his eyes locked on to my puddle of watery potatoes. "Gonna eat those?" he asks.

"You know I'm not," I say, pushing the tray between us and wondering how he could possibly have finished his lunch already. I'm not a picky eater, but I draw the line at anything with the consistency of baby food. "Consider it taxi fare."

A pale girl with freckles approaches, her dark-rinse jeans speckled with rhinestones, her leather jacket tattered from wear. She slides her tray onto the table and swings her legs through the opening above the bench. "Hey. How's your dad?"

"I don't know you," I reply, never raising my eyes from the chicken patty sandwich in front of me. She smells of pomegranate and mint, the mass-manufactured scent of chemicals imitating nature. Preppers don't wear perfume. Stranger danger.

"I'm the girl you elbowed in the face at the accident. You fractured my eye socket." She sniffs at her chicken patty and prods it with the edge of her pinkie. "Do you think this is actually chicken?"

Well, that's one hell of an introduction. I peek in her direction and absorb the purple bruises around her eye, how the swelling piques her eyebrow, giving the impression that she's in a constant state of confusion. "I'm sorry," I say, wincing. I don't even remember hitting her, though that does explain the lingering tenderness of my elbow. "Does it hurt?"

"*You broke my eye hole.* Of course it hurts." She laughs and rubs the bands of medical tape plastered diagonally across her eyebrow next to a silver hoop. "But I'm totally blasted on Vicodin right now, so that's a fair trade to me. No hard feelings."

Even though she probably knows us as the doomsday freaks, I tell her my name and Roy's in the hopes that she'll offer hers. It's a bit embarrassing to realize that we ride the same bus and live practically next door to each other, but I still don't know even this basic piece of information.

"I'm Sydney, like Australia."

"Cindy?" I joke. "I'm bad at geography."

"Don't make me break your eye socket," she warns. "You know what they say—'An eye socket for an eye socket leaves the whole world without eye sockets.'"

8

THE SECRET TO SNEAKING INTO A HOSPITAL WITHOUT
registering for a visitor badge is to go through the emergency
room. Roy drops me off and disappears, mumbling about filling
up the bike at the gas station we passed on the way here. I wish
that I had some money to pitch in, but since I couldn't even
afford to pay for my lunch today, I don't bother pretending to
search my pockets.

As I'd hoped, the waiting room is full enough to distract the
triage nurses and the desk attendants from my presence. A news
channel crackles through the speakers of the television in the
corner, the closed captions warring with the banners at the bottom of the screen. Most of the patients appear to be intensely
bored rather than sick or injured. *Please rate your boredom on a
scale of one to ten.*

I keep my head down as I cut through the reception area

and slip into the radiology wing, my brain conjuring plausible excuses for being here. I can't remember which shift Mom is working, but I know she'll have a coronary if she catches me checking on Dad before he's authorized for visitors. Good thing we're in a hospital.

Since I don't know where he was transferred after surgery, I call the main line and ask for the patient liaison. She answers on the third ring, the sound of chewing dissipating as she gulps into the receiver. "Hello?"

"Hello," I say, imitating the serious tone that Ms. Garcia uses when students are playing on their phones in class. "I'd like to add money to the television account for George Aldaine. Which room is he in?"

"Hang on." She pecks a few computer keys. "He's in room 505. You can set that up with the gift shop."

"Thanks." The patient liaison isn't permitted to discuss medical information over the phone, but I'm willing to bet she's wondering why a dude in a coma needs a television account.

I ride one of the stretcher-size service elevators up to the intensive care unit, hovering at a junction in the hallway while I orient myself to the layout. A doctor and a nurse converse nearby, so I keep my arms folded over where my visitor badge should be, skirting the nursing station and sneaking into room 505 before they notice.

Dad's new accommodations are sparse, the starkness of the white walls and beige tiles offset by a plastic-covered blue chair and a painting of sunflowers in an earthenware vase, their stems curved from where the artist bent them into forced perfection. This choice of artwork perplexes me. The flowers are uprooted, their plugs pulled, grasping at a lifeline of stale water pooled in pottery. It's not exactly an uplifting selection.

"I'm crashing your party," I say to announce my arrival. "No pun intended."

Dad doesn't answer, of course. I chuckle at my gallows humor, the laugh tinny and weak as it squeaks from my throat. "Katie misses you."

I approach the bed like he's a wounded animal, perching on the edge of the armchair to examine the array of tubes and IV bags sustaining him. His veins ripple beneath skin as dry as parchment as I rub my thumb across the top of his hand. This shriveled-up mannequin is not my father. It has to be some trick of light, a case of switched files or incorrectly numbered rooms.

But the scar is there, that ugly line across his chin from when he tripped over Belle on the first day he brought her home. Back then, I was naive, assuming that he was changing into a better parent, conceding to my relentless begging for a creature that could love me without expecting anything in return. When I saw the bunker for the first time, its shelves devoid of any food for her, I was sick with the deception that he was capable of kindness.

Maybe his accident was karmic justice, the universe's retribution for always taking and never giving, his flaws outweighing his strengths like two mismatched kids on a seesaw. The idea of such fairness is comforting, but if it were true, there wouldn't be so many evil people who glide through this world unscathed, their misdeeds collected like trophies.

I lace my fingers together behind my neck, pulling my head into an awkward bow. "You're too stubborn to die," I whisper, the joke easing the pressure building inside my chest. I wish that I could flip a switch and stop caring, turn off my love like a light bulb and leave Dad in the dark where he belongs. As far as I'm concerned, unconditional love can go to the dogs, yet I give it back as quickly as I take it, playing hokey-pokey with my feelings to the tune of the birdsong drifting in through the window.

There's no word to describe having a dead father, if my father is destined to die. Plenty of men jump ship and leave their children fatherless; dying isn't a prerequisite for that. I guess I'd just be half an orphan, something else in my doomsday life to half-ass.

The ticking of the clock seems to grow louder the longer I sit here. I can't tell if it's counting down to the end of his life or counting down to the beginning of mine. In two months, I'll still graduate from high school, but unless Dad makes a miraculous recovery, I have no idea whether my plans will change.

"I applied to Carnegie Mellon," I confess, half expecting his monitors to go berserk as it turns out he could hear me after all. "After I get my diploma, I can finally get out of this town."

I used to imagine a terse phone call placed from Pittsburgh, the sound of Dad's voice as he said, "Don't bother visiting," or some other zinger that parents say to their ungrateful runaway daughters. Death is so permanent by comparison, leaving no opportunity for reconciliation, no chance that he'll whack his head on a chandelier and decide that he wants to turn over a new leaf.

In the end, I was always going to lose him one way or the other.

"I met with the guidance counselor earlier. He gave me some

paperwork to figure out if you're a shitty parent." Without knowing why, I take the guidance counselor's pamphlet out of my backpack and complete the Healthy Home Life Checklist aloud. "Do your parents-slash-guardians encourage you to pursue your dreams? No. Do you have adequate personal privacy in your home? No. Are your parents-slash-guardians receptive to your feelings? No."

I slide my hand beneath his and give it a limp shake. "Congratulations, Mr. Aldaine. You are a shitty parent."

I check the boxes with my tears, scraping the paper across my eyes because it's more useful as a tissue than as a mental health tool. There's no grand epiphany here, nothing that will cause me to leap from my seat, shouting, "Eureka!" My parents' apathy has been clear to me for years. The evidence is in the velvet-covered photo album on the bookcase in the living room, the plastic windows sticking to old prints of my father smiling while he holds me as a baby, the last time he's ever seemed happy to have me around.

It's so easy to love babies with their automatic adoration, the primal understanding of a family hierarchy in which the baby's role is to shit, cry, and worship her parents. As I grew older, I still shit and cried, not simultaneously, but I quickly learned that my parents weren't life-giving, chicken-nugget-providing gods. My birth was nothing more than a line on the to-do list and a mental note to add diapers to the shelves in the bunker.

Katie was the backup daughter, the redundancy in case I decided to play hide-and-seek in the oven or pour drain cleaner into my sippy cup. But something about her lit a spark in Dad, made him into the man who let her paint his eyes with makeup and ride on his shoulders as he hiked the hills. It didn't change us, though. I was always just the obligatory offspring.

It's not like I was neglected in the true sense of the word. In those early years, the kitchen cabinets were so stuffed with food that opening the doors risked an avalanche of crackers and mason jars. Mom would bring home hand-me-down toys from her coworkers and wash them in the sink to convince both of us that they were new. I was grateful for those things, but even though I always had *enough*, it wasn't enough, not really.

"You never took me out for ice cream," I say. "My favorite ice cream is peanut butter with rainbow sprinkles. Don't you like ice cream, Dad?"

He's always been a father in name and presence, but there's still a piece missing, a feeling beyond just wanting to protect me from the world and keep me safe. As a child, I used to search for it in symbols, wondering if his approval was a symptom of the weather or finding a praying mantis on the windowsill in summer. Even now I feel myself yearning for it, listening for love measured out in meter by the steady *beep, beep, beep* of his unfeeling heart.

9

I STAND IN FRONT OF THE HOUSE FOR WHAT SEEMS LIKE hours, examining the physical impact of Dad's absence. Aside from the empty place in the driveway, it's as though he could be home right now, his feet kicked up on the circular ottoman while he flips through an old copy of *American Survival Guide.*

He was never the one who had to care about retrieving the mail or fighting the rebellious weeds that invade the front yard after a decent rainfall. In his eyes, those duties were just automatically completed, like our family has an invisible staff of enchanted woodland animals that sweep and clean whenever he's at work.

If our places were reversed, this house would be a wreck already, with dishes overtaking the sink and the drains in the showers coughing hairballs because no one else bothers to clean them. Dad would miss having a live-in maid and landscaper, but would he actually miss *me*?

"Snap out of it," I mutter to myself, slapping my hand against my cheek as I stuff two days' worth of junk mail under my arm. "Your daddy issues are depressing."

Katie and I nearly collide on the stairs as she scampers through the front door without looking where she's going. I balance against the railing, absorbing the fact that she's voluntarily wearing a coat and her hair looks freshly washed. "Are you sneaking out? You're, like, four years old. Get back in the house."

"Everyone is going to Roy's house," she says. "I think we're late. I was waiting for you."

I fish my phone out of my backpack. Six missed calls, a voicemail, and five text messages asking where I am. "Did something happen?" Dread creeps into my heart, stilling my breath. "Is it Dad?"

"I don't know," she snaps, sashaying away, hips swinging. "No one tells me anything."

I drop the mail and run ahead to Roy's property, banging through the side door of the barn like I'm in a footrace with the Grim Reaper. I double over with my hands on my knees, gasping. "What's wrong? What happened? I just saw my phone."

Tamara spins around in my direction, her legs wrapped through the top railing of a stall gate. "Nothing's wrong. We were worried that something was wrong with you. You're late for training."

"Sorry." I scroll through my text messages. We were supposed to assemble fifteen minutes ago. "I forgot to turn on my ringer after school."

"Funny how Roy was also late," she adds, waggling her eyebrows.

I'm too relieved to rise to the jab. Roy buries his face in his hands, his cheeks redder than a two-alarm fire in a ketchup factory.

"Why are we having a meeting?" I ask. Based on the attendance, it's an all-hands-on-deck situation, not a committee meeting or a few neighbors gathering to hash out a dispute. Ronald hardly ever leaves his house, but there he is, chatting with Mom in the corner.

"We'll explain once everyone arrives," Mrs. Hepworth says. "There are a couple of other stragglers. Don't let Tamara give you any grief about the time."

Tamara hops down to the dirt floor, straightening the hem of her taupe Carhartt jacket. "I wasn't giving her grief." She pats the top of my shoulder. "How are you holding up? Do you guys need anything?"

Sure. I'd like two non-comatose parents, a full scholarship, and a pony. "We're fine. Thanks."

Katie sneaks inside and dodges around our neighbors on her way to the kids' area. The barn only has three intact stalls, one of which is designated as a corral for children. Much like Roy's man cave, the space is full of secondhand furniture dragged in from the curb or purchased at the Tri-City Flea Market that operates an hour outside of Tin Peas.

She flops onto a moldy love seat and observes the crowd over the lip of the armrest. I excuse myself from Tamara's doting and duck through two slats in the fencing to reach Katie. "Can we talk?"

"You're talking right now." She rolls onto her side and curls into a ball with her back to me. "Are we having a meeting because of Dad?"

"I don't know," I reply, sitting on the ground and speaking over my shoulder. "His condition hasn't changed."

She sighs. "I want him to come home. I think Belle is sad."

Crap. I forgot to walk the dog this morning. She's probably leaving brown presents on the floor and howling declarations of revenge to the Doberman next door.

"Listen, I know we don't keep secrets from each other," I say, my pulse spiking with the lie, "but there are certain things I don't tell you because you won't understand. You're only ten."

"I'm not an idiot," Katie snaps. "I know what dying is. You go to sleep and you never wake up and then everybody sends flowers and wears black dresses and goes to the cemetery to say nice things."

It's a pretty decent description. I suddenly think of Faraday, how Ms. Garcia mourned his death for three seconds and then used him as a prop. He's been flushed down the toilet by now, his body wrapped in toilet paper streamers. It's not like Faraday's fellow fish are holding elaborate funeral rites and bringing each other fish food casseroles. In the animal world, death is inevitable. I envy that level of detachment.

A redheaded boy breaks away from the gaggle of children and toddles closer with a bouquet of crayons in his fist. Worry lines crease his forehead, his eyes squinting in concentration. "Can you help me?"

"Sure," I reply, sparing one last glance at Katie. I wonder how long she's going to wallow. "What's up?"

"I want to name my picture," he says, rubbing his chin in thought like a tortured artist. "What's a word for the best place ever?"

I think about Carnegie Mellon, imagining the weight of the acceptance packet in my hands. I can taste the heavy city air, feel the smooth rush of warmth as I step out onto the sunlit quad and know that I can go anywhere, but I never have to come back home. My mind latches on to it like a prescient vision, a fantasy so powerful that it drowns out this grubby cowshed, the gnawing rage of forfeiting my future for the sake of my sister's. "Paradise?"

His lips pop audibly on the first syllable while he tests out the word. "Can you write that on my picture? I'm a bad speller."

I pick out a crayon and follow him over to the rickety coffee table that doubles as a coloring station. "If you don't try to spell it, then you won't get any better."

He holds his drawing up between both hands and I almost punch straight through it out of reflex. In the background, a range of brown triangles stands for mountains, the sky blackened with thick curls of smoke. Stick-figure families stand below in their bunkers, holding hands and smiling with apocalyptic righteousness. The trees are doodled sideways, toppled onto the roofs of our houses, their branches burning. I tremble as I write Paradise *by Elijah Cooper* in the corner.

"Do you like it?" he asks. "Mommy says that we'll live underground one day. I hope there aren't worms."

I almost lose my shit. For the first time, I feel deeply unsettled by these children, their unquestioning commitment to any idea that's presented to them. I could draw a square on a piece of paper and tell them it's a circle. One by one, they would breathe matching sighs of revelation, their eyes glazing over with it, and someone would remark that the corners did look a bit round, didn't they? The herd instinct would take over after that, the thoughtless, furtive nodding of little empty heads spinning circles.

Katie and I are among the luckiest kids here, the unintended beneficiaries of Mom's ironclad refusal to quit her career just because plus signs turned up on the pee sticks. She doesn't have time to homeschool us like most of the other mothers, and she doesn't teach at the high school like Roy's father, so we're only part-time brainwashed.

Aside from Katie and Roy, I can only think of two others who haven't been withdrawn from the public school system over safety concerns. The community is closing itself off.

A new fear seizes my heart as visions of rough hands and barred doors swim into focus. By the time Katie is an adult, our opportunities to leave could be limited, especially if we aren't permitted to venture into town alone. They could force us to stay, confiscating our money and belongings, handing out essentials as we need them. No one would ever think to look for hostages in a neighborhood packed with half-baked isolationists.

Elijah reaches out a hand to steady me as I stumble sideways against the fence, my knees buckling with fear and exhaustion. "Are you sick?" He lays his palm across my forehead. "Should I get a grown-up?"

My head is a water balloon, my throat a concrete tunnel. I nod, blinking away tears as my entire body pulses with panic. "Sure." I grab his arm before he thinks of getting Mom, clarifying, "Go find Roy."

He drops his picture at my feet and scurries into the forest of legs, his tiny form swallowed by the group of adults towering over him. I pinch the corner of the construction paper and dangle it in front of my eyes. This propaganda piece is a testament to my family's legacy, the foul mark that we have left upon three generations of devotees.

I never met my paternal grandfather, but I want to dig up his skeleton and stage a *Hamlet* remake where I stand in the graveyard screaming at his disembodied skull. He started this. While other people's ancestors were busy being groovy or pioneering civil rights movements, all four of my grandparents were building bomb shelters in their backyards. Maybe they weren't geography aficionados, but it doesn't take a genius to realize that Cuba isn't going to launch a missile into northeast Ohio. There's nothing here worth destroying. *Soybeans* aren't going to spark an international crisis.

Roy kneels at my side, his eyebrows knitted in concern. "Are you dehydrated? Is it, um, hygiene problems?"

"I'm just a little dizzy," I mutter. In spite of the cold, sweat pools between my shoulder blades, my shirt sticking to my skin like the backing of a temporary tattoo.

Roy's eyes bulge as his gaze falls to Elijah's forgotten drawing, his sharp inhale almost a gasp. He crouches and paws at it without touching the paper.

"Are *you* okay?"

"No," he says, balling his hand into a fist and slamming his knuckles against the ground. "I've been trying to find a way to tell you. I don't . . . I don't believe . . ." He scrutinizes my face for a moment, then lets his gaze drift back to the drawing. "I don't believe that your dad isn't going to wake up."

I stare at Roy, wondering where this sudden burst of support is coming from. Maybe he cared more about my dad than I thought. "Thanks." I close my eyes until the room stops spinning, wishing that I'd had the chance to eat something before the meeting.

"No problem," he mumbles.

Using a combination of Roy's arms and the fence railing, I manage to wobble to my feet, my legs as sturdy as two soaking wet Slim Jims. Tamara beckons from the main room, her finger tapping the face of her wristwatch. I hobble over and slide into the niche that used to house a feedbox. Katie sidles alongside me, her lips set into a thin line to ward off any protests about her presence in an adults-only audience.

Ronald, one of our grandparents' original followers whose body looks like pulled taffy left in the sun to melt, steps to the front of the assembly and rolls out a partition to keep the children separate. "Thanks for coming," he says, fiddling with the zipper of his coat. "As many of you know, George is in the hospital."

Mom blows her nose into a tissue and sniffles as Mrs. Hepworth wraps an arm around her. I squint at her, confused by this sudden display of emotion when all she's done at home lately is sleep. The assembly is momentarily quiet, everyone shuffling their feet and looking anywhere except at Mom.

Roy dangles his hand next to mine, his fingernails grazing against my knuckles. I latch on to his hand and use it as a stress ball. He squeezes back, his thumb tracing patterns on the edge of my palm.

"We need to have a vote about who's going to take over," Ronald continues. "We don't know for sure that George will ever recover, so we can't count on it. Filling his shoes is a lot of responsibility. Does anyone have any nominations?"

I watch as the assembly congeals into two distinct groups with a few undecided neighbors trapped in the middle. I'm unsurprised to see Tamara favoring the hardline isolationists while Matt steps forward to represent the more permissive minority.

"Matt is the most qualified!" someone shouts from within the latter group. "He understands that sometimes we have to work with the outside world to get things done!"

"Matt is an asshole!"

"I'm standing right here! Don't call me an asshole! You're an asshole!"

"I nominate Tamara!"

After that, it devolves into a forty-person squabble as the rest of the adults start to realize that there's a power vacuum for the first time in decades. Katie wraps her arms around my legs as expletives go whizzing through the room, the squawking and bickering rising into a vortex of sound around us. I clamp both hands over Katie's ears, whispering reassurances that sound as hollow as they feel.

A cloud of white suddenly explodes against the floor. I stumble back, shoving her entire head underneath my sweatshirt as the smell of chemicals invades my nose and forces its way deep into my chest. My tongue explores my mouth in slow circles, tasting poison.

"ROY KANG!" Mrs. Hepworth yells. She straightens to her full height of department-store elf. "You know better!"

I wipe the tears from my eyes and see the blurry outline of Roy standing on the table, a fire extinguisher held loosely in his hands. "Need order," he grumbles. "Can't argue so much."

He steps down and sets the extinguisher by the door, hanging the pin on a hook to show that it's been used. His mother rushes out from the crowd and clotheslines him against the wall with her forearm at his throat. "Do you know what kind of chemicals are in that?"

"Nontoxic," he gasps. "Monoammonium phosphate. Mild skin irritation."

Katie wiggles her head free and starts scratching at her arms. The itching, real or imagined, spreads from one person to the next like a contagion.

"I nominate Tamara," the same woman announces, bringing focus back to the real issue of the night. "She knows how to order supplies."

A call picks up for more nominations. In the end, it comes down to three candidates: Tamara, Matt the Asshole, and, much to my dismay, Karen, my mother. There's an uneasiness in the room that wasn't there before her name was added for consideration. I can sense it in the shuffling of feet, the sighing, the flaring of nostrils as my neighbors look at one another.

"Well," Mrs. Hepworth stage-whispers to her friends, "George would want us to vote for his wife."

Once that's out in the open, the vote is just a formality. My mother is unanimously elected interim leader of the Doomsday Dimwits.

She steps onto the stage still clutching the wad of tissues and dabbing at her cheeks. When I look closer, I notice that her skin isn't wet. She wasn't crying at all. "Thank you so much for your support during this difficult time," she says, making a show of wiping her eyes. "George's accident was a wake-up call. We haven't been devoted enough. I'll be the first one to admit it. I wanted to be reasonable, balancing integration with the outside world against being prepared for the worst. But I see now that I was wrong. It's time for a change."

Mom turns her head a degree at a time to give the appearance that she's smiling individually at every single person in the room. "In that spirit, I'd like to propose a change to get our younger members more involved. I believe that we should lower the minimum training age to ten years old."

The silence is instantaneous as we collectively absorb her words. The hardliners can hardly contain their glee. "I'll second," Elijah's mom announces. "That'll allow my son to start participating."

The vote isn't unanimous, but it's hardly a contest. Mom's new measure passes. She claps quietly. "Thank you again for your support. This is what George would want."

She locks eyes with me over the top of the crowd.

I'm the only one who knows it's a lie.

10

I THOUGHT THE LOSERS IN THE ELECTION WOULD SEEM deflated, but if anything, they only act more determined to prove themselves. It's been six minutes since Mom took over and they're already sucking up to her.

Tamara herds the community out of the barn and indicates that we should follow.

"We put this training together in honor of your dad," Matt the Asshole tells us as he sets a quick pace toward her property. "We figured it would be good for people to have closure after the election."

Mentally, I fill in the end of the sentence: . . . *in case he dies.*

"Your dad would want us to make sure you've learned something from his accident," Mom explains. "I know it's not your birthday yet, but this is the best gift he could ever give you."

"He's going to be back as soon as he gets better," I say, my voice sounding tinny and weak even to my own ears.

"We can't count on that."

"This training is going to be so amazing," Tamara gushes.

In graph form, the lines contrasting my enthusiasm with my neighbors' would make an X. I mop my forehead with the edge of my sleeve, my brain spitting possibilities at random. The promise of escaping this life used to keep me going, but suddenly that's not enough. I can feel it slipping away. And now that Mom's in charge and Katie is going to start training . . .

We file onto Tamara's property like a row of ducklings and follow the horseshoe driveway that winds around the greenhouse. When we reach the rear of the building, I stop so abruptly that Heather slams into my back. "No way," I breathe, my chest tightening with panic at the sight of a blue sedan, its driver's side collapsed in on itself.

"Yes! Way!" Tamara cheers, slapping me on the back. "We were able to get *the exact same* make and model as your dad's car for our vehicle-safety scenario. How cool is that? I mean, I know it has to be a little upsetting, but it's going to be so authentic. Your dad would have loved it."

A shiver passes through me, like ice water dripping down my back. I grind my canines together and bite down on my tongue. I won't let them see me cry. "Supercool," I croak back before jamming my mouth closed again.

Mom steps to the front of the group and waves her hands for silence. It seems odd for her to be up there alone. "Most of our exercises are group training activities. However, in light of the tragedy that's befallen my family, I decided that an individual exercise was best. Becca, we designed this one just for you."

My stomach fills with the same sour, heavy feeling that I get when it's my turn to give a presentation in class. I step in front of Katie to separate us. I don't want her to be caught in the fallout of whatever this is.

Mom circles around the far side of the trunk and gestures like a gameshow host. "Let me set the scene. You've been in a hit-and-run and you're injured. You smell fuel leaking, but the doors won't open. No one is coming to help you."

I jump as Heather's mom presses her hand against the small of my back and guides me to the passenger-side door. Before I can open it, she pulls out a pack of zip ties and secures my right wrist to one of my belt loops. I'm too dumbfounded to move in my own defense. "You have a broken arm," she explains. "Just like your dad."

I crawl over the console and allow myself to be buckled in before I really start to panic. My legs are shaking so much that it takes them two tries to strap the weights around my ankle, simulating Dad's compound fracture. I have no idea what's going to happen next. They wouldn't hit me with another car, right?

The last touch is Mom strapping a pair of goggles over my face. "They're drunk goggles. Since you're supposed to be disoriented after a crash. We'll start the exercise in just a second. You'll know when."

"What's that supposed to mean?" I narrow my eyes to slits to maintain some semblance of sight as the goggles distort my view, forcing me to see the world through the eyes of a drunk driver.

She ignores me as she turns the key and closes the door. A blurry figure—Mr. Kang, judging by his size—opens the hood. I lean back in the seat to get a better vantage point as the doors shut around me. An upbeat Bruno Mars song trickles through the radio. Every other note hisses with static.

I don't see headlights yet. That's probably a good sign.

With a sound like a gunshot and a similar smell, the airbag explodes out of the steering wheel faster than I can see. The brunt of it hits me in the side of my face, but enough catches my nose that I can taste blood pooling against my upper lip.

From outside, I can hear Mr. Kang whooping in surprise. "Damn! That's even louder than I thought it would be!"

I try to lift my dominant hand before I remember that it's tied behind my back. I push my left arm around the airbag and gingerly poke at my nose. It doesn't feel broken, but many thanks to whichever jerk decided to move the seat up this far.

My neck is aching and loose, as though it's lost some essential structure meant for holding up my head. I open my eyes a little wider, wincing as I attempt to focus the six blurred dashboards into the one I know is real. I try not to think that this is what Dad must have seen, the way he must have felt. Trapped. Alone.

I concentrate on the throbbing pain at the center of my skull and push those thoughts away. I need to get out of here. I assess the situation as well as I can with only four fully functioning senses. The seat belt is the first step.

I reach across my body and push the button, but of course nothing happens. Training would never be that easy. But if this is truly meant to mimic my father's car, then there will be tools in the glove box.

I almost dislocate my shoulder stretching to reach it with my left hand. I run my fingers across a manual and a handful of napkins before I feel the smooth metal of a rescue tool. Bingo.

After cutting through the seat belt and wriggling free, I contort around the indentations in the door and press my cheek to the window. "Everybody stand back, okay?" I shout, just to make sure that Katie isn't anywhere in the vicinity. Once I'm sure, I slam the point of the tool against the far corner of the window, the only spot I can apply any useful amount of force.

I keep hitting the window long after I hear the glass break. I move methodically, checking each portion of the window with the tool until I'm reasonably sure that I won't gut myself on a glass shard. I'd prefer to go feet first, but I'm supposed to have a broken leg.

I take a few preparatory breaths before I just go for it and dive through the window. My stomach slams against the rough patches of glass, but none of the remaining pieces on this side are long enough to puncture. I wave my arm toward the ground, kicking out with my "good" leg for that last push to propel me forward.

"Come on," I grunt, swinging my foot blindly behind me.

Finally, I connect with what feels like a headrest and flop out of the car in a heap. I'm so happy to be free that I don't even mind the scrape on my scalp or the glass fragments embedded in my palm.

Tamara helps me stand and beckons Katie to her other side. Once, Katie might have fussed about the blood or cracked a joke, but now she struggles to maintain the same impassive look as everyone else. Tamara points to each of us in turn. "George Aldaine might not make it, but his daughters will carry on his legacy."

It sounds too much like a promise for comfort.

Mom pats me on the shoulder and removes the goggles from my face. I rub the sore indentations in my skin where the force of the airbag pushed against the thick plastic rims against my cheekbones.

"You're next," Mom says to Katie, scrubbing the blood from the goggles with her shirt. "Obviously we can't fix the window or put the airbag back, but you can try everything else. Are you ready?"

Katie looks around at the encouraging faces, the smiles. I reach for her arm, but she shrugs me off. "Would this really help if I got in an accident like Dad? What if I was on the school bus instead of a regular car?"

Mom crouches beside her. "Absolutely. It's the same idea." She takes Katie's hand and leads her over to the passenger door.

I find my spine somewhere in the next few seconds and spring forward to intercept Katie before she can climb into the car. "Mom, this is danger—"

I yelp as Roy catches me around the waist and pulls me back into the crowd. "Have to let her start sometime," he mumbles. Quieter, he adds, "Pick your battles."

The brief interruption is enough to quash my impulsivity. I can't protest here in front of all of these people. They'll sniff me out in a second. The only way to protect Katie is to change her mind and convince her that this doomsday stuff is stupid. I'm not going to accomplish that here.

I chew on the end of my knuckle as Mom buckles Katie into the seat. She lets her keep the use of all of her limbs, but she does make her wear the goggles. Katie's head swivels to the side as she tries to regain some semblance of vision.

She watched me do the original exercise, so it only takes her a minute to find the glass breaker where I dropped it in the footwell. She simulates smashing the window. Her hands are so tiny that she uses both of them to hold the tool.

I suck in a breath and peek through my fingers. "Watch the edges on the right," I mutter quietly enough that I doubt anyone else can hear. "Oh, those are sharp. Be careful."

I see the potential for injury rapidly aligning into reality. Katie presses both palms over the sill and tilts her chin up to see as much as she can of the ground in the sideview mirror. The moment she puts any weight on her hands, the glass is going to shred them.

I shove past Roy and dash over to the car. "Katie, Katie, Katie. You have to watch out for the broken glass. It doesn't look sharp, but it is. Go out the other part of the window."

"Stop interfering!" Tamara barks, shoving me out of the way.

"I'm just teaching!" I whip around to face Mom, gesturing to the jagged shards. "Are you going to let her get hurt?"

I was hoping that Mom's nursing instincts would override whatever zombified, brainwashed stupor she's in, but she only scowls and pushes me farther to the side. "Pain is the best teacher."

Katie taps along the window with her fingers, her head tilting in the air like a snake sensing prey. She checks that there are no glass fragments on the left side of the window and scoots forward until her legs are hanging out. She's just short enough that she can slither through without getting stuck or bending her spine at unnatural angles.

She doesn't exactly stick the landing. Her butt slams into the pile of glass shards, but she's up on her feet before I can worry too much. She brushes off her pants and looks at the surrounding crowd. "Did I do good?"

There's a slight pause before the entire community erupts in cheers and applause. I whistle and clap and scream and stomp and pretend that I'm crying tears of joy.

11

THE FOLLOWING DAY, I WAKE UP GASPING FOR AIR, MY BODY pinned against the mattress by a warm weight. My hand lunges out and connects with a fur-covered leg. I follow the curve of Belle's body to where it intersects with Katie's. I don't remember a dog pile being part of our birthday traditions. "Why are you guys crushing me?"

"Get up!" Katie swats me on one side of the head while Belle's tail wags against the other. "You've been sleeping forever."

"Go away."

She pinches my cheek and digs her fingernails into my arm fat. Not cool.

"Seriously. Go away. You're only allowed to wake me up this early on Christmas."

Katie presses something cool and flat against the tip of my nose. I open one eye as she illuminates the screen of my cell phone. "It's noon," she says. "People are coming over soon for your birthday party."

I leap out of bed and accidentally launch the dog sideways into the air. She hits the ground and flails to her feet, trotting off without a backward glance, as if to say, *You win this round, human.*

Katie dissolves into a fit of giggles.

"Glad you think this is funny," I snap as I hop around the room with one leg in my jeans. I was supposed to wake up early and vacuum before Mom got home from work. She's going to kill me if I try to do it while she's sleeping.

The first thing I notice about the main part of the house is the smell. It isn't the usual mixture of dust and the lemon disinfectant that sticks to Mom's scrubs. I sniff the air, following my nose into the kitchen where the smell is stronger. It's gas.

I rush to the offending burner and click off the knob. Three eggs and a packet of cheddar are penned in a frying pan on the corner of the stove. "Katie! Come here!"

PHYSICS PROBLEM: Gas has been leaking in your house for an unspecified period of time. If it explodes and launches your 63 kg burning corpse into the air with an initial velocity of 20 m per second, how far away should they wait with the body bag?

Bullet-resistant windows don't have locking mechanisms, so there's no way to ventilate without opening the front door. I kneel beside Belle and hold her collar for emphasis. "You can go outside, but if you chase Mrs. Hepworth's goat again, I'm going to lock you in the laundry room for a month."

Her ears perk at the mention of the goat, a skinny, bow-legged creature that couldn't outrun a turtle with a cinder block strapped on its back. I open the door and kick her outside, not wanting to be the girl who indirectly killed her father *and* asphyxiated the dog.

"What'd I do now?" Katie asks, appearing at my side. Her jaw falls open with shock when she sees Belle peeing on a bush. She dashes outside and retrieves her, a steady stream of pee leaking onto my foot as they scurry back inside. "There isn't a fence in the front yard! Belle could get hit by a car!"

"We had an agreement that she could go out front as long as she doesn't chase the goat." I shake my foot and splatter the hardwood with urine, sighing at the official start of my adult life.

"She doesn't speak English!"

"Right. Her name is Belle. She must speak French. Anyway, I wanted to talk to you about the stove situation. If you leave the burner on, gas leaks into the kitchen and it can then explode and kill everybody. *C'est mauvais.*" Those French classes finally came in handy. "Just keep your mitts off the stove, okay?"

Her head sags against my chest. "I wanted to make you breakfast for your birthday. I thought I knew how to do it."

"I'll teach you sometime."

"Really?"

"Sure," I drawl, scrubbing my foot to a raw pink with dish soap and a raggedy sponge. "But first, you have to help me clean the house."

To her credit, Katie doesn't whine about helping with chores.

She mops the foyer while I prepare a cheese platter and a few pitchers of juice for our guests. My cake is on a shelf in the fridge, a bunch of sliced vegetables stacked in a circle with dip spread on top as frosting.

"Ew!" Katie cries, poking the dip with her finger. "A vegetable cake?"

"It's cheaper than making a real cake. Best I could do."

"Cake can't be that expensive," she insists. "We have cupcakes at school all the time."

"It's cheap and healthy. If you don't want any, then don't eat it."

Grand total, I think the whole spread will cost three bucks if I wash the plastic cups and plates after the party. The blobs of cheese are from Mrs. Hepworth's goat, the vegetables from the communal greenhouse on Tamara's property. Without Dad's income from the weld shop, we need to take advantage of the free food that's available to us.

We pile miscellaneous clutter into the closet and close the doors to our bedrooms. After a quick scrub of the countertops and picking up the tumbleweeds of Belle's fur, the place looks presentable enough for company. The real eyesores, the cheap brass chandelier and the green pinstripe wallpaper, can't be helped.

I retreat to my room to finish some homework and surf the Internet as much as I can without bumping into Mom's draconian child filter. In my inbox, I find an e-mail from Ms. Garcia outlining her plan of attack for the science fair. I almost write back asking her not to harangue me while my life is going to shit, but then I notice the time stamp—sent at two o'clock in the morning the day of Dad's accident. She hasn't e-mailed since, not even to ask why I missed her class yesterday while I was malingering in the nurse's office to avoid the substitute physics teacher.

Ms. Garcia always seems to know what I need, whether that's solitude or a cup of coffee smuggled out of the teachers' lounge. With a sigh, I close the lid to my laptop, recalling the day she dragged me to the library to apply to Carnegie Mellon, her alma mater.

"Go Tartans," I mumble.

Mom wakes up right before the first guests arrive, wiping her finger along the surfaces of the furniture like a disapproving governess. She looks well rested and composed, her hair hanging in spirals of blond curls. "It's filthy in here. I thought I told you to clean."

I bite my tongue. Of course she would pick out the one thing we didn't clean and criticize it. "Do you really think this is appropriate?" I venture, gesturing to the plates and food, our meager attempt at festivity. "Shouldn't we be going to visit Dad?"

"He's not going to know if we're there or not. Life goes on."

"Mom." I block her path, gripping her shoulders with both hands. "I think you need to talk to someone about what happened. Is there someone at the hospital I can call?"

She scoffs. "I don't need to talk to someone. I'm thinking clearly for the first time in years. And the logical, objective truth is that your father is unlikely to recover. We need to move on and start planning for the future."

In the procedure about what to do if my parents die, the first step is to dispose of their bodies away from water sources and predators. The last step is to calculate new rations.

"I always told you girls not to get attached. Love makes you reckless." She pops a square of cheese into her mouth. "Do we have any cheddar?"

▲ ▲ ▲

Our guests arrive with eerie precision, ringing the bell just as the hour hand clicks to one o'clock. Belle completely spazzes, her paws skittering on the floor as she bounces between Tamara and Mrs. Hepworth. Matt the Asshole tries to pat her head, but she growls in warning, prompting the quick withdrawal of his hand.

"She doesn't like men," I explain. I'm not sure if she came home from the pound that way or if Dad had anything to do with it. Neither would surprise me.

Tamara kisses her nose. "Smart dog."

Mom sweeps into the room wearing a ridiculous low-cut dress covered in pastel sunbursts. She could be the spokeswoman for a cotton-candy company. "Thanks for coming!" she exclaims, hugging her way around the room as though everyone traveled from New Zealand to be here. No one has the gall to comment on her new outfit, despite the fact that it's both a waste of money and completely impractical. What if the apocalypse started *right this instant*?

"How are you holding up?" Mrs. Hepworth asks, resting her tiny palm on Mom's exposed shoulders.

"It's been terrible," Mom replies. She catches a tear on the tip of her index finger and presses it against the hem of her dress like she's saving it for later. "I don't know what to do without George. I'm barely sleeping, between work and caring for the girls."

Most of our neighbors are an enigma to me. I can't understand what drew them here, though I suspect that Heather's family had a bad experience with flooding, judging by their insistence on having an inflatable boat stashed in every building.

It's different with Mom and Dad, since they were born here, the offspring of the first founding couples. I can't tell if this detached version of Mom is her true self, or if she's just bouncing between different facets of her prepper-approved persona, unmoored by Dad's sudden absence.

With a shake of my head, I start distributing glasses of juice while Katie ushers everyone to various seating areas in an uncoordinated game of musical chairs. The couch is too soft for Ronald's back, so he switches with Roy in the dining room. Matt the Asshole stands in the corner, but Roy's mom doesn't like him hovering over her. Elijah commandeers Katie's seat from the kitchen, prompting a screaming match.

I'm already exhausted and they've only been here for five minutes.

I despise these informal gatherings. They always have the stuffy feel of a dress rehearsal, a cast of two-dimensional characters parroting lines. It's a symptom of having the same conversations over and over for years. Unless there's an exotic new virus or a natural disaster strikes, our discussions are limited to five core topics: supplies, training, maintenance, threats from the outside world, and whether Bunker One or Bunker Two is the better assignment.

Finally, when I really can't take it anymore, I retreat to the kitchen to retrieve the vegetable cake and a fresh stack of plates. I reach into the drawer and heft the cake knife, wondering if it's sharp enough to give myself a lobotomy.

"Don't forget the candles," Katie whispers. She says it so innocently, as though everyone else in the world puts their birthday candles into pieces of zucchini.

Tamara conducts with her index finger while the rest of my neighbors assemble around the cake to sing "Happy Birthday" in a caterwauling, off-key chorus.

"Make a wish!" Katie shouts at the end.

Please, Wish Fairy, fix my father and then get me the hell away from this town as fast as you can. I blow out the candles, click my heels together, and open my eyes. Still here. Damn.

Mrs. Hepworth steals glances at the pile of presents under the window. I think she wants me to open them, but I'd rather do it in private, especially since I suspect that my neighbors have been overly generous in light of my family's recent misfortune. Usually my gifts consist of a homemade jar of sugar scrub or a new set of flannel base layers. Today, there are more cards than boxes, the envelopes thick and straining against their seals.

While I feign interest in a debate about whether North Korea has sufficient firepower to bomb California, I mentally compile a list of things to do with my birthday money. Katie is going to need new shoes and school clothes, plus I have to settle my debt with the cafeteria. If Mom didn't pay the electric bill, there's that, too. The pressure builds against my temples like two magnets demanding to be reunited.

Roy rests his hand on the small of my back and nods his head toward the door. "Can we talk outside?"

I close my eyes and dream of Carnegie Mellon, the curve of the Allegheny River as it snakes through the city. On nearby

Craig Street, there's a restaurant called Crepes Parisiennes that looks delicious even as an icon on Google Maps. My mouth waters with the phantom taste of whipped cream, candied walnuts, and freedom.

"Becca?" Roy says. "Feeling sick again?"

"No, no," I reply, fixing my ponytail and leading the way into the backyard. "I'm fine."

Out on the patio, he thrusts an enormous wad of recycled brown paper and tape against my stomach. The sunlight flashes across his black hair, slicked back with too much gel and curled over like a wave. "Present from my parents. Happy birthday."

"Oh. Thank you." I bite through the tape and spit pieces of wrapping onto the concrete. My excavation efforts reveal an orange mesh pouch containing three self-propelled aerial signaling flares. I examine them in great detail, resisting the urge to light my house on fire. "They're waterproof *and* approved by the Coast Guard. Wow. Fancy."

I pinch the extra mesh at the edge of the pouch where it looks like there should be another object to flesh out the space. I guess giving someone a used pack of flares isn't any weirder than giving them flares as a birthday gift in the first place.

"Sorry," Roy mutters when he notices. "Korean superstition about the number four."

"Like thirteen?"

"Worse." He kicks a pebble across the lawn and runs his tongue across the uneven ridgeline of his teeth. "Have something else for you, too."

"You didn't have to do so much." I'm already in his debt for the kind words and chauffeur service, for sticking by my side in spite of my irritability and general unpleasantness. The guilt wrings my heart like a dirty sponge.

He reaches into his back pocket and slaps a thin blue box into my palm. It's sturdier than a dollar store gift box, about the size that a normal person would use to wrap a gift card. Roy wouldn't give me a gift card, though, not unless a Cabela's opened in town. His fingers pull back reluctantly, his chest swollen with the pressure of a held breath. "I've been waiting a long time for your birthday."

Without another word, he turns on his heel and vanishes inside, a nervous exhale trailing in his wake. I shake the box and hear something small shifting between the sides. It sounds like a carabiner. No, it's too light for that.

I shrug and lift the lid a few inches. There's a silver chain inside held in place by two velvet-covered tabs. A compass pendant dangles from a delicate bail, its surface covered with fine black etchings that indicate the cardinal directions. I flip it over and squint to read an inscription there, spinning the pendant in a slow circle to keep the text upright.

THERE ARE NO SHORTCUTS
TO ANYWHERE WORTH GOING

I tuck the necklace inside my pocket and slam-dunk the box into the garbage bin by the door. It falls neatly into a gap between a couple of empty jugs and disappears from sight. I shuffle the rest of the trash just to be sure it's buried. My heart lurches and thuds faster than the bass beat of a dubstep mix. No one else can ever know about this.

I return to the party before I can be missed, scrutinizing the women in the room to see if the restrictions on jewelry have eased without my notice. Their necks are bare or hidden by turtlenecks, their hands empty except for plain wedding bands, which have always been an exception. Matt the Asshole has a fitness tracker strapped on his wrist and an NRA pin stuck through the front of his NRA ball cap. Besides that, no one is wearing so much as an earring.

It occurs to me that the necklace could be a test of my commitment to the rules, an elaborate scheme to discredit my family in light of the recent political upheaval. But if that were true, the gift would have come from someone who wanted to increase their standing in the community by proving that I had accepted contraband in direct violation of the commandment that Thou Shalt Spend All Spare Money on Survival Crap.

My paranoia eventually subsides, replaced by confused anger as I puzzle the underlying meaning behind Roy's gift. The logical conclusion is that he's a poser, a fellow nonbeliever, but my brain protests this idea, spitting out past examples of his devotion to the community. We've had so many tedious conversations, days at lunch that consist of nothing but discussing sustainable farming and bioterrorism. It couldn't have been an act. Anyone that good at bullshitting should either be at a poker table or on the red carpet.

Yet Roy is still while others move about him, silent while others speak. He fades into the background like a stain on a rug. There's a certain safety in shyness, at least for someone with a secret to keep. Did we used to be friends before we were forced to be a couple? I can't remember. Obligation has clouded so much between us.

He backpedals a single step as I approach, hanging his thumbs over the waistband of his jeans. "You were faking it this entire time?" I ask, fighting to keep my voice low.

He nods his head by looking at me, then the ceiling, and back again. "Not here. Talk later."

I weave my arm around his chest and dig one of my knuckles in between his ribs, smiling as Mrs. Hepworth snaps our picture with a boxy old Canon. "I'm going to murder you," I snarl through my teeth. "We've been dating for five years, Roy. You couldn't have dropped a hint in *five* fucking years?"

"Been trying for the past week. I almost said something at the meeting."

"I just thought you were being a weirdo."

"Look at you kids," Mrs. Hepworth gushes, flipping her camera around to show us the grainy screen. Roy managed to appear happy rather than pained, more proof of his prowess as a liar. "You're both eighteen already! All grown up! I can't stand it."

"Yeah, we're adorable." I shove past her and stomp to my bedroom, kicking the door closed with my heel.

My cramped room resembles a prison cell, and today, it feels like one. I stand against the wall and survey everything that is mine in this world: a twin bed with a metal headboard, a closet of secondhand clothes, a battered nightstand, and a lamp that only works if I jiggle the cord. Add in a toilet and it might as well be Rikers.

Regardless, I climb into bed fully clothed and take solace in the solitude. It lasts for thirty blissful seconds before Mom barges in. "Don't just laze around. People are leaving and there's trash to pick up."

Katie appears in the doorway clutching a roll of trash bags and a shower caddy packed with cleaning supplies.

"Once you're done cleaning," Mom continues, "we'll have to sit down and review the maintenance plans. Your dad usually takes care of those, but his brain scans are terrible. He's probably not going to surv—"

"MOM!" I stick my fingers into my ears. "SHUT UP! JUST SHUT UP!"

In the hallway, Katie sits cross-legged on the floor, the trash bags unfurled over her knee like a scroll. She crawls into her bedroom and collapses onto a pile of dirty laundry. I shoulder past Mom and join her, pulling her into my lap even though she's heavier than she looks. "Hey, Katie Cat. Dad's a fighter. He's going to be okay."

"Stop it," she orders, shoving free of my embrace. "I'm not a little kid. You don't have to lie to me."

She stands with purpose and opens a trash bag. Before I can speak, she straightens her hand and knocks her action figure collection into the trash, including Iron Man.

"What are you doing?"

She jumps onto the bed and tears her posters down, scattering pushpins onto the carpet. Her comic books are next, then the Batman backpack that I bought her for Christmas. "Superheroes are stupid. They can't save anybody. That's why we have to keep ourselves safe so we don't end up like Dad." She pauses. "Can I see the bunker?"

"Why do you want to see it? We used to make fun of how silly it is, remember?"

"I want to see the bunker!" Katie shouts to Mom.

Mom emerges from the hallway, holding out her hand. "Come on. I'll show it to you."

"And it's safe in there?" Katie asks.

"Safest place in the world."

I scramble for my phone as the back door swings shut, but there's no one to call, no one to swoop in and deliver us from this insanity. The phone falls from my grasp and clatters to the floor. I've lost my edge, whatever grip I had on Katie that kept her skeptical, cracking jokes over breakfast about how the dinosaurs didn't waste their days waiting for a meteor. I underestimated the power of fear.

I watch through the window as they disappear into the forest, holding hands and smiling like Elijah's picture come to life.

12

MOM WAKES ME IN THE HALF-LIGHT OF DAWN, A PAIR OF teal chemical gloves tucked in the crook of her arm. My eyes drift to the coffee in her other hand, and in a moment of extreme naivete, I actually think it's for me. "You have greenhouse duty in ten minutes," she says, draining the mug in a single prolonged swallow. "Take Katie with you. You can start teaching her about sustainable farming."

"Fine." I'm too exhausted from the weekend to offer much in the way of resistance. Besides, as far as doomsday chores go, taking care of the greenhouse is far from the worst assignment. Plus, it's not dangerous, so I don't have to worry about her wandering off and decapitating herself by accident.

I throw a light jacket over my T-shirt and leave on my pajama bottoms. Katie does the same. This early in the morning, the air is still brisk, but frost season has finally ebbed away.

The greenhouse is situated on Tamara's property, a hulking structure meant to house enough food for all. The door is unlocked when I arrive, thanks to an earlier start by the others. Heather spots me through the glass panels and waves. "I didn't know you were coming," she says to Katie as we cross the threshold.

"Neither did I," I grumble under my breath. "We'll do the water testing and the paperwork."

Katie scuffs her shoe against one of the non-slip mats. "Paperwork sounds boring."

"Good observation. It is boring."

My mood further declines when I notice Roy on the far side of the greenhouse. He spots me and offers a smile. I make a show of greeting Candace instead. "Can you keep an eye on the time for me? I don't want to miss the bus."

"Doesn't it make you nervous being around all of those other kids?" Heather asks. She draws a line in the air between Candace and herself. "We like being together all the time. You should drop out and be homeschooled with us. It would be fun to hang out more!"

I'd rather drop dead. School is the only escape I have, my personal bastion of freedom. "It's my last year, so it would be weird to change it now."

I grab the daily maintenance procedure and start ticking off various steps. I send Katie to do the easy ones that I usually don't bother completing, like making sure the aisles are free of tripping hazards. It gives her something to do while I check the pumps that cycle water from the tiered grow beds down to the fish tanks below.

"How come there's no dirt?" Katie asks, pressing her nose against the tank and startling the squirming tilapia.

"You don't need dirt when you have a setup like this. The fish make the food for the plants. It takes up less space."

Meanwhile, Roy carries a pail to a nearby fish run and tosses in a handful of worms, chirping, "Breakfast time! Look alive!"

I ignore his attempt at attracting my attention. The conversation I want to have can't be done in front of the others.

"Want one?" he asks, dangling a worm from his outstretched finger.

Candace and Heather share a muted giggle from behind the tomato plants. They don't know that Roy is nothing but a liar, a fraud capable of running a five-year-long con.

I pinch the worm between my fingers and hold it out toward Katie. "You seem to be taking this doomsday stuff pretty seriously lately. Part of that is learning how to find food in the wilderness. Like worms. Here. Try one." I stick it in her face.

She keeps eye contact with me as she snatches the worm and swallows it in one gulp.

Roy gasps in surprise and turns back up the aisle. I dunk a test strip into the closest trough, startling the nearby fish. I'm still frustrated when I finish collecting the samples an hour later. She ate the worm. She ate it. This is infinitely worse than I imagined.

I watch Katie until it's time for me to head to the bus stop, hoping that I'll see some kind of delayed reaction. A gag, a wrinkled nose. Anything. She doesn't so much as drink a glass of juice before I leave the house.

On the bus, Roy and I sit in silence amid the clamor of twenty other students. We take turns attempting to speak, our lips flapping on mute like two mimes in a screaming match. He rubs his palms against the sides of his jeans, pausing at each stoplight to scrutinize my face in profile.

At lunch, I can't decide if it's worse to join him or avoid further tension by scouting a new seat. Sydney appears to sense my dilemma, giving a short wave and indicating the space next to her. Her table is lively and boisterous, filled with a hodgepodge of athletes and artists. A goth girl with pink hair shares a slice of pie with the junior prom queen. Snippets of their stories and jokes reverberate throughout the cafeteria.

I summon my courage and melt onto the bench, my knees trembling. Sydney offers an encouraging grin, the sentiment somewhat lessened by the gruesome line of bruises adorning her skin. "Welcome Becca, Breaker of Eye Sockets."

A linebacker or quarterback or something-or-other-back jerks his chin in the air. There's ketchup dribbled down the front of his white-and-red mesh jersey. "Hey. What's up?"

I lick my lips and stuff a piece of burger bun into my mouth, shrugging. The girl on the other side of Sydney elbows her with a quick jab, her eyes never leaving the screen of her cell phone. She tilts it slightly to the side, just enough to angle the camera in my direction. Light explodes in my vision and the linebacker crumbles into a fit of laughter.

I can already imagine the caption attached to the photo: *Ew! Freak alert!*

Sydney smacks the phone out of her hand and sends it tumbling into the gray sludge that's supposed to be chocolate pudding. "What the fuck, Mel?"

Within seconds, I'm running back to Roy. He radiates safety

from the two-person table with freestanding chairs, a former outpost for the security guard who used to monitor lunchtime back when Tin Peas High could afford that sort of staffing.

He helps himself to one of my fries, gnawing it to nothing with small, thoughtful bites. "Still mad at me, huh?"

I squirt ketchup onto my tray in the shape of a frowny face with angry eyebrows. "Exhibit A: My feelings." I'm so mature. "You can have my lunch if you're still hungry. I've lost my appetite."

"Half," he says, slicing the burger in two. "Eat something. You'll regret it later if you don't."

I flatten the cheeseburger in a sudden fit of rage, crushing it into a puck of crumbled beef and tufts of bread. "You know what I hate about this place? All of it. I hate those stupid bitches over there who think they're better than us just because they were born into normal families. I hate this end-of-the-world bullshit every minute of every day. I hate that my dad is dying. I hate that my mom is a useless parent. I hate this school. I hate being home. I hate my life. I hate it.

"And all this time, I've been working on a grand master plan to get accepted to a school in Pittsburgh and move away and now it can never happen because of Katie. She's getting brainwashed. The worst part? I hate her for it. I hate that she doesn't trust me anymore. I hate you because you should have told me a long time ago that you didn't believe and then I wouldn't have been alone, hating."

As soon as I speak the words, I wish that I could snatch them from the air. Pain flickers across Roy's face like sunlight glinting on glass. "I'm sorry," I say. "I don't hate you. I don't know why I said that."

"Sorry for not telling you sooner." He wraps the chunk of meat in a napkin and shoots it into the trash can in a neat arc. "I was afraid to uh, break my cover. Once I told you, I couldn't take it back if I was wrong. Wasn't even sure that you didn't believe until—"

"Until I accidentally went on a hypothermic rant while trying not to die in a duck pond?"

"Yes. That."

"I was just going to pack my stuff and bounce. Go away to college and get a job. Maybe even fall in love. No offense." My giggle snowballs into a laugh, then into a raw, hysterical howl. "I mean, isn't that priceless? I actually thought I could be somebody."

"You are somebody," he says, his hand darting across the table until our fingers are a hair's breadth apart. "Somebody to me. The only somebody."

I raise my head and smile with genuine happiness, the muscles in my face perplexed by their unusual configuration. "You spoke in, like, three complete sentences without me yelling at you!"

"Not making a habit of it," he mumbles. "That's part of *my* grand master plan. My parents always assume I'm too dumb to disobey the rules. They won't even notice that I'm missing until I'm long gone."

"Can you do me a favor?" I ask.

"Sure."

"Can you just talk normally when we're alone? Now that I know you're mumbling and using two words at a time on purpose, it's making me want to strangle you even more."

He shrugs. "I've been trying, but it might take a little while. It's kind of a habit by now."

"I can't believe you've been hiding in plain sight for this long without slipping up. Where will you go when you leave?"

"Anywhere." He leans forward and reads my palm with his lips, planting a delicate kiss above my wrist as though he's afraid of breaking it. We've touched before, but never with such tenderness. I intertwine our fingers, holding tight.

I'm so tired of being strong, not like a piece of steel, but like a sidewalk—cracked and trampled, but enduring nonetheless. "It sounds nice in Anywhere."

He nods, biting his bottom lip hard enough that it flashes white. "Never rains in Anywhere." He spreads his fingers on the edge of the table and presses down until his knuckles are nearly concave. "Never have to keep a secret in Anywhere. Never have to lie. Never have to wake up knowing that the worst can always get worse."

I envision a quaint little town dipped in the colors of sunlight and grass, swaying branches, endless sky. The houses are clean and well kept, their owners exchanging niceties in the morning before they head off to work on safe, sleepy streets. "Tell me more."

With tears dripping from his eyes, he does.

▲▲▲

The locker room is a dungeon of half-broken cubbies and showers that dribble yellow water into slimy tile basins. I avoid Sydney's groupies, sitting on a bench in the corner as I change into a one-piece bathing suit, shorts, and a T-shirt. I lift my feet in the air, stuffing them into shower shoes before I can catch a disease from touching the floor.

A line forms at the sinks where girls are throwing water onto their shirts to pretend that they've showered. We file down the hallway between the locker room and the pool, our flip-flops snapping against our heels.

As enticing as it sounds to flail around in a pit of chlorinated bodily fluids with thirty other teenagers, I can't quite bring myself to follow the rest of my classmates into the water. I flag down Roy's dad, my eyes locked on my big toe as I open my mouth and say, "Can I be excused from swimming today?"

He folds his arms against his chest where a silver coach's whistle dangles from an Ohio State lanyard. His tanned biceps are two pork loins straining against the confines of his sleeves, his calves so defined that he must sleep in a leg press. I bet he never missed a day of gym class. "What's your excuse?" he asks.

I was planning on mentioning Dad's accident, but something about Mr. Kang's austere demeanor suggests that it wouldn't be well received. There's a decent chance that he'll just spout doomsday dogma and toss me into the pool. "Um. I have my period."

His eyebrows rise in slow motion. "As I recall, you're not a fan of water survival," he says, as though anyone enjoys the thought of imminent drowning, "so it's awfully convenient that your period is only a problem when it's time for swimming."

"Actually," I reply, "it's more of a monthly thing."

"You don't get special treatment because you're marrying my kid," he whispers.

Marrying, not dating.

"Do I get special treatment because I'm leaking from my bodily orifices?" After seeing Roy, his pent-up helplessness mirroring my own, I can't help but lash out at this man who is complicit in ruining our childhoods like some deranged storybook villain. Not for the first time, I wonder if my neighbors are irreparably brainwashed, swept up in a hive-mind power trip without a single independent thought beyond what to eat for breakfast. "I'm not swimming. You can't make me."

"It's not going to matter that you have your period if there's a flood or you're sucked up in a riptide," he retorts, his neck bulging. *Yeah, there are so many riptides in the duck pond.* "Roy never pulls this crap."

"Yeah, well, Roy doesn't have ovaries." I should probably be terrified that this guy is my Health and Sexual Wellness teacher. Half of my classmates probably think babies come out of your nose if you kiss a boy when Mercury is in retrograde.

"I'm writing you up." He reaches for his notebook, this little yellow pad that he uses like a pocket-size black book. "Talking back. Sarcasm. Slacking off. And don't think that your mom isn't going to hear about this."

"Good," I snap. "I'll tell her that you're harassing me over my menstrual cycle."

He freezes. "Fine. Go sit on the bench with Cyclops. *She* has an actual excuse."

"I have an excuse too," I say over my shoulder as I waltz away, stretching the waistband of my shorts in the front. "I told you that I have my period. Are you going to check?"

Sydney swivels to straddle the bench as I approach. She kicks up her turquoise Doc Martens and adjusts her glasses with a pointed stare. When her hair moves, a stray lock falls forward to reveal a line of stars tattooed behind her ear. She doesn't look like anyone I've ever met before or anyone I could conceivably think of meeting again. She doesn't take anyone's shit, either. "That was awesome," she says.

"You heard that?"

"Everyone heard that," she replies, banging the metal buckle of her bracelet against the bleachers to demonstrate the echoing properties of the aquatics wing. "I can't believe he called me Cyclops."

"You should put that under your yearbook picture. Sydney Cyclops."

"Yeah, if I want people to think I'm named after a one-eyed homicidal stripper." She sighs. "Also, I'm really sorry about lunch. If it makes you feel any better, I ripped Mel a new asshole after you left."

I absolve her with a flop of my hand. After everything that's happened lately, a few mean remarks are the least of my worries. "How's your eye doing, by the way?"

"It hasn't fallen out yet."

For the remainder of the hour, Sydney amuses herself by filming her friends in the pool and providing a comedic voice-over. Four of the girls are playing chicken, splashing and hooting as they dunk each other beneath the water. I recognize them from the bus stop. All of them are Sydney's neighbors, the people she probably had sleepovers with in elementary school. Maybe they still hang out together, joking about the old times as they hunt down bargains at the mall or swap secrets in late-night texts.

If I had been born a mile to the west, we might have built a friendship like that, comparing our bedazzled sneakers on the first day of kindergarten. But even before anyone understood *why* I was different, they still seemed to sense it, their parents whispering cautions and withholding invitations to birthday parties that I wouldn't have been allowed to attend anyway. In the end, I guess we can't all have a fairy tale. Some of us are just born on the wrong side of wonderful.

Sydney turns the camera on me next. "And here's Becca keeping me company on the bench. I know she doesn't look like a boxer, but trust me, folks, she gives a mean elbow."

I brandish my elbow at the lens, growling under my breath.

She stops filming and watches the playback, smiling. "Do you have Facebook? I'm totally posting this later."

"My parents won't let me."

"Oh." She sucks in a breath. "Is it because of the whole Rapture thing?"

I burst out laughing, both hands pressed over my aching abdomen. "We're not waiting for the Rapture," I choke. "Just the plain old end of the world."

13

MS. GARCIA IS WAITING FOR ME IN THE HALLWAY, HER NAILS scratching at the sides of her arms. She sees me and scratches harder. "I'm sorry about your dad."

"Thanks." My brain conjures images of a man in a hospital, a victim slouched over the seat belt that didn't save him. I shake my head like a snow globe until the memories fragment and vanish. "Sorry for cutting your class the other day. I hid in the nurse's office."

"Take as much time as you need."

Well, in that case, I'll just take off for the rest of the school year.

"Besides that, how are you holding up?" she whispers. "Any news?"

I'm not sure if she's referring to Dad's condition or my pending acceptance to Carnegie Mellon, but I don't want to talk about either. I can't scrape Mom's words out of my head or keep my inner voice from crying out in response. *Coma. College. Brain scan. Carnegie Mellon. Bad melon.* "No developments."

"Katie was a mess when she got to school for the field trip, but I talked her down on the bus ride. The teacher was threatening to call home and I didn't think you wanted that."

I suck in a breath. "Yeah, that would have been a disaster."

"I'm here for you as much as I can be without getting fired, all right?"

"Thanks."

"You can withdraw from the science fair," she adds, but her tone drips with thinly veiled disappointment. Aside from her daughter and a well-stocked aquarium, I don't think Ms. Garcia has much of a social life. If I renege on our deal, her plans for the end of the year will probably consist of guzzling boxed wine during a marathon of gut-wrenching Lifetime movies.

God, I'm such a sucker. "I'm still going to enter. I could use a distraction."

"Really? You're an angel." She leans down as if to kiss my forehead, rethinks the idea, and settles for a pat on my shoulder. Her shampoo smells of citrus and cotton, a scent I could recognize in a crowd. I wish she would have hugged me instead, wrapped my sorrows in sweet-sounding lies and promised that everything would be okay. I'd almost believe her if she did.

It has to be some kind of cosmic joke that Ms. Garcia is my teacher and Karen Aldaine is my mother. Two women born in the same town, breathing the same air, yet they're as different as a sun shower and a storm.

With Mom, there's always a catch, a string attached to her love like an umbilical cord. I'm nothing but a hamster, a caged animal that she can poke at her leisure, dropping a few pellets of food between the bars as a reward for keeping the wheel turning.

I simmer all the way home, nearly ripping the door off the mailbox as I check for college correspondence, mostly out of habit. I balance the stack on my forearm while I flick through the letters. The majority of them are medical bills or claim forms from Dad's auto insurance.

A circular logo sticks out from a thick envelope at the bottom of the pile. I'd recognize that crest anywhere. It resembles a pineapple stuffed inside a halfpipe and it belongs to Carnegie Mellon University. I suck in a breath, stunned. Ms. Garcia always says that scholarship offers add padding.

It's Mom's day off, so I hide the envelope under my shirt, tucking the bottom into the waistband of my jeans. My skin prickles against the cool paper, the logo pressed against my skin like a brand.

I force myself to appear calm as I enter the house, chucking the junk mail in the recycling bin and tossing the bills on the kitchen counter for Mom. When they scatter, I see a sealed bundle of papers that I didn't notice before. I hold it up to the bare light bulb of the ceiling fan, struggling to discern its contents through the privacy lining. I check the return address stamped in the corner. It's from Katie's school.

I guess I'll give her a chance to explain herself before I assume the worst. I chuck the Carnegie Mellon envelope into my closet like a Frisbee, then barge into Katie's room without knocking. She snaps the lid of my laptop closed, but not before I catch a glimpse of a Hurricane Katrina conspiracy page. I nod at the computer. "You should ask for permission before you borrow my stuff."

"Sorry," she says, her voice rising at the end. She twirls the power cord into a black braid around her finger. "I was just playing games."

I wave the envelope, fighting the urge to throw the laptop out the window and lock Katie in her room until she detoxes from the doomsday propaganda. If there was ever one constant between us, it was the truth, but now even that is gone. "Did something happen at school?" I ask, struggling to tear the perforated seals without ripping the entire document in half.

"That's my report card. I got good grades."

"Oh. I'll take you shopping to celebrate," I say, mentally calculating how much birthday money I have stashed in the lockbox under my bed. "Think of something special that you want."

She massages the ends of her toes where the skin is rubbed red and raw. "Can I pick out new shoes?" She nudges her sneakers with the side of her foot. I can't imagine how painful it must be for her to wear them. They have to be at least a size too small by now. "Dad was supposed to buy me new ones, but Mom says we don't have enough money."

"I can use my birthday money, Katie Cat. You can pick out whatever you want."

I close the door and press my back against it, pinching my fingers across the bridge of my nose. She deserves better than this, than us.

"Oh, Katie's report card came," Mom observes, plucking it from my grasp before I can finish opening it. "Let's take a look."

I follow her into the kitchen, eager to see the feedback from Katie's teachers. Mom tears the rest of the seals, letting the tabs drift to the floor. Her eyes flick down the page, a muscle in her neck twitching as she smiles. Her fingers tap against the back of the paper, her nails bitten down to pinkish stubs.

I take the report card and scan the comments, all of them stating "pleasure to have in class," except the one for World History. The teacher's remarks direct us to an enclosed note, which Mom is currently hogging. She finishes it and passes it to me, an assembly line of guardianship.

In careful script, the teacher explains that Katie keeps disrupting his classes on World War II, raising her hand to tell the other students that France was only invaded because their citizens weren't prepared for a fight. The words might have come from her mouth, but I read them in Dad's voice. "Katie?" I shout toward her bedroom. "Can you come here?"

"Why do you sound grumpy?" she whines from down the hallway, her huffs and stomps growing louder as she approaches. "I got straight As."

"You can't say things like this," I tell her, quoting passages from the note. "It's hurtful to blame a country for being attacked. The Nazis were bad men. They killed a lot of innocent people in France."

Our conversation is ended by an abrupt squawk from Mom. She flaps a newsletter in my face. The picture on the front shows Katie and her friends gaping at a tiger shark, their hands clutching disposable cameras. In the background, Ms. Garcia smiles over the shoulder of her daughter, but her eyes are trained on Katie, keeping up her end of our science-fair-for-chaperoning bargain.

"You went to the aquarium and you didn't tell me," Mom accuses.

Katie takes a step back, bumping into the edge of the table. "It was my field trip."

"And how many visitors were there besides you? You could have been kidnapped! We don't have enough money to pay a ransom. You know that these tourist traps are magnets for shooters and psychopaths." She pauses, throwing up her hands. "I should just talk to Ronald about getting you homeschooled like Candace."

"I don't want to be homeschooled! I'm sorry!" Katie hangs her head, her wispy bangs soaking up her tears. "Becca signed the permission slip. She said it was okay."

Little fucking rat.

"You're so irresponsible," Mom snaps at me, one hand perched on her hip. "You're not her mother."

"Somebody has to be!"

Her hand whips out faster than a python strike, slapping my cheek hard enough that the sting is secondary to the shock of blunt force impact. My body tenses as adrenaline spikes my bloodstream. I square up automatically, my reflexes shaking off the blow faster than my heart. We stand there, frozen, our arms outstretched toward each other. Her hands. My fists.

"Stop it!" Katie runs in between us and spreads her arms into a blockade. "Stop it!"

"Here's your latest lesson," Mom says, grabbing Katie's arm and drawing her forward. "If you want something for yourself, like going to the aquarium, it's wrong."

Maybe it's the anger, but I can't stop myself from blurting out, "Like all those dresses you bought? Or the fancy latte mix? Aren't those selfish and wrong too?"

"I've made enough sacrifices that I've earned a few splurges. I didn't want to live in my parents' house forever. Be a nurse. Have two kids before I was thirty. But I did it. You know why? Because I did what I was told. And so will you."

I lock eyes with Mom over the top of Katie's head. I hope she knows that I will put her in a coma if she ever touches me again. Maybe the hospital gives multiparent discounts. It could be like a second honeymoon for them. Couples' respirators.

I stalk down the hallway and into my room, kicking my door closed behind me. The mark from my bare foot intersects with the muddy splotch I left behind doing the exact same thing on my birthday. I sigh and rub the knob in apology. It's not the door's fault that my life is a circus.

I retrieve the Carnegie Mellon envelope and burrow beneath the covers, my bloody fingers picking at loose threads. My right cheek burns with the memory of Mom's palm, my left with shame. I shouldn't have reacted after she slapped me, not in front of Katie.

But I've spent my whole life not reacting, biting my tongue as I endured endless scenarios and training sessions, lectures from Dad that outlasted my patience. Everyone and everything has a breaking point, and I'm starting to feel broken.

I pin the envelope between my teeth and tear off the corner with a snarl. My tongue sizzles with the taste of glue and resignation. The first page is my official acceptance letter. The second page is my financial aid award, stapled to a waiver for admissions fees. I don't make it to the final page because I'm reeling with shock, the blood in my body blasting to my brain in geysers. I lean back on my pillows, light-headed and disgusted.

A full-ride scholarship to Carnegie Mellon is worth more than our house.

But I can't go. Not now, when Mom has become Queen Control Freak on planet Doomsday and I can't even trust Katie to keep a simple secret. Above all else, I need to protect my sister.

My future, that long-held dream of freedom, will simply have to wait.

I hurl the admissions papers across the room and stomp them into the carpet as I turn off the lights. I climb back into bed and drift off to sleep, chasing dreams that stay where they belong.

14

THE SOUND OF BELLE'S BARKING WAKES ME FASTER THAN
the sirens do. I crack my eyes into slits and nudge the blinds
apart, expecting to see equipment staged for a surprise night-
time drill. Instead, the neighborhood is bathed in red from
the floodlights on Tamara's porch. Another high-pitched wail
pierces the silence.

"Oh my God," I huff as I throw off my blankets and leap for
the door.

Mom reaches the hallway at the same time, her bathrobe tied
hurriedly around her body. "We're under attack!" she shouts,
slamming a fist into Katie's door. "Wake up! Code red!"

She hustles into the living room and stuffs her bare feet into
boots. I glance away for a moment to guide Katie down the darkened hallway. When I look back, Mom has already slung a rifle
and donned a tactical ensemble befitting a SWAT commander.

"What's the threat?" I ask, bewildered.

Mom doesn't answer because she's already yelling orders into a portable radio. Based on Tamara's terse replies, someone tripped several of the proximity sensors. Her cameras picked up footage of a man crawling next to the greenhouse. "He was wearing a yellow bandanna!"

"And this isn't a drill?" someone else interjects.

"No!" Mom yells. "This is not a drill!" She shoves past us and out the door, pausing only to call over her shoulder, *"Get to your station!"*

I slip my feet into sneakers and pull a rifle from the rack in the living room, one of the spares that isn't kept loaded. I don't even bother to take any magazines. At least this way I'll be able to prove my lack of involvement if the police arrive. "Stay here and don't move," I tell Katie. "I'll come back as soon as we're done."

Statistically speaking, it's far more likely that some idiot decided to wander through the wrong woods than it is for this to be part of an apocalyptic ground invasion by bandanna-wearing bandits.

I grab a bag of gear and sprint across the backyard, my lungs burning with exertion. The trees seem to swallow me whole as I vault over the wall of vehicle barriers and smash through tangled branches. Once I'm fully concealed by the darkness, I slow to a lazy walk. No one can see me shirking my duties now.

By force of habit, I continue following the path that leads to my emergency station by the river. A stick snaps behind me, but I dismiss it as a passing animal. When it happens again, I whirl around, lifting my useless rifle, and scream as Katie bumps straight into my chest. I steady her with one hand and press the other over my pounding heart. "You scared the crap out of me! What are you doing here?"

"I wanted to help," she replies, holding up the pair of binoculars dangling around her neck. "I can be a lookout!"

"You could have helped by following directions." It's closer if I leave her in the bunker instead of sending her home, but there's no guarantee that she'll stay put in either location. As much as I don't want her out here, it's better than losing her in the dark. I sigh. "Fine. You can be the lookout as long as you're quiet. And if I tell you to run, you run and you don't stop until you find someone you know, okay?"

"I promise."

True to her word, Katie is silent as I navigate to the wooded slope that juts up against the river and scan the mud for footprints. Finding none, I maneuver onto a rocky outcropping and tuck her into a nearby thicket. Aside from the gleam of her white shoelaces in the moonlight, she's almost invisible. I settle opposite her with my back against an overhang.

"Why are we guarding the river?" Katie whispers. "No one is going to steal the river."

I jerk my thumb in the direction of the metal monstrosity rolling in the water. "That's the turbine that powers the bunker. It's worth a pretty penny. Plus, if someone steals or destroys it, we won't have any electricity down there unless someone's riding the bicycle generator." And by *someone*, I mean me. My legs shudder at the thought.

"Is that a . . ." Katie pauses and wobbles her head to the side. "Is that a 'high-value target'?"

I somehow manage to choke on my own saliva. "What did you just say? Where did you hear that?"

"When we went to the bunker, Mom was talking about what the bad guys would need to blow up if they wanted to kill us. She said life-sustaining systems are high-value targets."

"Do you even know what that means?"

"I'm learning!" she snaps. "Mom says that it's important for me to know the official terms so that I can understand the procedure books."

I groan and roll onto my side, letting the chill breeze wash across my burning cheeks. After all these years of shielding her from the worst of the doomsday doctrine, I'm still losing. I peek at her in my peripheral vision, disturbed to see the intense eyes and dilated pupils of a believer. "Don't believe everything you hear, Katie Cat."

She scoffs. "Maybe if you paid more attention in training you could have helped Dad."

The crackle of the radio covers the pained cry leaking from my throat. I bite my sleeve to muffle the noise as I fish the handheld from my bag and press it to my ear. *"Three-nine-seven, this is three-six-four."*

My thumb trembles against the transmit button. The only reason anyone would contact me directly is if the pursuit is leading them in our direction. *"This is three-nine-seven. Go ahead."*

"Pursuing one adversary—"

The radio falls from my grasp as someone crashes through the brush to our left. Katie shrieks in surprise and dives over the nearest ledge, tumbling into the grass below. I stand in between her and our assailant with my empty rifle held like a baseball bat. I mentally berate myself for refusing to bring ammunition until the adrenaline narrows my focus to single-word thoughts.

Katie. Threat. Katie. Generator. Katie.

. . . Goat?

Goat. I lower my weapon and approach the terrified animal snuffling around on the riverbank. Her coat is matted with mud and covered in burrs. A yellow bandanna hangs around her neck. "Come here," I mutter through my teeth in the nicest voice I can muster. "I'd really like to make you into stew right now."

Katie hauls herself back onto the rock and starts digging through our supplies. She holds up a granola bar in triumph. "She'll come home if we have food. She knows me."

I pretend to scowl at her, reveling in the chance to dispel the tension from a few moments ago. "Yeah, you're the reason she's overweight."

While Katie tears open the wrapper and offers the goat a few bites, I retrieve the radio to inform our neighbors of my heroic apprehension of the intruder. *"All units, this is three-nine-seven. I have detained the adversary on the south side of the river. Her description is horned, hooved, and wearing a yellow bandanna. Makes excellent cheese."*

After a long pause, Tamara breaks the silence with a nervous laugh. "Um, great job, everyone! Surprise training exercise!"

I can almost feel my neighbors rolling their eyes inside the defensive positions hidden in the woods. I turn to the goat and whisper, "In case you were wondering, the official doomsday term for that is 'bullshit.'"

15

I DON'T BELIEVE IN COINCIDENCES, BUT I FIND IT ESPECIALLY intolerable that Aiden Pilecki received his acceptance letter on the same evening that I received mine. And given that I slept a whopping two hours last night, I'm not exactly in the mood to listen to his gloating.

"Do you know that I'm the first Tin Peas grad to be accepted to an Ivy League?" he asks a crowd of admirers before the start of Advanced Placement French. I eavesdrop from the doorway, rolling my eyes as his groupies coo like it's some mind-blowing revelation. Our town's biggest claim to fame is a second-rate flea market. We can't even make it into the lofty annals of the local travel guide, never mind earn a reputation as a hotbed of academic prowess.

"I've been waiting for this day for so long." He's swapped his usual jeans and tattered T-shirt for business casual, as though he anticipated giving this acceptance speech. "I couldn't have done it without all of your help. We're in this together."

I suppress a snort. Aiden makes a lone wolf seem like a party animal. I'm positive that he'll grow into the kind of tailored-suit-wearing jerk who is rude to waitresses and calls an Uber to bring him to the grocery store because driving is too bourgeois.

When he walks deeper into the classroom, other students reach out to touch his shoulder like he's a prophet or an Ivy League rabbit's foot. He adjusts the collar of his azure dress shirt, running his thumbs around his waistband to smooth out the wrinkles.

I attempt to fight my way across the classroom with gentle nudges and strategic turns of my backpack, my head bowed in the hopes that my hair will serve as a screen to conceal my face. It doesn't work. Aiden spots me and waves, standing taller as he approaches. "Hey, Becca. Did you hear the news? I got into Columbia's neuroscience program!"

I wonder if he's going to wear matching shirts for the rest of the year or if that's another coincidence. I observe his arrogant smile, his swagger. He wore that color on purpose. "I did hear that."

"And?" he prompts, waiting.

If he rubs it in any harder, he'll displace my inferior frontal lobe. "Yay," I mutter, shaking my fists like maracas on either side of my head. "You did it."

"Thanks." He scowls and dips away from my limp-wristed high five. I don't know what he expected. It's not like he's a gracious winner.

Meanwhile, our classmates are staring at me like I just bad-mouthed their mothers.

> **PHYSICS PROBLEM:** If you pretend to be excited
> for your classmate and everyone realizes that
> you're really seething with jealousy, what is the
> coefficient of friction?

Monsieur Wheeler begins the lesson by congratulating Aiden in a series of blubbering English-language compliments. Apparently, Aiden is so awe-inspiring that he shocked the French out of the French teacher. I thump my textbook onto the desk.

"I think we can spare a few minutes," Monsieur Wheeler says, "for everyone to say a few words about your plans for after graduation. This is an exciting time for the senior class. You're about to start your new lives. I can't believe that it's almost time to say goodbye."

Jeez, Monsieur Wheeler, we're graduating, not dying.

A ripple passes through the rows as my fellow students stand to summarize their futures, their eyes glazed with far-off visions of dorm rooms and lecture halls. A few simply point to their chests where the names of colleges or branches of the military are embroidered in boxy letters. I squirm lower in my seat, dreading my turn like the approach of a toxic cloud.

I can just imagine the look on my classmates' faces if I said, *My plan is to proceed with an arranged doomsday marriage, then have doomsday children, then throw my doomsday children into duck ponds to prepare them for, y'know, doomsday.*

When it's time for me to speak, I grip the edges of my desk

and force my knees to straighten. The air wheezes out of my lungs. After an inordinate amount of time, someone coughs, then giggles. "I'm not ready to disclose my plans yet." I wink at Aiden, fighting arrogance with mystery. "I don't want to jinx it."

I permit myself a peek in his direction as I sit, pleased to see the reddening of his ears. I'll let him stew over that for the rest of the day, wondering if he's about to be one-upped.

On the way to lunch, I revel in winning this battle with Aiden, even if I've lost all of the other battles, the war, and the crown. The joke will be on me soon enough when Aiden dons his vale-dictorian's sash and then vanishes to New York to eat overpriced bagels and debate artificial intelligence with his fellow geniuses.

I frown at the sloppy joe and soggy carrots on my tray. Car-negie Mellon seems less impressive now, but not any easier to sacrifice.

"Is something wrong?" Roy asks as soon as I sit down. As usual, the table in front of him is bare. He must hold the Tin Peas record for fastest eater. I wonder if there's a scholarship for that.

"I'm just tired from last night."

"Liar."

"Fine. There's also this." I fish the acceptance letter out of my pocket where it's burning a hole like a stack of hundred-dollar bills. I drop the folded square of paper onto Roy's lap and stare out the window while he opens it.

"A full ride," he breathes. "That's amazing. Congratulations."

"I'm not going." I try to say it with conviction, but the sound barely seeps past the lump in my throat. Now that I know I've been accepted, it's like holding a chocolate cake and refusing to eat it. Marie Antoinette would be disappointed. "I'm staying here."

Roy gesticulates like a malfunctioning robot, his eyebrows cranking up and down in unison with his flailing arms. He settles into a deflated lump and presses his knuckles against his cheekbones. "No," he says. "That's . . . no."

"No?"

"It's stupid to ruin this opportunity. There's nothing worthwhile left in Tin Peas."

"Katie." My entire life summed up in two syllables. With Dad in the hospital and Mom working double shifts, I'm Katie's chef, chauffeur, teacher, maid, and companion. I have to be her everything, which means that I can't be anything else. "She's getting brainwashed."

"Not even she is worth it," Roy says, spoken like an only child. "You can't stay here."

"You can't stay here or I can't?"

"Both." He shrugs, gesturing to the sprawl of the run-down cafeteria, the symptoms of economic depression evident in duct-taped gym bags and margarine containers used as Tupperware. Our town isn't glorious, but it's home, a mark on the map that some people spend their entire lives searching for. "Especially now that you have a way out and money for school. Maybe you'll even find a job that you like. It's a chance to start a whole new life."

I throw my sloppy joe back onto the tray, my mouth sour for reasons that have nothing to do with the food. Roy is asking me to hang a price on Katie like a toe tag. "This isn't up for discussion, okay?" I'm sick of dragging around everyone's expectations like a set of chains on my intellect and my heart. I'm a rational adult capable of making my own choices, not the Ghost of Childhood Past.

The muscles along Roy's jaw flex with each clench. "That's so wasteful."

I suck in a breath as fuel for a scream. "Don't ever say that word to me again." *Wasteful.* If my neighbors had a favorite adjective, it would be that one. Education? Wasteful! Just read tabloids and crappy websites for all your learning needs. Entertainment? Wasteful! Working on your bunker is the ultimate pastime.

Love? Wasteful!

Fulfillment? Wasteful!

Becca Aldaine? Wasteful!

Instead of conceding to my obvious anger, Roy is the opposite of chagrined. I extricate myself from the bench and stomp through the doors into the hallway. Without anywhere else to go that's guaranteed to keep Roy from following, I turn into the nearest bathroom to sulk.

Except that the bathroom is occupied by Sydney, who is dangling her phone out of the window on speakerphone in a futile attempt to get service. "I can barely hear you. Why can't you just text me, Mom?" She glances up and notices me hovering. "Oh, shit!" Her shoulder slams against the metal frame as she lurches to her feet. "You scared the crap out of me."

I scramble into the nearest stall and slide the latch into place, my world currently measuring three feet by five. The confinement is an instant comfort, even with the sound of Sydney's conversation ricocheting off the tile. It's amazing how the right mindset transforms a cramped box from a cell into a haven.

A bunker.

My eyes widen with the realization. The pale green walls warp and swell in my vision. Thick lines of graffiti proclaim epithets and love notes, filth and nonsense. I stare at the covert messages, signed only with initials, wanting to scar them from the steel as my own contribution to this pathetic tribute. I am *not* a bunker-dwelling coward. And yet, my feet remain frozen.

I don't know what I am anymore. Am I becoming one of them?

"What's wrong?" Sydney asks, crouching down.

She coaxes me out with more questions, if only because it's a terrible annoyance to shout a private conversation into the eight-inch gap at the bottom of the door. I seize one of the sinks, resting my forehead against the cool glass of the mirror above it. "I'm a freak," I mutter. "You know how animals raised in captivity can't be released into the wild? That's me. I'm like a fucked-up antelope. I have no idea what I'm doing with my life."

She clicks off her phone and stands, her eyes flicking down the length of my body. "You're more of a porcupine."

"Why am I a porcupine?"

"Because you walk around acting tough and breaking people's eye sockets, but you're really a big softie on the inside." She darts over and crushes me in a backward hug. "Come on. Hug it out. You know you want to."

It's literally impossible to reciprocate a backward hug, so I just lean against her torso, forcing a smile in the mirror. "Why are you so nice to me? I elbowed you in the face."

"Yeah, well, karma's a bitch."

I turn around and fold my arms. "What's that supposed to mean?"

"I egged your house freshman year," she admits. "Mel dared me to sneak into your neighborhood."

Unless she goes into detail, it's impossible to know which one of the numerous egg-related pranks and gags she was responsible for committing. Our community is popular on Mischief Night, more insidious and real than any haunted house. We should open a gift shop with kitschy souvenirs and completion badges. "Thanks a lot. Every time that happens, I end up cleaning scrambled eggs out of the gutters for a week. It smells like a sewer inside of a bigger sewer inside of a breakfast buffet."

"If it makes you feel any better, I thought your dad was going to shoot me."

"I'm not surprised," I grumble. "Last night my neighbor's goat set off some alarms and everyone acted like a horde of demons was coming to wipe out Ohio."

"You're pretty normal for living with a bunch of weirdos," Sydney says, pushing her bangs to the side. "I know that sounds awful, but my parents told me not to talk to you or that droopy dude you hang out with at lunch. They said you were dangerous. I guess I always thought you guys sat at home making quilts out of human flesh or something."

I point to the dissolvable blue stitches dotting her face like a treasure map. "You're my first square."

She laughs and extends a delicate hand bedecked with fine silver rings. "Are we even?"

I ignore it and wrap her in another hug, nodding my head against her collarbone. Tears well in my eyes. I finally have a friend from the other side of the stop sign. "Yeah. We're cool."

The bell rings throughout the halls, signaling the end of lunch.

Sydney turns as if to leave, then calls over her shoulder, "Come to my house tonight at midnight. It's the only one with hedges."

"Why?"

She pauses, the door balanced on the tip of her high-heeled ankle boot. "Because I'm releasing you into the wild."

"What does that mean?" I ask. The analytical part of my brain screeches with displeasure, demanding to know specifics and details. "What's the plan?"

Sydney smiles and locks her lips with a pretend key. "It means that you're going to do something spontaneous for the first time in your preplanned life."

The door closes behind her and I still don't know what's coming next.

I like it.

16

LATER THAT NIGHT, AS I HURRY DOWN THE STREET TO rendezvous with Roy, it occurs to me that maybe Sydney was planning a girls' night. I invited Roy along as a weak apology for bailing on him at lunch, but I don't think cucumber facials and pillow fights will help smooth the rockiness between us.

I'm surprised to discover that I'm the first to arrive, especially since all Roy has to do is walk outside. I hunker down behind the cowshed, peering into the darkness for any sign of movement. His heavy footfalls betray his presence before I discern the hazy outline of a figure hustling across the lawn. "Sorry," he mutters. "My parents wouldn't go to bed. Did you have any trouble sneaking out?"

"A little." I raise the leg of my jeans and show him the angry scratches from Belle's nails. "Katie conked out around nine o'clock and Mom's at work. I couldn't get the dog to shut up, though. She was jumping all over me."

Roy laughs, his black hair ruffled by the wind. "You need to buy a bark collar."

"That's inhumane!" I protest, slapping his shoulder. "And even if I did buy a bark collar, I'd put it on my mother instead."

I loop my arm through his as we walk toward the end of the street. In the distance, the stop sign is the lamppost leading to Narnia, promising adventure beyond an invisible divide. We cross the boundary with purposeful steps, entering foreign territory as we pass one ordinary home, then another.

"Do you ever wonder what it would have been like to grow up here?" Roy asks.

I peek into living rooms bathed in the glow of television sets and upper floors darkened for sleep. The front doors are adorned with springtime wreaths and polished knockers, the innocent facades of happy homes. I eye a minivan with a stick-figure family pasted on the back above magnets with snarky honor-student jokes. It's basically a four-wheeled biography.

"I think about it all the time." Maybe I'm being naive about the idyllic perfection of these strangers' lives. Happiness is more than a Dodge Caravan and high-definition television. "But I'm sure they have their own problems."

A breast cancer flag waves from the next garage. I nod to myself.

Roy isn't nearly as philosophic. "I'm going to guess that chasing a goat around the forest at two o'clock in the morning isn't one of them," he grumbles.

We give a wide berth to the rusty van idling on the right side of the road. Strips of white paint hang from its fenders like a peeling sunburn. The loading doors are held closed by a bungee cord and the rear windows ripple in the wind to reveal themselves as nothing more than plastic wrap duct-taped around the frames.

To my knowledge, Tin Peas has never had a serial killer, but there's a first time for everything, right? I scamper closer to Roy, clinging to his forearm as we drift into the center of the street to avoid the Creepy Murder Van.

"Hey, dingus!" I whirl around and see Sydney backdropped against the interior lights, one hand propped on the edge of the open passenger door. She gestures to the hedges beside her. "I said the house with the hedges!"

"You didn't mention the Creepy Murder Van with plastic-wrap windows."

"Would you have agreed to come if I told you our ride was a Creepy Murder Van with plastic-wrap windows?"

"Touché."

Roy and I pile into seats in the second row. When I raise my head, I recognize the mousy-haired girl in the driver's seat as Mel. I wonder if this is her chariot or Sydney's.

Sydney pulls down the sun visor and dusts her cheeks with blush. When she catches me watching, she grins and puckers her stained lips. "Do you like my sexy face paint? I need to snag a date for prom."

Mel interrupts us by shoving a handful of colorful straws in my face. "Pick."

"For what?"

"Designated driver," Sydney answers. "Do you guys have

licenses or is that against your principles as Civil War reenactors?"

"We're allowed to drive. And we're doomsday preppers, not Civil War reenactors." I pick the orange straw. Roy chooses green. "Or waiting for the Rapture."

"Guess it doesn't matter," she says, sparing Mel a pitying glance as she comes up with the short blue straw, "because Mel's DD and we're about to party like it's 1861, bitches."

▲ ▲ ▲

I thought Sydney was kidding about the 1861 part until we pull into the driveway of a Southern-style colonial walled in by knee-high red brick. Ancient trees tower behind it like old watchmen, tall and timeless. I peer at the faint outline of white railings on the upper balcony, half expecting to see an antebellum belle staring back through the darkness. The house seems displaced in Ohio, lacking lush gardens and fountains of sun-bleached stone, as though it's a dollhouse discarded in the wrong section of a shop.

Mel steers onto a patch of pea gravel, the van silent except for the slight twinkling of her keys and the guttural sputtering of the engine. She takes a deep breath. "You know, it's not really fair that I have to be designated driver when my boyfriend is throwing the party."

"The straws have chosen," Sydney replies with a ceremonial air. "All straws are final."

"But—"

Sydney twists around in her seat, shooting Mel a peripheral glare. "Brock's parents are out of town, so don't worry about making noise. Everyone here is cool. No weirdos and perverts, unless you're into that sort of thing, in which case you should consider investing in a Creepy Murder Van with plastic-wrap windows."

"Which one's Brock?" I can never tell the athletes apart. Between their identical haircuts and matching uniforms, it's like trying to distinguish a whippet from a greyhound. "Is he the tennis guy?"

"Football. He sat across from you at lunch the other day."

I think back to Sydney's odd assortment of friends, vaguely recalling a boy with wind-burned, baby-fat cheeks, and shoulders as wide as a surfboard. It was like talking to a freshman's head screwed onto the body of a Calvin Klein underwear model.

"He's the starting quarterback," Mel brags, smearing a fresh coat of ChapStick on her lips and smacking them together in an air kiss. "He wants to go pro."

"Hope he has a backup plan," I mutter. Though the Tin Peas football team dominates in our tiny corner of America, there's little to suggest that any of our players have attracted the attention of national scouts. I don't mean to disparage another person's ambitions, but my tolerance for fantasy is low these days.

"Brock doesn't need a backup plan," she says, which is what every high school athlete thinks until they break their femur on a mistimed tackle. "He's going to college to play football, not study."

I can't help but snort. Reality is going to sucker punch that guy like a drunk coward.

"Is something funny?"

"The only thing dumber than a box of rocks is a box of Brocks,"

Sydney interjects, clearly growing impatient with our banter. "That's what's funny."

As we trudge through a series of iron gates and across the backyard, I realize that I haven't thought about Katie or Dad or Carnegie Mellon since I left my house. It's heartening to know that I can shrug off my worries like an unneeded coat, even if it's just for tonight.

We emerge into a man-made clearing no wider than Brock's beloved football field. Its surface is dotted with stumps, the grave markers of the trees that stood here before. Dozens of other students are gathered around a pile of planks, their hands planted on their hips in collective confusion. A junior kneels on the stones that line a makeshift fire pit, his thumb clicking at a plastic cigarette lighter. Even from here, I can tell that it's never going to work, not without some proper kindling underneath. I glance at Roy and he's wearing the same smug, knowing smile.

Brock thumps his chest and shoves the junior out of the way. "Let me do it."

I enjoy watching him wear the pad of his thumb raw against the flint of the lighter. Most of the partygoers fall silent, sensing that the mood of their host has shifted. As Brock continues to struggle, the bartender guarding cases of booze and water bottles full of siphoned liquor stifles a laugh. Sydney taunts Mel in loud, irreverent whispers.

"Brock," I interject before he hurts himself. "Why don't you let me and Roy take care of that for you?"

He looks around the circle and his face hardens with decision. "Yeah." He throws the lighter at my feet. "This is nerd work."

Roy retrieves the lighter, shaking it next to his ear to check for fluid. He gives a single nod of approval. At least we don't have to bust out a flint and steel, which I'm 100 percent certain Roy has on a key chain along with his house keys. *That* would be very 1861.

I wander into the woods and search by the light of my cell phone until I find a birch tree nestled among the oaks. I work the blade of my pocketknife beneath a strip of bark and slice a segment free, scavenging for twigs and sticks on my way back. Roy has rearranged the planks of wood to allow for better airflow and carved out a hollow suitable for kindling. I break the bark down the middle, scraping the fuzz of the inner lining into the gap. Someone contributes the cardboard from a six-pack of beer.

Without further ceremony, Roy lights the cardboard and the kindling. We lean closer on opposite ends of the pit, our breaths bringing the flames to life. In that moment, we are two shadows in perfect accord, four eyes gleaming in the night. Even though I can't see his face, I know he's pleased to be here. His contentment radiates like the revival of a long-smoldering coal.

A cheer erupts around us as the first planks catch and bathe the clearing in dancing orange flickers. Sydney raises Roy's arm in a victor's salute. "Always bring a Boy Scout to the party!" She slaps him on the back. "*Roy* Scout!"

I'm too busy laughing to bother correcting her.

A radio thumps to life, the music a feeling more than a sound. Couples interlace arms and sway to the bass line, adding percussion in the form of fizzing bottles and the clicks of caps whizzing into the forest. As smoke drifts across the crowd, they become fractals patterned around the witchy light of the fire, like planets to a sun.

Sydney shoves a red plastic cup into my hand and pours in a brown liquid that smells like caramel-flavored nail polish remover. I take a tentative sip. My tongue flops out of my mouth, my teeth bared in a repulsed snarl. "Nope. Nope."

She fills another cup with pop and offers it to me in between guzzling the contents of the first bottle. "Chug that and then chug this."

In a flash of unthinking compulsion, I empty both cups in quick succession, surprised by the sweetness of the aftertaste. "It's not bad with the pop right after," I admit.

Sydney takes that as a cue to refill my drinks before she goes flitting off to join a gaggle of people, presumably the top candidates for her prom date. I swallow another mouthful of booze, enjoying the fluid warmth trickling through my body like hot soup on a snow day.

I give a short wave to a few kids from Advanced Placement Physics, those rare hybrids who straddle the line between popularity and geekiness. They're huddled over a stump with a notebook and pen, apparently calculating the optimal trajectory for trying to jump over the fire. "Brock bet me fifty bucks that I can't make it without getting burned," Brian boasts when he sees me examining his subpar calculations. Maybe he shouldn't have slept through Ms. Garcia's lecture on projectile motion, though I doubt it included a variable for drunkenness.

"An ambulance costs five hundred dollars," I point out.

"YOU ONLY LIVE ONCE!" Sydney howls, tagging my back with her hand as she leaps into view. "Do it. Do it. Do it. Peer pressure." She leans closer to me, her breath ripe with the sour smell of cheap liquor. "What are we doing?" she attempts to whisper in my ear, though it comes out as a yell.

When I don't answer, she plants both hands onto Brian's shoulders and hops side to side behind him. "DO THE THING!"

Roy calls my name from beneath a nearby tree. His voice is disembodied, accompanied by an old pair of boots poking into a swath of moonlight. As I approach, his face emerges from the shadows, his cheeks reddening in shades like the shell of a crab under a slow boil.

Roy holding a beer does not compute in my brain. He throws his drink back in a single slurp, holding the can with both hands. "This is the best night ever," he slurs, giving me a sloppy kiss on the cheek as I sit beside him. "Beer and Becca."

"How many of those have you had?"

"Three." He giggles. "Maybe four. I've lost count."

"Roy, you should really slo—"

He shoves a bottle of hard lemonade into my hand and smacks a fresh can against it, shouting, "ROY SCOUT!"

Sydney hears his call and sprints over, her sheer black skirt billowing in the slight breeze. Silhouetted by the fire, she looks ethereal, an angel who smells like wood smoke and hair spray. She grabs Roy's arm and lifts it in the air again, beer overflowing onto their triumphant fists.

My heart swells in my chest at the sight of his unguarded smile, his infectious happiness over this morsel of freedom. Sydney gives me a reassuring pat on the head before dashing into the woods after one of her friends, their girlish shrieks blending with the laughter and the music and the stomping and the whisper of my breath. Here, I see only the true faces of my classmates, their pretentions washed away by booze and the anonymity of the night.

When they look back at me, am I still the daughter of a dying man, the product of years of brainwashing? I like to think that it's possible to transcend my past in these final weeks before we toss our caps onstage. Aside from the odd glance or timid smile, the other partiers outright ignore my presence. I am unnoteworthy tonight in a way that I have never been before.

I smooth Roy's hair and run my fingers along his jawline, feeling his heartbeat pounding beneath his skin. The touch between us is so familiar; it's the wanting that's new. "You're my best friend," he mutters. "Don't be mad at me."

I lie on the leaves beside him and think how impossible this would have been a year ago. Roy nuzzles his cheek against me and abandons his beer to snake an arm around my waist. I lean into his touch, finding comfort in the warmth and the closeness. "You must really like me if you'd rather snuggle instead of drink."

For just a moment, everything else fades away, until it's just the two of us, this tree, this feeling of contentedness that I've never known enough to want before. I tip my head down and search for Roy's lips in the darkness, smelling damp earth and the tang of alcohol. I've kissed him a thousand times for show, but this still feels different somehow. Instead of kissing because everyone's watching, now it's because they're not.

But then Roy sits back abruptly and digs the palms of his hands against his eyes. "I swear, I don't usually cry like this."

"What's wrong?" Oh God, I'm such a bad kisser that I've made the only boy I've ever kissed burst into tears.

"I'm just really happy. And really drunk." He hiccups and looks away. "Because you're about the only part of this horrible, shitty, goddamn awful life that I ever wanted to keep."

Suddenly, Brian Wendland sprints toward the fire and soars above the flames, his untied shoelaces dangling from his sneakers like fuses. In that moment of magnificent stupidity, I believe in the fallibility of doubt, just as Brian's feet touch solid ground.

17

IF MY PARENTS WEREN'T COMPLETELY USELESS, THEY MIGHT have imparted some adult wisdom onto their eldest daughter. For example, never drink milk with a hangover.

The high-pitched pinging of the doorbell yowls across my eardrums. I groan, clutching my sloshing stomach as I shuffle toward the foyer. The deliveryman is already climbing into his truck by the time I peel open the door with my eyes half closed against the punishing glare of the sun. A cardboard box totters on the edge of the porch, naked except for a shipping label slapped on one side. I drag it into the house and park it against the umbrella stand, because my house is lame enough to have an umbrella stand.

I snatch Mom's keys out of her purse and stab through the packing tape. The latest doomsday fad must be earthquake preparedness. I paw through packages of picture hooks and furniture straps rated to withstand seismic tremors. There's even a set of metal braces to bolt the hot-water heater to the wall. Darn. I really wanted to be the first person in Tin Peas to be crushed to death by a hot-water heater. I've always had aspirations of fame.

Katie rounds the corner and raises her eyebrows at the keys in my hand. "Can we go to the shoe store today?"

"Maybe," I reply, rubbing my bloodshot eyes. "Just give me a few minutes, okay?"

I return to my room and flop my feet through a wobbly field sobriety test. I can't drive in this condition. I won't even make it to the end of the street. Roy is probably hurting as much as I am and waking up Mom just isn't an option. It's safer to light a bear's fart on fire than it is to rouse a sleeping swing shift nurse.

I call Tamara without thinking. She answers on the first ring. "Hey, Becca," she says. "Everything okay?"

"Yeah, I'm fine. Katie needs new shoes and I don't want to wake up my mom. Can you drive us to the mall?"

She replies with a derisive snort. "Is this a joke?"

I sigh and amend my request to include a doomsday-appropriate location. "Can you drive us to a tactically defensible store that also happens to sell shoes for children?"

"I guess. Hang on." The sound of her unlocking her gun safe filters through the line. "I can be there in ten minutes."

"Thanks."

I'm never touching another drop of alcohol for the rest of my life. I run a brush through my hair, still unruly and tangled from going to bed without drying it after my shower. The waistband of my pants strangles my bloated midriff and my toes are swollen from stumbling back to the car in the dark, one arm around Roy and the other around Sydney. The drunk leading the drunker leading the drunkest.

Katie is waiting on the couch in her best outfit. She bounces up and down and checks her plastic wristwatch. "Are you ready yet? Can we go now?" We don't get out a lot.

"I'm feeling a little sick," I confess. "Tamara is giving us a ride."

In my earlier daze, I didn't notice the plastic bin by the back door or the wall stripped of our family's lone portrait. I pad across the carpet and lift the edge, recoiling as if a fist had reached out to strike me. Dad's clothes and shoes are jumbled in the bottom, the contents of his desk tossed on top. I scrape a nail over the lies I painted on the pale rock he used as a paperweight: *World's Best Dad.*

"You kept it," I whisper, lifting the rock I gave him for Father's Day and cradling it to my chest. Even though I was Katie's age when I made it, the words were more of a wish than a fact. I wanted the kind of father who deserved that rock. I still do.

I sprint to Mom's bedroom in an icy rage, the scabs on my knuckles cracking as I twist against the resistance of the knob. The blood seeps through the gaps between my fingers. I slam my palm against the white door, leaving behind a red smear of accusation. From within, I hear a faint groan. "We need to talk, *Mother.*" I glance at Katie waiting at the end of the hall. "I'll be back once I'm done doing your job for you, like always."

I pull Katie onto the porch by her sleeve, leaning against the railing until I regain control of my breathing. I jam the rock into my pocket, comforted by its presence for reasons that I don't fully understand.

After a few minutes, a white hatchback pulls into the driveway. Katie runs to the car and clambers into the back, watching me drag my useless body in after her. I steady myself on the roof rack and fall into the passenger seat with an audible thud.

Tamara pushes a button on the steering wheel and reverses onto the street. Katie and I jump in unison as the radio jolts to life with an eight-thousand-decibel blast of Mozart. I wince and rub my palm over my hair to confirm that there isn't actually a ballpeen hammer protruding from my skull. If I weren't in so much pain, I'd laugh. Only Tamara would listen to *classical* music loudly enough to make the vents rattle.

"I talked to your mom!" she shouts, her voice deafening as the song transitions to a softer sequence. I seize the opportunity to slap the volume dial into silence. "Since you're graduating this year, we had a meeting to discuss your future career."

That's a terrifying sentence.

"We need an electrician and a mechanic," she continues. "Talk to your mom about signing up for the electrician's apprenticeship exam. Roy's dad is signing him up for the mechanic program."

"What if I don't want to be an electrician?" I blurt out before the filter between my brain and my mouth can intercept the transmission. "What if I want to be a physicist?"

Tamara shrugs and reaches for the radio. "What if I want to be a princess?"

"Please leave the music off. Have mercy on my soul." My fingers dig into the corners of my eyes, then my temples. "I have a headache already. I'm dying here."

"Oh, right," she mutters. She gropes for her thermos and pries it free of the cup holder, passing it over to me as she whips onto the highway. "I think you need this more than I do."

I guzzle the coffee, ignoring the fact that it's akin to drinking acid, the heat scorching against the rawness of my throat. "My hero."

Tamara parks and escorts us to the front of the small shopping complex. "I'll stand watch out here." She pats the front of her waistband where her pistol is holstered. "Let me know if you see anyone suspicious already inside."

"Yeah, okay," I mutter.

Katie veers into the shoe store with a blip in her gait that might have been a skip of excitement. She ignores the brand-name sneakers and makes a beeline for the clearance section.

I meander through the aisles, pausing to examine the floor model for a pair of sandals that costs forty-five dollars. I don't even see the shoe, its delicate buckle and pastel beading. I see ground beef and fresh bread, electric bills and school supplies.

I find Katie crouched near the bottom of the shelf where a row of white boxes contains recent customer returns, their sizes and colors scribbled on the front in permanent marker. I stand out of her field of view, watching as she tries on a pair of neon shoes. She smiles and twirls in them until she sees the price. She looks both directions, her expression close to guilt as she stuffs them back in the box and chooses another pair from among the meager selection.

"Becca?" she calls.

I step around the corner. "I'm here. Did you find something you like?"

She nods and pushes the box into my hands. I glance at her mismatched socks and back at the shoes. "Are you sure these are going to fit you? They seem a little too big."

"I'll grow into them," Katie replies, flexing her toes against imaginary constraints. She bites her lip. "They're on sale. Is thirty dollars a lot of money?"

I suppress a sigh. "No, that's fine. Buy whatever you want, Katie Cat."

She hugs the box to her chest like a cherished stuffed animal and waddles across the store to the checkout counter. The girl behind the desk rings up the shoes and then scans a coupon from their circular that reduces the price by five dollars. I sigh with relief.

"Can we go visit Dad?" Katie asks as she plops onto the nearest bench to change into her new shoes. Her fingers wiggle through the loops of her laces. "Mom told me to forget about him because—"

"Love makes you reckless," I finish. "Let's talk for real, okay? If you still want to go see Dad after this, then I'll take you as soon as he's allowed to have visitors. I promise."

"Okay."

"Tell me your last memory of Grandpa."

She considers the past with a blank stoicism wholly unbecoming of a child. I can almost see the memories flicking through her mind like a filmstrip, her head nodding along with the scene changes. "He was in a hospital bed."

"And your last memory of Grandma."

"She was cooking ham in our kitchen." Her lips rise into a smile at the thought, then plunge into a frown. "No, wait. That's not the last time I saw her. She was in a hospital bed, too."

"What's your last memory of Dad?"

"He was leaving for work. He took me to Mrs. Hepworth's house to wait for the bus. He told me to be good."

I place my hand over hers, my thumb tracing circles on her skin. I know for a surety that no one, not even Dad, has ever loved this girl as much as I do. She didn't grow within my body or wail her first cries against my chest, but she is mine. "If we go to the hospital, I'm afraid that your last memory of Dad could be him in a hospital bed. Are you sure that you want to do that?"

Her chin wrinkles and quivers. A solitary tear wobbles on the edge of her eyelid. "I don't want him to be in a hospital bed at all. I want him to come home."

I pull her against me, rocking her gently and glaring at the cashier for daring to gape at us. "I know, baby. I know."

▲ ▲ ▲

A hooded figure waits on the bottom step of the porch when we return home. Tamara hesitates with the wheel halfway turned to steer us into the driveway. I crane forward in my seat and recognize the double-knotted boots and serpentine surgical scar winding down the side of one knee. "It's okay. That's Roy."

"Nice Grim Reaper costume," she mutters.

"I don't think the Grim Reaper wears shorts."

Tamara wags a finger in his direction. "When is that boy going to learn that you don't wear shorts with sweatshirts and you definitely don't wear boots with shorts?"

I can see the wheels grinding in her head already. Before long, we'll have an apocalyptic dress code. As if reading my mind, she grumbles that shorts expose your legs to ticks.

"Thanks for the ride."

She lays a firm hand on my arm to keep me from exiting. "You can return the favor once you're an electrician's apprentice. I really need someone to do periodic testing of Bunker Two's lighting. It's been on the fritz for months."

Maybe if I chew on the wires I can shock myself straight into another universe. My teeth gnash together as I storm past Roy and into the foyer.

When he follows, I whirl on him with unjustified annoyance. "What are you doing here?"

"Nothing. I just wanted to see you." My anger wilts at the sight of his gentle smile, the way he grazes the top of my shoulder with his fingertips in greeting. I wonder if he's thinking about last night.

"Sorry," I say, shaking my head, and then wincing at the motion. "I feel like dirt today and Tamara's been rambling about how I need to become an electrician."

His nose crinkles with distaste as he removes his boots and sits them on the shoe rack beside Katie's new sneakers. "Yeah. Mechanic for me. Because I'm too dumb to be an electrician, according to my dad."

"I heard."

He scowls at the crusty dishes overflowing the sink and the laundry swaying on the bars of the exercise bike. "Anything I can help you with?"

"You can do my science fair project for me," I joke. I haven't even bothered to mark it on the calendar in the kitchen, the one that still says February. A tri-paneled white poster board forms a lean-to against the wall beneath it.

He shrugs. "Okay. Have you started it yet?"

Before I can answer, Katie shuts the fridge and waves in our direction. Her scavenging can't have yielded much. She gnaws on the corner of a square of cheese. "I'm hungry."

"Um." I run through a mental list of our available groceries. "How about some buttered noodles?"

She crumples the rest of the cheese into her mouth and shrugs. "Whatever."

My eyes droop as I attempt to remain conscious and not fall face-first into the pot of boiling water. When I hand over her meal, Katie carries the bowl into the dining room without a word. Her bright eyes lift in a challenge, daring me to order her to the kid table in the kitchen.

"Use a place mat," I scold. "You're leaving heat rings on the wood."

I'm willing to permit her small act of defiance, but only because Roy is nearby, surveying my domesticity with a wry grin. Plus, if I treat her too much like a child, she'll find worse ways to try to prove that she's capable. She might be willing to sacrifice her childhood, but I'm not going to hand her the knife.

I turn my attention back to Roy. "What were we talking about?"

"The science fair."

"Right. Yeah, I haven't, uh, started it yet. I've been meaning to get around to it."

"Want some help?" he offers. He sounds almost eager about it. "I can make posters or do some research for you. Despite my excellent acting abilities, I'm not actually an idiot."

"I'll take any help I can get. School is killing me lately." When I move to retrieve my laptop from my bedroom, Roy remains rigid, his eyes tracing a straight line down to the floor. His expression is impassive, but the muscles of his cheeks flex and curve into two parentheses around the thin line of his mouth. "Actually, I kind of need to ask you something else, too, if that's cool."

"Sure." I linger with one foot poised to fall. "What's up?"

"Will you run away with me after graduation?" he blurts, his shoulders rising into a shrug as his hands fall to his sides, palms upraised. He shuffles his feet as the silence stretches into uncomfortableness. "Because you don't hate me anymore." He phrases it like a question. "Last night—"

"I remember." The chill in my voice could frost glass. Inviting Roy to the bonfire was a mistake. I didn't intend to give him the wrong impression. "Listen, just because I kissed you doesn't mean that I'm not standing by my decision. I'm staying in Tin Peas. Someone has to be responsible." I giggle, the phantom threat of hysteria threatening to overwhelm me. "My mother sure isn't going to do it. My father *definitely* isn't."

I don't blame him for it, though. A coma is a good excuse for being an absentee parent.

Roy glances toward the dining room where Katie is eating. Jealousy and resentment flash behind his dark eyes just long enough for me to detect.

"Do you know what I did today?" I snap, spinning around to snatch the collar of his shirt. "I spent my birthday money on new shoes for Katie. Hers haven't fit for weeks. My mother always says we don't have enough money. 'Not right now, Becca. We need *seismic-rated picture hooks*, Becca. You should get a job if you want luxuries, Becca.' Are you seriously asking me to leave my little sister alone with that frigid bitch?"

"We can send money home once we get settled. Maybe Mrs. Hepworth would agree to help."

"And what happens if we don't have any money?" This isn't a cutesy theoretical discussion that ordinary eighteen-year-old girls have with their ordinary eighteen-year-old boyfriends. We'll need a car and an apartment, not to mention furniture, food, and utilities. "If one of us gets sick or injured, we're screwed."

"You have free tuition and free housing," he reminds me. "You're not going to get a bigger break than that."

"First-year students are required to live on campus. You won't be allowed to live with me." I never thought I'd want to share a home with Roy, cooking dinner together and sleeping in the same bed, but it sounds safe—homey, even. It's amazing how much our shared history is a source of comfort now that I know he was always on my side.

I find that string of longing and wrench it from my heart like a loose thread from a sweater. It will not unravel me.

Roy shakes his head. "I already checked online. You can apply to live off-campus."

"Oh, I'm sure that conversation will go well. I'll just waltz in and explain that we're fleeing a community of heavily armed doomsday freaks, but they're probably not insane enough to storm the campus and demand my return. Probably."

"Might work," he offers, his voice hopeful. "It can't hurt to try, right?"

Roy's words are a river eroding my rock-solid resolve. "It can't be this year. Katie doesn't even shower without me nagging her. You can move out on your own. Maybe I'll be able to follow when she gets older."

"No," he spits through his teeth, grabbing my arms and dragging me closer. His dark eyes smolder with intensity and panic. "We go together or we don't go at all."

"I'm not leaving without Katie, and I can't take her with me until she's eighteen. The last thing I need is an interstate kidnapping charge." I swat away my tears, frustrated with their pointlessness. I've cried enough in the past month to make a sixth Great Lake. It hasn't changed a damn thing. "I'm not your keeper. Don't dump that responsibility on me."

"I'm in love with you," he chokes. "I'm not just saying that because it's what our parents want. I fell in love with you by accident, the way you're supposed to fall in love with someone. We'll take care of each other."

My chin rises in the air. I glare at him down the pinched slope of my nose, inherited from my perpetually sneering mother. "You don't even know me." I cling to those words, ignoring the gutting ache that takes root in my heart, the fear that maybe he does know me. And that would be even more terrible.

Roy is as still as a rabbit sensing a predator, his chest frozen halfway in between a breath. His exhale is a sigh. "I know that your favorite color is purple." He kisses my cheek. "I know that you keep the necklace I gave you in the front pouch of your backpack." He wraps his arms around my waist, pressing his hands into the small of my back to pull me against him. "I know that you sneak out of your house sometimes to take walks in the middle of the night." He bows his head against my collarbone.

"Okay, maybe you know a thing or two," I whisper in his ear.

"I know that you're ugly on the inside. I am too. It's the only way we survived living here. I love you because you're the only person who could ever love me back." He wraps one fist in my hair. "You have no idea how fucking angry I am, Becca. I want to burn this town to the ground. I will *kill these people* if they try to stop me from leaving. Come with me. Please."

I imagine our escape, sitting in a stolen truck as we speed out of his driveway in the dead of night, spilling gravel behind us like a line of bread crumbs that we will never follow home. But then I think of Katie darting through empty rooms, her voice shouting my name as she discovers that I'm gone. I'd miss the most formative years of her life, my love nothing more than a name on a check and a pair of thumbs behind a text message. "You make it sound so simple."

"It is that simple. We leave. The end."

"Right. Nothing terrible has ever happened because Stupid Girl ran off with Stupid Boy."

Roy flips my hair back from my face like a veil, his lips grazing mine and finding them as shuttered as my heart. "Leaving without you is worse than not leaving at all. Please, Rebecca." He nuzzles his nose against my neck. "Say something. I love you."

"I'm sorry." I can't help but wonder how long those words have been trapped inside him, like a fly caught between windowpanes. "I will never love you as much as my sister."

I kiss his cheek to ease the pain of tearing off his wings.

18

OVER THE NEXT FEW WEEKS, I SEARCH FOR A NEW RHYTHM
to help orient my life. Without Dad's routine naps and clock-
work demands for snacks, I feel off-pace and stilted, like a flip-
book animation without anyone around to turn the pages.

Mom is working extra shifts, so I don't even have scenarios at
predictable intervals to punctuate my evenings. I'm not complaining about that part, though. She sleeps during the day, leaving plenty of time for me to wallow in misery and contemplate
how much I hate myself for hurting Roy.

Those lengthy respites make it harder to focus when she
has the occasional night off. "Are you paying attention?"
Mom asks, impaling an orange on a kitchen knife and fling-
ing it across the dining room table. "Try a vertical mattress
suture."

I catch the orange before it rolls off the edge. The cut in its side is jagged and gaping, revealing the tender inner core. She isn't making this easy.

I reach for my suture kit and arrange my fingers through the grips of the needle driver. Katie is my assistant, picking up each item and asking, "What's this?"

Mom explains in an exasperated, condescending tone. I kick her in the shin with all of my strength. "I didn't realize your leg was there," I croon, as if her leg would be anywhere else but in front of her chair. "Sorry."

I sigh as I rub the needle driver over the peel of the orange. I can't shake the image of Dad on a steel operating table, the doctor's fingers curled around the same device as he sews my father together, like mending the battle scars of a child's beloved doll.

Katie grows bored after a few minutes, wiggling her butt in what I call the Antsy Pants Dance. When she was a toddler, she was never still, always crawling after a toy or climbing on the furniture. Even though I was only eleven years old at the time, I couldn't sleep when she graduated from her crib to a bed. I was terrified of waking to a loud thump in the night and finding her crumpled body on the floor. "Can I use your laptop?" she asks, her eyes drifting to its usual place on the coffee table.

"Go ahead." I don't want to know for what purpose. I'll check the browser history later.

When Mom and I are alone, I set down the half-stitched orange and eat the rest of it, careful to avoid the thread. If only every scenario included snacks. "What's up with all of Dad's stuff? It's been sitting in that box forever." Except for the rock I stole, but I doubt she's going to inspect my shoes for rogue paperweights anytime soon.

"I've been meaning to throw it away." She helps herself to a remaining sliver of orange, sucking it between her teeth. "He doesn't need it where he's going. It's just taking up space."

"You don't have to phrase it like that. You're talking about my dad."

"I don't believe in euphemisms. People don't 'pass away' or 'go to a better place.' Humans die the same way that bugs do. Life over. I don't understand why you want me to be one of *those* widows, always moping around and wailing. I'm not wearing black, either." She flips her golden hair over one shoulder. "It makes my skin look pasty."

I hold back a scathing comment about her crow's feet and the gray hiding in her bangs. Only she would be concerned about the fashionableness of mourning clothes. "It's like you don't even care about him. So, what, you just throw all of his stuff in the trash and forget that he ever existed?"

"I'm focused on the future," Mom replies. "He'd do the same, if our positions were reversed. We'll have to review our procedures. A lot of them reference work that he's supposed to do. You're probably strong enough to handle most of it. You're very, uh, you know, *sturdy*."

"And what does this glorious future look like?" I ask as I struggle to ignore the insult.

"For one, we're not burying another member of our family. We'll be ready from now on. For anything." She picks a crescent of dirt from beneath her fingernail. "On a practical level, I suppose I'll keep working and you'll train to become an electrician. Did Tamara talk to you about that? We had a meeting the other day to discuss you and Roy."

"Let me get this straight. I'm supposed to become an electrician and marry Roy and that's my entire life."

"In a nutshell," she replies, oblivious to my horror. "I'll still need you to babysit while you're completing the apprenticeship. We'll find you somewhere else to live once you get married."

Hell is starting to sound like a nice option.

In eight years, Katie could be sitting in this same rigid chair, one of its legs too short to quite reach the floor without tilting. Or maybe it's the world itself that's sloping beneath my feet as I imagine her stripped of choices, marching into my mother's version of her life because it's the only path left unblocked. Even if I stay and fight, I can't suck the poison from her mind like a snakebite, can't glue together the breaks that are already forming in her tiny sense of self.

"Speaking of which," Mom segues, excitement filtering into her voice, "I just finished negotiating a match for Katie."

"What?" I deadpan. "She's ten."

"I know, but it can't hurt to set them up early. I chose Elijah. He's the closest to her age from Bunker Two. I'm pulling her out of public school next year, so they'll get to spend more time together in homeschooling."

A sudden flash of movement in the reflection of the china cabinet catches my eye. I cock my head to the right and see the tip of Katie's nose extending past the door frame. It disappears as I scrape my chair back from the table and dart through the kitchen to stand behind her. "I don't know how much you heard, but—"

She cuts me off with a shove to the chest. "You only talk about important things when I'm not around! How would you like it if I talked about you behind your back all the time?"

"I didn't even know there was anything to talk about!"

I try to pull her into a hug, but she dips under my arm and rushes back into the dining room. In the dim light, I can barely discern the sheen of tears glistening on her cheeks. She stands by Mom's shoulder. "I don't want to marry Elijah. He's mean to me."

"Let me just talk to Mom, okay?"

"I don't want to!" Katie shouts.

Mom drops the tool in her hand and grabs a handful of Katie's hair, wrenching her head viciously to the side. "I don't care if you don't want to marry Elijah. I don't care if you don't want to have kids. You're going to do exactly what I had to do." She tosses Katie away. "I didn't get a choice and neither do you. End of story."

Not for the first time, I find myself pitying my mother for turning into this hateful, sour person who doesn't know how to do anything except hurt, and hurt, and hurt. I stare at her in profile, wondering whether the lapses and loopholes—her fashionable outfits that aren't technically against the rules—are just glimpses of who she might have been. "Maybe you could give her a couple of years to decide who she likes."

Mom slams both hands flat onto the table, upsetting the delicate instruments arranged on the tray. "There is a procedure to ensure the genetic viability of children if the world population is eliminated! She needs to know what her life is going to be like before she starts to get *ideas* about things."

"Are you listening to yourself? You really think that anyone can have a stable marriage based on *genetic viability at the end of the world*?"

"It's easy for you to be so lofty about it," Mom retorts. "You're marrying a Chinese kid with genes from the other side of the planet. You'll never have to worry that your great-granddaughter is accidentally shacking up with her cousin because the entire population comes from the same handful of families."

"Roy's not even Chinese. There are other countries besides China."

"Whatever."

I intercept Katie as she dashes into the hallway. She slams full-force into my body, crumpling against my stomach. "I miss Dad."

"Do you want to visit?" I ask, even though I refused to take her before. Maybe the best way to repair our relationship is to just give her what she wants. I miss the days when all she begged for was another hour of television. "I'll do it. Whenever you want, we can go."

"I don't want to go anymore," she says, her voice dropping to a hoarse whisper. "I want to help. I want you to teach me everything so that no one gets hurt again, but I don't want to marry Elijah!"

"We can't prepare for everything, Katie Cat. Dad was wearing his seat belt. It was a freak accident." I smooth the rough patches of her hair. "You don't have to marry Elijah. I won't let that happen to you."

"You're a liar." She runs to her room and shuts the door, leaving the faint click of the lock as the final word between us. I stand in the hallway with my fist half raised, but I don't knock. It won't help. She's closed her ears to me, and her heart.

I wander back into the dining room in a daze. "Are we done for tonight?"

Mom wears a smug smile as she toys with a crescent of orange peel. "You should be proud. Katie is much more invested than you were at her age. I'll have to start thinking of some simple training exercises." She stifles a yawn and points to the thin chain leash dangling from the hook in the entryway. "Take the dog for a walk and make sure my lunch is packed for tomorrow. I'm heading to bed."

Belle trots over at the word "walk," her tail thumping against the hardwood. When I stop to consider it, we're more alike than I'd care to admit. I sit, and stay, and wait for a kernel of happiness to break the monotony. With a resigned sigh, I buckle her harness and lead her outside.

The moment we step onto the porch, Belle lunges for a grazing rabbit. She reaches the end of her leash and snarls, her iridescent eyes shining with fury. I drag her down the driveway, pausing by the mailbox to consider our course. Part of me wants to turn right and follow the road to Sydney's house. She would listen, even if she didn't understand. Between her tattoos and piercings, odd clothing and combat boots, Sydney is the last person to cave to the pressures of convention. She wouldn't let someone else, least of all her parents, stuff her into a convenient career, a convenient life.

But I turn left, because I have always turned left on these miniature sojourns. I walk toe-to-heel along the seam where the curb slopes to meet the asphalt. A wooden signpost swims into view, blank except for a phone number and FOR SALE stuck on both sides in peeling vinyl letters. If I were a few years older, maybe this would be the home that I'd move into with Roy.

The lawn is tended with care and the exterior seems well kept, but location is everything, right? It isn't meant for an ordinary family, the kind of people who come with swing sets and yard sales. A buyer will bite eventually, rolling into our corner of Tin Peas with trailers full of equipment, like frontiersmen with covered wagons.

Once they unpack their equipment, then they'll unpack their stories. They were robbed and now they're too paranoid to live in a regular neighborhood. They're deathly afraid of wombats. They think that Wichita is going to be ground zero of a massive rabies outbreak and you would have left, too, if you knew what was good for you.

Or, worse, they'll be just like Roy's family, who showed up here for no discernible reason. There was no catastrophe that made them afraid, some supreme instance of bad luck that I can at least sympathize with. Instead, it was just the slow rot of knowing that *anything can happen, so you better watch your back.*

I remember the day Roy moved in and the entire community came together to help his family unpack. His belongings seemed so strange at the time. I remember holding a pair of soccer cleats and wondering what he intended to use them for.

Tamara is our real estate agent. She posts vacancies on the prepper boards, touting the benefits of our neighborhood defense plan, the mutual aid arrangements held between families. Walk-in closet. Solar generator. Original hardwood floors. Short-wave radio system.

As I stare through the darkened bay window, I know that my neighborhood will forever be a scar slashed across my skin. Even when I am old and withered, the memory of the forced stillness, the silence, will remain. It is the absolute quieting of life, a perpetual anticipation of the comet, the bomb, the plague, the answer to where we go next.

The apocalypse is supposed to be the literal destruction of the planet, an existential ignition point that renders us all down to bleached bones, fragments in space. I dispute that definition. The true end of the world, of *my* world, is losing the ones I love. I clutch Belle to my chest, hoping that if I just hold tight enough, I can ward away the hopelessness that burns through my veins like a slow-moving toxin.

I turn away from the house as a light drizzle begins to fall on the heels of the spring breeze. The damp air is a harkening of summer that used to mean late mornings snuggled in bed and board games with Katie in the afternoons. Now it signifies bobbling around in arc flash gear and learning about inductive circuits while Roy dives into engine components and oil changes. No matter how much I rail against it, change is coming. Only I can decide what that change will be.

Belle yelps as lightning ripples across the sky, its golden fingers reaching to ensnare the moon. I tuck her under my arm like a four-legged football, kicking the tips of my boots against the railroad tracks as we cross. Beneath the violent sky, the streetlamps are mock stars in the distance.

When we reach the gas station, I tie Belle's leash to the frame of a metal trash can out front, scanning the immediate area for signs of dog-snatching criminals. Aside from a tired-looking employee with a cigarette dangling from her lip and a couple of people fueling their cars, the parking lot is deserted. Belle is too loud to kidnap, anyway. I could say the same thing about Katie. "Stay, all right? I'll just be a minute."

She lifts her ears and whines. In dog language, that means, *Buy me a hot dog, if it isn't too much trouble.* Semantic cannibalism.

A bell jingles as I step inside the convenience store. I weave through the aisles, my fingers sliding along the glossy packages of gummy bears, the individually wrapped muffins that are more preservatives than food. The coffeepots gurgle like cauldrons beneath the windows, a half-burnt aroma wafting through the air. I pause in front of the ice cream dispenser with a paper cup dangling from the tip of my pinkie.

After a second thought, I trade the cup for a peanut butter and chocolate cone, piling on sprinkles and peanuts from the plastic containers nearby. The food warmers are empty except for a few shriveled hot dogs and a single piece of pizza wilting over the edge of the rack like a Salvador Dalí painting. I extract the least pathetic of the hot dogs and roll it in a napkin. The cashier only charges me a quarter for it. I think I overpaid.

I pull my jacket tighter around my chest, backpedaling through the door. Belle whines and pins her ears flat, finally barking when I don't toss over the hot dog.

"Yes," I mutter, tapping her head, "you're very ferocious."

I drop the hot dog onto the sidewalk as I perch on the edge of the curb with my feet on the storm grate. I peer down into the murkiness, the dim store lights reflecting on the water below. In that serene moment, I consider death, whether it's otherworldly light or all-encompassing darkness that will greet my father at the end. My thoughts are tainted by sorrow, a deep discontent that hovers over my head like a halo.

I trace the lines of my life, my heartstrings, until they fade into bleakness and doubt. There isn't a fortune-teller alive who could craft the truths I want to hear. I rub my palm, wishing it contained a future rather than a ridge of calluses above a handful of scars.

Suddenly, I remember the inscription on the necklace that Roy bought me for my birthday. "There are no shortcuts to anywhere worth going," I recite to the dog. She strains against her leash as she attempts to crawl into my lap. I fold her body against mine, tugging at tethers of my own. "I hate this place, Belle." I gesture to the cracked road weaving beyond the lot, its surface pocked with potholes. "Is that wrong? There are people who would kill to live here. I know that you're a dog and all, but I think even you can understand that we've got it made. We don't have to worry about war or being homeless or finding clean water. I'm so ungrateful."

She lifts a paw and scratches at my stomach as I drop fat, heavy tears onto her fur. I think about Dad, the crest and fall of his heartbeat on the hospital monitor, as tremulous as a clothesline whipping in a storm. He never asked for his fate, yet I blame him for it. That's proof enough that I can't expect Katie to forgive me if I toss her aside to clear my own path. In the end, it doesn't matter why we leave; it's the leaving that matters.

But I can't stay. I can't subsist on this life that is just life.

I chew the edges of my nails while ice cream melts down my arm in a cascade of rainbow sprinkles. I bite through the top of the swirl, a sharp pain stabbing through my teeth as the sugary cream melts across my tongue.

It tastes cold and sweet, but not like a memory, and it doesn't remind me of anyone at all.

19

ON THE WAY HOME, I FIND MYSELF WALKING ONTO ROY'S property, as though my feet have commandeered the ship without consulting the captain. I permit my body to take control, shutting down the inner voice that preaches of responsibility and convictions.

I tie Belle's leash around the nearest tree with a wide enough canopy to shield her from the rain. She curls into a ball and rests her head on her paws, eyes drooping. I sigh, wishing that I could be so easily placated, my worries erased by a full belly and a soft patch of grass.

I approach the shed and knock against the wooden doors. A chain rattles on the inside followed by the click of a padlock. Roy's head appears in the gap, his cheeks sallow, his eyes framed by shadows. He smooths back his hair and steps aside. "I didn't know you were coming," he says, illuminating his cell phone screen with his thumb to check for the call I never placed. "I would have cleaned."

I snort and kick over a pyramid of empty pop cans. They fall onto a heap of shoes, not to be confused with the heap of food wrappers beside it. "Yeah, right."

Roy pivots the space heater to blow in our direction as he relocates to the couch. Before I can sit, he stands again, consulting the shelf that appears to function as his pantry. "Do you want anything to drink? Eat?"

I run my tongue over my teeth, feeling the grainy film left behind by the sprinkles. I would love a can of Sprite, but one of my molars is already throbbing, and I'll rip it out of my mouth with pliers before I waste any money on a dentist. "Water, if you have it."

He tosses over a bottle and cracks open an energy drink. I steal his seat on the couch; he sits across from me in a metal folding chair, forearms balanced against his knees. "Are you okay?"

"I've been thinking." I sink lower into the sagging cushions. "Maybe you're right. It's time to leave."

"Really?" he breathes. "Did something change?"

"While I was sitting there sewing fruit," I say, grinning as Roy nods in understanding, "I had this thought that if no one ever leaves, how are these kids supposed to know that it's possible? Maybe we could get back in touch with them before they turn eighteen. We could offer to help them." The emptiness in my heart fills with that purpose, feeling the rightness of it. "If we stay, we just show them that giving up is the only option. I honestly think that's what happened to my mom. Maybe that's why she's so bitter about everything. I want Katie to have choices. I owe her that."

Even to my own ears, my words sound too adult, too calculating. If there are any remnants of a childhood within my memory, they've fallen through the crevices formed by years of purposeful forgetting. I feel cheated.

Roy opens his mouth and closes it again, perhaps sensing that my rant isn't quite over. "Our parents have our entire lives planned out. No one cares if we're happy as long as we're contributing." I dash a tear from my eye. "I thought about what you said, about dying if you stay here. I can't do it anymore, either. I can't just suck it up for decades and decades until I'm too old to do anything else except be an apocalyptic electrician."

Roy glowers at the ground, his hands clenching and unclenching in his lap. His features soften as he lifts his gaze, fixing me in place with an unwavering stare. "I just want you to know that I don't expect anything. If we leave." He clears his throat. "We don't have to stay together. It would just be easier in the beginning if there were two of us to pay the bills."

His reassurances cool the rage roiling in my blood. A future away from here, once a distant delusion, is now an insurmountable challenge looming before us. In spite of my posturing and denials, I'm afraid. I'm not only afraid of failure, but of what I will do to ensure our success. I will break laws, break *myself*, to see us leave this place for good.

PHYSICS PROBLEM: You're trapped in a tug-of-war match between your dream life and your sister's well-being. Your sister weighs 33 kg and exerts a force of guilt and obligation. Your acceptance letter weighs 0.028 kg and exerts a

force of fulfillment and success. Determine the
tension.

"We can't go until I know that Katie is safe," I say, squaring my
shoulders to exude the confidence I don't quite feel. "We have to
find a way to do that. Promise me."

"Promise."

I search his eyes for sincerity. "Once we figure out how to deal
with Katie, where are we going to get money?"

"Sell stuff," Roy says, pointing to the laptop tucked underneath
the table and the rescue ropes stuffed in colorful bags. "All of it."

I run through a mental inventory of my belongings and
their approximate worth. It won't make us rich, but it could be
enough if we subsist on bologna sandwiches and act like two
kids trained to survive off the absolute minimum. I can name
over a dozen edible plants, though I doubt that I'll find any of
them in the treeless streets of Pittsburgh.

"We should start stealing things from the bunkers." It's the
only option, and the least of what we deserve from this community. "I consider it compensation for years of babysitting
and chopping wood and doing laundry and cleaning rifles. My
parents act like I enjoy being Outdoor Adventure Cinderella. I
never saw a dime for any of that shit."

"No."

"No?"

Roy grimaces and wrings his hands until his joints crackle like
a line of Bubble Wrap. "We can't break any laws. It just gives
them an excuse to file charges, drag us back here." He stands
and crosses the small space in a single step, pausing before the

tube television that looks better suited for an archaeological exhibit than a source of entertainment. He sinks into a crouch and pokes his fingers into the built-in VCR to retrieve a bundle of papers.

"That hiding spot is epic."

"Thanks." His cheeks redden as he rises and spreads a series of maps and lists onto the table. I peer over his shoulder, angling the desk lamp to illuminate the research. "Carnegie Mellon," he explains, indicating a black star. He traces routes with the tip of a pen, pointing to red circles that mark cheap apartments and blue squares that stand for bus stops. "We can live anywhere in here and still have quick access to the school. None have credit checks. I've already talked to a few of the landlords. Lots of vacancies."

"With my housing scholarship, we won't have to worry about paying rent, but we'll still need to find jobs before our money runs out."

"Got it covered," Roy says, flipping over the map and producing a list of job openings. A few even sport smiley faces and exclamation points, the margins decorated like a schoolgirl's diary.

My heart sinks. The postings are for dishwashers and unskilled factory workers. I don't want Roy to sacrifice his dreams because he's too busy packing glass or scrubbing pots to finance mine. "You should apply to college. I know it's late, but maybe they have rolling admission at one of the community colleges."

"No way." He lifts his knuckles and skims my cheek, his eyes softening. "You need to focus on your degree first. Then mine. I already found a part-time position. Guy needs help making specialty fishing tackle. He told me to stop in for a trial after I sent him some pictures."

"Fly fishing?" I ask, knowing that Roy's flies are always the best when we practice making lures for our weeklong summer survival challenge. Mine end up looking like hair glued on goat food. His are lifelike and delicate, a perfect blend of colors and neutrals.

"Yeah, I'm pretty good at it by now."

"What do you want to be when you grow up, Roy Kang?"

"Teacher," he mumbles. "History teacher."

I kiss him. I kiss him to taste the hope that fills him like an eternal well. I kiss him as I imagine how much sooner we might have allied if I hadn't been so cruel, so sour, so isolated and determined to remain that way. Here, with my lips against his, I learn that a person can feel like home. "I'm sorry for everything," I say. "I was never fair to you. I never gave you a chance."

"I don't blame you. Our parents kind of forced us into this, huh?" He cradles my neck in one hand and tips my head back for another kiss. "It seems to be working out all right, though. I love you, Becca."

The guilt is a stone in my stomach. I care about Roy, and he's the muscles-and-tractors kind of handsome, but some element is missing, blocked by my staunch refusal to love anyone ever again. I love Katie and it has devastated me. I just want to be safe and free and my heart can't fight for so many wishes at once. "I'm sorry," I repeat. "I don't know what to say. I—"

"Stop," Roy interrupts, clamping a hand across my mouth to stifle the words. "You don't have to explain yourself, okay?"

I nip at his palm. "Okay."

Even as I deny it, I can sense the vulnerable newness of the connection braiding between us, its warmth like a long-sought spell. For me, to speak those three words is to drown a sprout and poison its roots. With the nurturing of time, our relationship will grow, but not now. I'm too messed up for right now, hardly capable of coping with the punishing pace of the present. But what else is there, if there isn't *now*?

Thankfully, Roy seems unfazed by the muddled emotions that squirm in a tangled ball within my chest. There's no tension in his shoulders, no trace of entitlement in his touch. He is patient and unrelenting, resilient and strong. We are two jagged stones smoothed by our shared trials. Together, we will weather many more. I wouldn't want anyone else by my side.

Maybe it's that thought that causes me to toss aside caution, forget my own hesitations, and blurt, "I might be falling in love with you, too." I've never felt this way before. I can't be sure that it's love, but I know that Roy and I are two sides of the same scarred coin, passed from hand to fist and taken at face value by everyone who holds us. We are the only ones who see each other as we truly are and as we wish to be. "If you ditch me for some ditzy airhead in Pittsburgh, I'm going to murder you."

"Declarations of love and death threats," he jokes. "How romantic."

As I hold his gaze, a sparkle of joy glimmers in his eyes, like light flooding a tomb. I used to think that this shed was just Roy's hangout spot, the grounded version of a child's treehouse. Now, I see that it's a sanctuary for his secrets, perhaps the only place that he can shed his shell. It isn't a man cave; it's a war room.

"What's all this?" I lift the edge of one of the papers on the table to reveal chemistry calculations for determining molarity. The next page is a history essay written on notebook paper in careful blue pen strokes. I shuffle the entire stack, finding everything from handouts on volleyball techniques to diagrams of the human anatomy. "What *is* this?"

"Homework," Roy replies.

I skim through a page of algebra problems and recognize them as the ones I finished for him on the bus all those weeks ago. "Why did you ask me to do your homework if you already knew how? These answers are correct."

"I couldn't let my parents know that I have more than two brain cells," he explains, tapping a finger against his temple. "I needed a crappy report card, but that doesn't mean I don't want to learn. I just had to play dumb. 'Roy dumb as caveman. Roy too dumb to use complete sentences. Roy too dumb to run away.'"

"No offense, but it was pretty convincing," I muse. "Not bad for a caveman, though I always thought you sounded more like Frankenstein."

He laughs, but the bitterness behind it twists my guts into a stopper knot. In the yellow light, he looks sickly and weak, nothing but skin stretched over sinew and bone. I remember the feel of Dad's hand when I visited the hospital, the way his body had retreated into itself. Here, staring at Roy in the silence, I realize that there are many different forms of dying.

20

IT'S NOT STALKING IF THE PERSON WANTS TO SEE YOU. AT
least that's what I tell myself as I hover outside the teachers'
lounge waiting for Ms. Garcia. I cup my hands around my face
and strain to see through the frosted glass window. Since her
first class isn't until later in the day, she comes here most mornings to eat her bagel and play games on her phone. If I listen
closely on my way to homeroom, it usually sounds like a space
battle. It's silent today.

The door whips open, the glass shaking in the frame as the
knob collides with the brick wall behind it. My gaze flicks from
two red sneakers up to a pair of black shorts, then the face of
Roy's father. He steps forward and fills the doorway with his
broad, disproportional shoulders. "What?" he snaps, his eyes
cold.

"Oh, um, hi." I blink away a wave of sudden panic, as though he can sense my escape plot like a scent. He and my mother are walking fortresses, impenetrable to hope or laughter or any of the beauty in this doomed, lovely world. "I just wanted to see Ms. Garcia."

"Well, she ain't here."

"Okay. Sorry." I press my chin to my chest in a nod as I back away, my steps soft on the slippery white tile. He regards me like a lazy predator, his head turning to follow my path. Even the thought of living beneath his thumb, of bearing the title *daughter-in-law*, is abhorrent.

I straighten my backpack on my shoulders and command my spine to follow suit. I'm not afraid of Mr. Kang. I don't have to be afraid of anyone anymore. I'm leaving.

Yet despite the comfort of my impending escape, I can't help but feel that I'm gaming the system, shirking some cosmic misery imparted on me for unknown reasons. I've never believed in providence, but I can't stomach the idea that Roy and I have suffered for nothing.

On second thought, that's absolute crap. None of this is part of a plan or some great hidden purpose. Everything that we've endured was caused by the selfishness of the people who raised us, who made us from their own flesh and then felt entitled to our lives. I wouldn't keep company with a leech just because it shared my blood.

After a few more minutes of meandering through the halls, I find Ms. Garcia in her classroom eating an onion bagel behind her desk. I say "behind" because she's kneeling on the floor like a carbohydrate-munching monk, a red felt-tip marker twirling around her thumb. She bows closer to the nearest exam and scribbles checkmarks in the margin at each stage in an equation. I pause at the line of papers spread before her and clear my throat. "Hi."

"I recognized you by your shoes," she replies.

"What does that mean?"

"Your shoes are always muddy." She jousts with her marker and pokes the cap against the sole of my sneaker. A few flakes of dried dirt fall to the floor. "The other kids are too obsessed with their shoes to walk around like that. You should hear how often I have to tell parents that physics and sandals do not mix."

I lift my foot, examine the bottom, and frown. I didn't realize I was the village foot slob. "If you're busy, I can come back later." I feel a little better when I notice that Ms. Garcia isn't wearing shoes at all. Her black loafers are hidden underneath her desk, the sides faded where she pushes to kick them off.

"No, it's fine." She scribbles faster. "I was caught up watching my shows last night and I didn't finish grading these tests for second period."

"I went to the teachers' lounge first," I explain, not sure if she's actually listening, "but no one was in there except for Mr. Kang."

She rolls her eyes and hoists herself into a standing position using the handle of a locked drawer, the one I assume contains her bottomless supply of energy drinks and canned espresso. "What an unpleasant human being. It must be something they learn in college. All coaches must be gruff, intolerable little snots. It's a rule."

"Mrs. Fletcher is nice," I offer.

"She never replaces the jug in the water cooler," Ms. Garcia grumbles, nose wrinkling. I've never seen this side of her before—the person capable of holding a grudge. I'm suddenly thankful that I didn't back out of the science fair. "Anyway, enough about those ignoramuses. Do you need something?"

I twist the hem of my shirt. "I got a full ride to Carnegie Mellon."

Ms. Garcia's mouth opens in a silent shriek of joy. She slides closer and drums an off-kilter beat against my shoulders, accompanied by the rapid stomping of her stockinged feet. "I am so proud of you!" She hesitates a moment and then throws her arms around me. I take a deep breath, inhaling the scent of citrus and cotton that has come to signify belongingness. "What are you majoring in?"

I blanch at the question, pained that she even felt the need to ask. "Physics."

"I just wanted to hear you say it," she squeals. "Is your family happy about it?"

"They don't know," I admit. "My mom wouldn't approve."

Her lips draw back into a thin line. "It's none of my business, but I understand that you have some special considerations at home."

"You were the only one who ever cared."

"Well . . ."

"I mean it," I mumble to my ratty sneakers. "Half the time, you were the only reason I wanted to come to school."

Ms. Garcia examines a stray cuticle beneath the lab lights strung above our heads. Her nails are painted with pink crackle polish. We remain in those exact positions, my head bent, hers raised, until I say, "If gym teachers are rude, then physicists are social rejects."

She bursts out laughing, and her relief is almost tangible. I manage a shy smile. "You know that I'm no good at this touchy-feely stuff." She smacks her palm against her forehead. "Almost forgot! I have a gift for you."

She hustles over to her desk and shoves aside the heaps of books and folders to find a crinkled foil gift bag with three reindeer on the front. "I know it's not Christmas, but I have a thousand Christmas gift bags and no plain ones. Sorry."

I reach into the folds of the tissue paper to discover a miniature stuffed dog wearing a plaid ribbon around its neck. The beady stare of its polished plastic eyes follow me no matter which way I turn it. "You bought me a dog." A possessed dog.

"Scotty!" she chastises. "The new CMU mascot!"

I swipe a finger at the dust clinging to the bag. "How long ago did you buy this?"

She shrugs. "I knew that you would get accepted. I picked it up while I was visiting Carnegie Mellon for my unspecified-year reunion. You're lucky the gremlins in my crawl space didn't eat it."

I shudder. The dog is horrifying enough without its body half eaten by mice and vermin. Its jaws are frozen in a spine-chilling snarl, its fur like spikey wisps of black wire. Maybe Scotty is supposed to be symbolic, a reminder that the future can eat me alive. "I'll bring him to college with me," I say. "I wish I could bring you, too."

Ms. Garcia scoffs and flaps her hand at me. "I love Carnegie Mellon, but I couldn't keep up with their coursework nowadays. When I was a student, we still used these old-fashioned gadgets called pencils and we didn't need any fancy-pants modeling programs to conduct experiments. I broke four ribs my freshman year because I fell while I was throwing paper airplanes off the roof of the Animal Science barn."

"Did you get in trouble?"

"No." She barks a laugh and runs a thumb over her rib cage. "The Animal Science professor came outside because he was worried that one of his cows was injured on account of the racket I was making." The bell rings and she jabs me in the side with her marker. "Enough reminiscing. I have papers to grade. Shoo!"

I turn around once I'm safely out of poking range. "Hey, Ms. Garcia?"

"Yeah?"

"Shouldn't you say 'Moo' instead?"

"I already regret telling you that story."

"I'm milking it for all it's worth."

"Go to class."

"I'll hoof over to homeroom as fast as I can."

"Puns are the lowest form of humor."

"I find them udder-ly hilarious."

▲▲▲

The levity of my conversation with Ms. Garcia ebbs as I confront the next task on my to-do list: e-mailing the Dean of Student Affairs. Contrary to my joking promise to Ms. Garcia, I have no intention of attending homeroom.

I pause outside the double doors of the library and rest my forehead against the cool bricks. All around me, the hallways are silent, the school nearly empty of students. Prom is tonight. Everyone else is primping and priming in downtown salons, gabbing with their manicurists about the color of their gowns and stretch limousines. Even in a small town like ours, there will be parties and celebrations until the sun peeks over the horizon, maybe after. Like every other special occasion, I haven't been invited.

I dig the heels of my palms into my eyes until static clouds my vision. I can't afford to be distracted by trivialities. Roy is counting on me to do this.

With a sigh, I push through the glass doors and approach the block of computer desks in the center of the room. Each blocky, ancient computer has a new flat-screen monitor and wireless mouse, the technological equivalent of gluing an antenna onto a trilobite and calling it modern.

I reel in the clipboard dangling from a length of twine at the corner of the nearby reference desk and pretend to sign in to a computer station. In reality, I draw a few smiley faces across the lines and turn the clipboard facedown against the fake wood paneling. The librarian is too busy reading celebrity gossip on her laptop to bother checking what I wrote. I'm not stupid enough to leave behind written evidence that I'm cutting class. Unless I attempt to hack a credit card company or research how to make a bottle rocket, the feeble Internet monitoring system shouldn't flag my account.

I sit at the desk farthest from prying eyes, my body scrunched behind the paper-thin partition as I access Carnegie Mellon's website. I scroll through the Residence Life pages, but there isn't a standardized form to apply for authorization to live in off-campus housing. They must not have many doomsday refugees in their incoming class.

Instead, I find the e-mail address for Kenneth Barton, the dean of student affairs, and open a new message. I type my contact information in the header, omitting a mailing address. It's painful to realize that I won't have one anymore. Until Roy and I settle in Pittsburgh, home is just a hope. I don't care if it's in a leaky basement apartment or a single room in the slums. It doesn't have to be fancy as long as it's ours.

With that in mind, I begin typing the most important letter of my life. I try to view each line from the dean's perspective, imagining how bizarre it will be to receive such an unusual request. I'll count myself lucky if he doesn't mistake it as spam and send it whizzing into his electronic trash can. The final product makes me sound desperate, but I *am* desperate, so I suppose that's accurate.

> Dean Barton,
>
> My name is Rebecca Marie Aldaine and I've been accepted to Carnegie Mellon for the upcoming fall semester. I'm aware that first-year students are required to live on campus, but I would like to apply for a waiver for nontraditional freshmen.
>
> I'm not sure how to put this, so I'll just say it. My family is part of a doomsday community, like the show on television, only with more brainwashing. You can contact my physics teacher, Ms. Eliza Garcia, at Tinker Peaks High School in Ohio if you want to verify that I'm telling the truth. I know how to pay bills and run a household. As you

can imagine, doomsday preppers are big on self-sufficiency.

My boyfriend and I intend to flee the state later this month, but I need to know that we'll be allowed to stay together in whatever housing we find in the city. We don't have enough money to live apart. If I can't live off-campus, then I can't attend college and I'll have to forfeit my scholarships. I won't leave him behind.

I just want to study physics. Please.

Sincerely,
Carnegie Mellon's least-traditional applicant,
Rebecca Aldaine

I read the e-mail at least a dozen times before I'm satisfied that it conveys both the absurdity and the direness of my situation. I wasn't bluffing when I said that I'm prepared to sacrifice my academic career if the dean refuses to grant his blessing. Now that I've sunk my teeth into the idea of starting over, I can't resign myself to stagnation. While dreaming of Carnegie Mellon has always been a source of tranquility, I am certain that there are many paths to peace. I will wring happiness from this world if it kills me.

Before I send the letter, I search the archives of the *Tinker Peaks Times* and attach the feature story that a bored journalist wrote about our community a few years ago. Though my neighbors declined to comment, my father is quoted as saying, "When you're sick and hungry and burned up by bombs, don't come knocking on my door. You don't get to act like I'm a whack job and then ask for my help."

The accompanying photograph depicts a tanned, stoop-shouldered man standing on the porch with his work-worn fingers curled around the barrel of a rifle. In the background, the curtains are stretched a few inches to the side, the only evidence that I was peeking through the window during the entire interview.

The day it was printed, I spent the afternoon talking to the social worker about my parents. She wanted to know if they were abusive, if they had ever hurt me with words or fists or the cumulative slights that sink into the psyche.

Maybe I shouldn't have lied.

Once my plea to Dean Barton is safely in cyberspace, I return to locker number fifty-seven for the first time in weeks, spinning the combination lock in lazy circles. The slotted door creaks open like a time capsule. I run a finger over the spines of my textbooks, laughing at how I've managed to limp my way through classes without them. By this point in the school year, there's more than enough apathy to go around. Now that we're accepted to colleges and the Advanced Placement exams are finished, my teachers are popping in DVDs and handing out optional homework just to maintain appearances.

In Physics, our current assignment is to build catapults out of Popsicle sticks, plastic spoons, and weaponized sugar cubes. Based on the exams from earlier, Ms. Garcia isn't cutting her General Physics students equal slack, so maybe building medieval contraptions is our reward for pretending to still care about high school. I'd bring mine home as a gift for Katie, but I'm afraid that

Mom will be inspired to commission a life-size equivalent. Still, I feel like I should leave behind a physical memento as a testament to our bond.

I'm stunned to realize that my locker doesn't contain any personal effects capable of fitting that bill. There isn't a magnetic mirror lined with photo-booth stickers or cutesy knickknacks from family vacations we never took. Part of me is petrified that Mom will prevent me from speaking to her and Katie won't even have a picture to keep my memory alive.

In a decade, will we recognize each other?

Will she still wear electric-blue shoes and eat candy corn by the handful?

Will she still need a sister?

As I shut the door, my eyes land on a thick, cream-colored business card poking out from the side of a textbook. I don't know why I didn't throw it away with the rest of the pamphlets the guidance counselor gave me. Maybe even then, I knew I'd need a pocket ace someday. I pry the card free and run my thumbnail over the embossed name: MELISSA TEAGUE, DISTRICT SOCIAL WORKER.

21

AT LUNCH, I'M SURPRISED TO FIND SYDNEY SITTING BY herself, the table forlorn without her usual assembly of boisterous compatriots. My hands are busy holding my tray, so I flap my elbows like a chicken to attract Roy's attention, jerking my chin in Sydney's direction. I've eaten lunch alone enough times to know that it's a particularly monotonous form of torture.

Roy crosses the room with deliberate steps, catching my arm and whispering, "Can we talk later? I wanted to chat earlier, but couldn't find you after homeroom."

"Sorry." I rub the skinny knob of his shoulder in apology. Up close, his skin is still waxy, his eyes rimmed by purple shadows. Even his spine seems curved beneath an invisible weight. "I skipped class to e-mail the dean."

"Sweet. Fingers crossed."

"My mom is working tonight. You should come over and we can brainstorm the next stages of the plan."

"If I'm not dead by then," Roy huffs, easing open a fist to reveal two caffeine pills. "I slept like shit like night. Lots to think about."

The mention of sleep almost has my legs collapsing as I reach the bench. Roy sits to my left and digs into a snack-size bag of nachos. I can't help but glance at his thin stomach, then the calorie count stamped on the label. Maybe not eating enough is another one of Roy's habits that I need to break.

"I'm surprised you're here today," I say to Sydney by way of greeting. "I thought the entire senior class was taking off for prom."

She glowers and draws her hair into a sloppy ponytail. "I have the last appointment before the salon closes. The principal said I can't miss any more days of school or I'm over the limit."

"That sucks."

"What about you guys? Extreme hoarders aren't allowed to go to prom?" She winks. I love how she mocks our lifestyle, never deigning to acknowledge our families' apocalyptic obsession. "Or are you both bounty hunters? I forget."

"Actually," I admit, "we are hoarders. We're superhoarders. We love *stuff* so much that we bury it in bunkers in the backyard."

She curls her arm around the lower half of her face, snickering into her elbow. She sobers when she sees my complete lack of amusement. "Oh, God, are you being serious? Do you really have a bunker in your backyard?"

"And security procedures," Roy adds. "Ones that say things like 'Don't tell kids at school that you have a bunker in your backyard.'"

"We also have a greenhouse, a small farm, a hydroelectric

generating system, three years' worth of rations, several dozen rifles, and enough ammunition to fill an Olympic-size swimming pool."

"Why do you need that many guns?"

"Shooting trespassers," Roy quips, slurping at a milk carton.

"You haven't actually killed anyone, though, right?"

Neither of us answers. I strangle the giggles forming in my chest before they can burst free. Roy's toes tap against the bridge of my foot in a silent laugh. I sandwich his boot in between my sneakers. Above the table, we remain unnaturally still, sipping at our beverages with cold, eerie expressions.

Sydney's eyes drift back and forth between us, her body rigid. The lace cuff of her sleeve is tangled in her earrings, but she doesn't seem to notice the awkward bend of her suspended arm. "Am I on camera?" She pivots to observe the cafeteria, her torso contorting with the movement. "Pre-prom prank?"

"Nope."

"So, like, all those boogeyman stories my parents told us about how you guys are psychopaths who eat human flesh and live underground and wear space suits as pajamas . . ."

I lean forward in an awkward half bow, my lungs close to exploding. "Welcome to being a doomsday prepper."

Roy sniffs at the burrito on my tray, spearing a piece of greasy meat with the tine of my fork. He holds it up to the industrial lights flickering overhead. "There's not enough human flesh in this, Becca. Doesn't taste home-cooked."

"Sometimes we add hair for extra crunch," I tell her, reaching across the table to release the snag before she rips her lobe in half. She flinches at the touch.

Sydney is as pale as a cooked chicken breast. Her chest swells with a shuddering breath, her nails clacking on the table as she drums her fingers against it with increasing speed. Behind me, the cafeteria is abandoned except for a few underclassmen and a pair of cafeteria workers hunched over the steel serving counter. It's the perfect atmosphere to complement the ominousness of this conversation. After another minute of tense silence, Roy reaches under the table and pinches my thigh.

"Just kidding!" I exclaim, throwing out my arms in a theatrical arc. "We *do* have all of that crap in our yards, but we're not cannibals. Don't you think you'd notice if a bunch of people randomly went missing?"

Sydney presses a trembling hand to her chest and leans backward until she's suspended in the air behind the bench. Her tongue sticks out toward the ceiling. "You totally got me." She rises and stabs an accusing finger in my direction. "You have a pretty sick poker face. You have a pretty sick *mind*."

"Sorry," I mumble. "I couldn't resist."

Now that her terror has subsided, Sydney looks prepared to pummel me with my own tray. "For the record, a lot of people have gone missing over the past year. There were, like, four joggers who went missing in Cleveland. The police never found all the bodies." She purses her lips and strokes her chin. "Sounds like cannibals to me. Yup, definitely cannibals."

A memory kindles in my mind like a long-dormant monster roused from sleep to rattle its cage. I fight to contain it, my teeth snapping together in a steel trap. It wriggles through until I can see my father sitting at the table reading the police beat in his slippers, his chestnut hair mussed and messy. His voice is a gravelly echo, now a foreign sound. *A young woman's body was found in Cleveland today . . . it could have been you.*

"My dad told me about that," I explain. "He used to read the police beat every night at dinner to warn me about all the horrific shit that could happen to me."

"That's completely insane."

"Ah, insanity," Roy remarks in between bites of burrito. "Our specialty."

"Like, hey, while you're enjoying your fried chicken, let's talk about serial killers." Sydney shakes her head. "Man, I am never complaining about my parents ever again. At least they shut up when it's clear that I'm not listening. Did you ever try changing the subject?"

My half-choked laugh is nothing more than a soft, strangled cough. "Honestly, sticking up for myself would have made it worse. My dad even blamed me for waking him up late the day of his accident." The guilt put itself to bed in my heart and made a home there among my hopes and my loves, twisting them until I couldn't see the truth around blinders of my own making. I see it now, as vividly as the truck that shattered steel and bone on a chill spring morning. "He'd blame me for dying if he wasn't so preoccupied with, you know, dying. It's the same thing at school. I let everyone think I'm a freak and a cannibal and a monster."

Roy presses his weight against my shoulder, a hand sliding down to grip my knee as if he senses that I need an anchor. Sydney inclines her head, her eyes glowing with an emotion bordering on pity. It's a look that I recognize.

"Poor doomsday girl," I say. "Crazy girl. Brainwashed girl. Minion. Fanatic. Pawn."

Sydney clears her throat and sighs through her nose, a faint whistle emitting from the hole of her piercing. "Hey, listen, I'm sorry. I was just messing around."

"Everyone is always yapping about how childhood should be full of wonder and magic and believing in the Tooth Fairy. They never think about kids like us. If a random lady burst into my house with dollar bills, a tiara made of teeth, and a wand, we'd shoot her."

Sydney clinks the beads of her bracelet together like a sterling silver Newton's cradle. "You'd be rich if you charged admission. People would totally pay fifty bucks to see a bunker. It's better than blowing eleven dollars on a movie ticket."

Suddenly, I turn to Roy, his arms jerking as my nails dig into his shoulders. My sadness and frustration vanish in an instant, replaced by manic inspiration. "I know what I want to do for my science fair project."

And I know how to save my sister in the process.

▲ ▲ ▲

I sprint down the hallway, whipping around corners on the way to the lobby. The soles of my shoes squeal against the tiles, the painted bricks gliding beneath my palms. Despite my speed, I take the longer route, blazing a course through the building like a heat-seeking missile. Shouts echo from the gymnasium and televisions flash through the open doorways of classrooms.

I slow to a walk as I approach the window at the front desk, rubbing my eyes with my knuckles until tears form at the corners. The secretary slides back the thin pane of glass and scowls at my straggly hair and splotchy cheeks. She makes a grand show of setting down her chicken salad sandwich. "Can I help you?"

"I lost my diary," I snivel, tilting my head in the direction of the locked closet to my right. My labored breaths become gasps of panic. I can feel the snot dribbling from my nose in torrents. "C-can I have the key to the Lost and F-found?"

On an ordinary day, she might have put more effort into discovering my true intentions. After all, I'm not exactly the journaling type. But with her chicken salad sandwich growing soggier by the minute and summer vacation looming, she plops a mayonnaise-streaked key onto the counter without further comment.

> **PHYSICS PROBLEM:** The door to the office is 400 m south of your location. If the secretary moves with a walking speed of 5 kph and leaves in three minutes to see what the hell you're doing, how long do you have to rob the Lost and Found?

I step inside the closet and behold the forgotten treasures of Tin Peas High School. The possessions closest to the door are more likely to be recent discoveries, so I shuffle to the rear, sorting through piles of discarded items that have lived in this trove for years. My moral compass may spin like a pinwheel when necessary, but I'm not taking anything that I think will be missed.

In a pink backpack, I find two glue sticks, a bottle of glittery clear-coat nail polish, and a black binder. The markers in the front pouch are ancient, too dry to leave more than a pathetic stripe as I test them on the skin of my forearm. A thin canvas satchel, obviously belonging to a teacher, contains paper clips and a sheaf of blue paper. A drawstring bag that smells like musk and unwashed feet yields a pair of scissors.

I sling my own backpack to the ground and stuff the supplies inside. Though the materials are a bit rudimentary, I'll make them work. Survivalist mentality isn't just roughing it in the mountains and hoarding supplies like a demented dragon; it's about conquering obstacles and finding creative solutions. I hoist my pilfered prizes onto one shoulder, standing taller despite the weight. I'm going to win this science fair with a budget of zero.

I might be broke, but I'm not broken yet.

Next, I return the key and barge into the staff lounge, upsetting the gaggle of teachers enjoying their break. Ms. Garcia stands immediately, sensing that I'm here for her. She sets her sandwich onto a strip of tinfoil. "Do you have a minute?" I ask.

"Sure."

"Sorry, I didn't know any other time you'd be free today."

She follows me out of the lounge and into the empty theater across the hallway. I take a seat in the front row, far enough from the door to shield us from any prying eyes. "You look upset," she observes. "Are you okay?"

"No." I run a hand through my hair, but it doesn't alleviate the pressure building against my temples. "I'm not okay. I need your help."

She nods, watching me with the intense focus she wields while solving a complex calculation. "Tell me what I can do."

I take a deep breath and pass her a cream-colored business

card, its edges worn from being stuffed in my pocket. "I found this in my locker and it got me thinking. I have to ask you for a favor." I shake my head at the cheapness of the word. "No, it's so much more than a favor. I don't—"

She rests her hand over mine and squeezes. "Whatever it is, you can tell me."

"I'm trying to find a way to prove to Child Protective Services that it's not safe for my sister to live in our community anymore. But she doesn't have anywhere else to go and I don't want her to be in foster care. I guess I just thought, you know, because your daughter is friends with her . . . that maybe . . ."

Ms. Garcia knocks the armrest out of the way and pulls me into a hug. When I try to back up to avoid crying onto her shirt, she doesn't let me budge an inch. Soon, I'm sobbing too hard to say a single word, but maybe I don't need to say anything else at all.

22

THAT NIGHT, I SCROUNGE TOGETHER A HALFWAY DECENT
meal by raiding the deep freezer in the garage and plucking a
few carrots from the community's greenhouse. The venison is
chewy and long past its prime, but Katie doesn't complain. I set
a place for Roy at the head of the table, his food growing cold as
he wrestles in the living room with Belle.

If there was flour in the pantry, I would have made dessert, too,
anything to distract me from the constant temptation to check
my e-mail again. I wasted so much time deciding to leave that I
didn't consider college deadlines. Today is National Decision Day.
If I don't hear back from Dean Barton by midnight, I'll have to
enroll without knowing for a surety that he'll allow me to use my
housing scholarship for a private apartment. Maybe I can pester
him enough over the summer to convince him to agree. I'd chain
myself to the wheel of his car if I thought it would help.

I flip my fork and stab it into my steak. Through the open doorway, I watch as Roy headbutts Belle like a triceratops and then crawls around the floor making high-pitched barking noises. "Would you come eat dinner already?"

"Belle won't let me," he grunts, his body transformed into a trampoline as Belle leaps onto his stomach. "Need to get a dog of our own when we mo—"

Silence falls like a guillotine.

I drag my eyes over to Katie. She hunches lower over her plate, her fingers tapping at my phone as she plays through another round of chess. Dad always insisted it would help us learn to maneuver against armed opponents, as though winning Monopoly makes you a Wall Street banker or sinking battleships is realistic practice for naval warfare. I wave my hand in the air to see how absorbed she is in the game. She doesn't move. I'm not even sure she's breathing.

Roy shields his face with Belle's body and peeks at me from around her leg. The ends of his mouth warp into an uneasy frown.

"You know the phrase 'stick your foot in your mouth'?" I ask.

He nods, wincing. "Yeah?"

"I'm going to stick my foot somewhere else if you don't eat dinner right now."

Roy deposits Belle onto the couch and joins us. His black shirt is covered in goopy strings of dog drool. "Sorry," he says, either for delaying his meal or for almost ruining the secrecy of our plan. He's lucky that my sister has selective hearing and she selects not to hear the vast majority of the time.

Suddenly, my phone explodes into a cacophony of bells and

drums, the specialized ring I set to alert me if a new e-mail arrived in my in-box. It better not be a Gander Mountain coupon.

Katie's hands shoot into the air. "What is that? I didn't do it!"

I snatch the phone and navigate to my messages. My heart drops to my feet when I read the first line.

> Ms. Aldaine,
>
> As you can see on our website, the appropriate contact for housing issues is the Student Housing office.

But then . . .

> However, I understand the uniqueness of your situation. Your request for off-campus housing has been approved on a tentative basis pending the receipt of your spring semester grades. If you fail to maintain acceptable academic progress, permission may be rescinded. Please see the forms below and return to the Student Housing office at your earliest convenience. Good luck.
>
> Best,
> Kenneth Barton
> Dean of Student Affairs

I send the phone whizzing to the head of the table. Every nerve in my body crackles with giddiness and excitement. Roy taps the screen and reads the e-mail, his eyes and his mouth opening wider in simultaneous shock. Without any explanation to Katie, we ditch her and bolt for my bedroom.

I almost break the lid of my laptop in my eagerness to complete the forms and accept my position in Carnegie Mellon's incoming class. My fingers fly over the keyboard as I type in the relevant data, thankful beyond words that my scholarship package included a waiver for the thousand dollars in enrollment fees. Still, reading the paperwork takes over an hour, never mind actually filling it out.

When I finish the final questionnaire, Roy points to the due date on the bottom of the screen. "You really waited until the last minute, huh?"

"Kind of?"

I hover the mouse over the button to submit my completed admissions package.

"It's not a nuclear launch button," Roy says after a minute passes, then two. He squeezes my shoulder, either as a comfort or to prevent me from running away. "Go ahead. Push it."

I almost lash out at him for pressuring me, but then I see the sweat beaded on his forehead, the slight tremble of his lower lip. I uncurl my index finger and stab it against the key before I can change my mind. The screen reloads and declares that my admissions package has been officially registered. "It's done." I feel so many emotions at once that it's almost the same as feeling nothing. "I can't believe it."

Roy wraps his arms around my waist and smothers my cheek in featherlight kisses. He chuckles. "Are you ready to be a freshman again?"

"Let's not talk about that."

The clock in the living room chimes eight o'clock, a reminder that I still have responsibilities, at least for now. I remove the batteries from the television remote, hide my laptop cord, and force Katie to change into her pajamas. She crawls into bed after our usual ritual of discussing the value of dental hygiene. Flossing the teeth of an unwilling ten-year-old is like trying to feed finger food to a tiny, enraged shark.

I pause by the light switch, noticing how naked Katie's walls seem without her superhero posters, carefully divided between DC and Marvel on either side of her closet. "Do you want to read a comic book before you go to sleep? I'll let you stay up another fifteen minutes."

"I threw them away." She smacks her pillow, stripped of its Wonder Woman case, on top of her head. "They're for little kids. Mom says that she's going to teach me to shoot a gun and then I don't need a superhero."

"You're too young to shoot a gun."

"Mom says that I shouldn't listen to you."

I storm out of her room and into mine, where Roy is busy pretending that he couldn't hear our spat through the paper-thin walls. "I have to get out of this house before I lose my mind." I turn my head to the side. "Is there brain matter leaking out of my ear?"

He points at the supplies scattered around the floor, rolling a marker beneath the arch of his foot. "You can't waste too much time. The science fair is in less than a week."

"Then let's go to your house and work on it. Katie will call me if anything is wrong."

"Too risky. My parents might be awake."

I gather as many supplies as I can carry and march into the hallway, through the living room, and straight out the back door. Roy jogs to catch up. "I'm going to the bunker," I explain before he can ask. "I know it smells funny, but it's quiet."

When we reach the entrance, I open the hatch and toss the smaller supplies inside. They plunk against the concrete like pebbles tossed into a dark pool. I shimmy down the hatch and reach up to grab the poster board from Roy. As he descends, I whip my hand through a few automatic motions at the control station to turn on the interior lighting systems.

We settle into two chairs at the metal desk bolted to the wall. Once I explain my plan for the layout, Roy wastes no time cutting blue paper to frame the photographs, diagrams, and snippets of text that I've already compiled. I paste the completed sections onto the poster board, painting the borders with the glittery clear-coat polish for extra sparkle.

After thirty minutes of work, plus the hours I spent on the project before dinner, my presentation is still plain and boring. "I know I have handouts for the judges, but I wish I had a model for the judges to manipulate. They love that kind of crap."

Roy brightens at the idea. "I'll make one for you this weekend," he promises. "Already have wire and a barrel of scrap metal."

Maybe our community's chronic inability to throw away trash is actually a boon in disguise. One man's trash is another man's science fair project. "Really? Thanks. That would be awesome."

I'm so excited about the model that it almost excuses the fact that I'm missing prom right now. I'm not a huge fan of crowds or most of my classmates in general, but prom is a rite of passage, one that I'll never have the opportunity to participate in again.

"What's wrong?" Roy garbles around the glue stick lodged between his teeth. I don't think he'd do that if he knew that I fished it out of a stranger's backpack in the Lost and Found.

"Everyone else is going to prom tonight and we're stuck down here doing arts and crafts. I just want one normal thing, you know? One normal thing to happen before we go."

"We could have our own mini prom down here," he suggests.

"Apocalypse prom," I scoff. "Sounds like a cheesy horror movie."

Without another word, Roy latches on to my shoulders and steers me into the makeshift bathroom, drawing the shower curtain partition between us. "Don't move. Ten minutes." When I start to protest, he glowers with such intensity that I recoil, plopping onto the antibacterial shower mat hard enough to rattle my teeth.

As far as bathrooms go, I guess there are worse ones to be sequestered in for solitary confinement. Not only is it seldom used, but it's cleaner than a quarantine center, mostly because an illness in an underground bunker is guaranteed to bounce between people like a viral ping-pong ball. What's worse than being buried alive at the end of the world? Being buried alive and having pink eye at the end of the world.

From beyond the curtain, I hear gratuitous amounts of banging and cursing, followed by a series of metallic thumps that might be chair legs striking the floor. At one point, the hatch opens, then locks back into place a few moments later. I rise to my feet, wondering if hiding me in the bathroom was Roy's inelegant way of stating that he wanted to go home. "Hello?" I shout.

"It hasn't been ten minutes yet!"

Well, at least he's still here.

Finally, with both of Roy's hands covering my eyes, he leads me back into the main living area. My eyelids flutter open. Chains of white printer paper slope from the ceiling like garlands. On the concrete floor, cans are arranged in the shape of hearts and stars, their labels covered by red cohesive bandages. Miniature origami animals assemble in a menagerie at the center of the desk, a pair of upturned flashlights serving as candlesticks. Our plates are circular chunks of cardboard. A pouch of freeze-dried cookies sits on top of each.

"Best I could do," Roy whispers, his voice washed away by the tinny techno emitting from his phone. He stumbles into an awkward bow and I notice the clump of muddy weeds taped to the front of his shirt. He slides a matching paper cuff adorned with glue-soaked leaves over my wrist. "Will you dance with me?"

The bass thrums to life as I take his proffered hand. Neither of us moves for a moment. I can't think of any way to dance to this music that won't make me look like an idiot. I clear the strands of hair from Roy's face, like searching for the eyes of an especially shaggy dog. When he smiles, I realize that it doesn't matter. No one is watching us tonight.

I spin away from him in a ballroom twirl, then we both launch into a graceless, head-bouncing flail to the beat of the music. Between the dimness and the speed of our movements, it's impossible to see my surroundings with any clarity. Unfortunately, the bunker just isn't wide enough to accommodate two uncoordinated goofballs at the same time. We knock over a suction-sealed container of linens attempting the tango and Roy almost breaks his elbow against a shelf while flapping through a hyperactive version of the Macarena.

Next, the music shifts into an upbeat pop melody. A singer I don't recognize wails about boys and broken hearts and the many other things that I, as a teenage girl, wish were my biggest problems. I snort, noting that Roy's Internet won't work in the bunker, so he must have had this song already downloaded on his phone. "I can't believe you like these corny love songs. I bet everyone at prom is listening to this exact same song and gyrating or rubbing butts or whatever it is people do at school dances."

"Like this?" Roy squats and shakes his butt in my direction, hopping backward like a demented rabbit. I retreat around the side of the desk, but he follows, bumping into my legs and sending me tumbling. I fall into a heap at his feet, laughing despite the pain pulsing through my knees. "Who are you and what have you done with the real Roy?"

He snakes his arm around my back and lifts me from the ground. "I've been here all along," he mumbles against my lips. Warmth floods my body as he steps closer, pressing his palms against the small of my back.

On an impulse, I lift the hem of his T-shirt and attempt to undress him, but the sleeves catch underneath his armpits and the middle smothers his face like a hood. My cheeks are still burning when he manages to free himself. "Smooth," he says, chuckling.

I hold out his now-wrinkled shirt. "Sorry."

He takes the shirt and launches it onto the desk, kissing me hard enough that my eyes close of their own accord. Our feet shuffle in time as we engage in a new kind of dance, moving as one across the bunker.

As I scooch onto the bed, I slap the closest set of switches, plunging the bunker into darkness. The springs of the upper bunk creak in protest as Roy's shoulders smash into them. He scrambles into the gap between my torso and the wall, hauling my body over his in a pathetic attempt to make a twin mattress sizeable enough for two people.

He kisses a line from my mouth to my navel and I squeal several octaves higher than my normal speaking voice. "Roy!" I bop his forehead with the heel of my palm. "I'm ticklish! You're killing me!"

He curves his fingers into claws and digs them into my sides. I twist and buck in the sheets, not exactly the kind of breathless writhing I was imagining when I dragged him over to the bed. When I'm too winded to continue my pleas, Roy relents, settling into a plank over my body and kissing me again. If he didn't stop when he did, that kiss would have become CPR.

I run my fingers across the muscles of his back, memorizing each curve and scar that scrapes beneath my nails like a code. "Is it okay if I take this off?" Roy asks, tugging on the first button of my blouse.

"Yeah," I reply, trying to sound more confident than I feel.

I shake my arms free of the sleeves and toss it on the floor by my shoes. Roy rubs his hands down my rib cage, across my back. "Your skin is so soft."

"I can't tell if that's really nice or really creepy."

He huffs a laugh against my collarbone. "I guess it is a little creepy to be commenting about your skin while we're locked underground in a secret doomsday bunker."

I can't resist the urge to fold my arms across my chest. "So, listen. No one has ever, like, seen me naked before. I've never even kissed another boy, someone who might have told me that my boobs are misshapen or my nipples are weird before they're, like, out there."

"Becca," Roy whispers, smoothing down my hair. "I promise that I will always love you, even if you have misshapen alien nipples that look like the state of Texas."

We lock eyes and burst into uncontrollable giggles. I don't feel so shy anymore. I reach for his waistband, just skimming my fingers along the edge.

"Actually," he says, growing serious and pulling away. "Hang on for a second. Stop."

He flounders for the closest light switch, his dark eyes blinking against the sudden brightness.

"What's up?" I ask.

"I don't want to do this with you."

My mouth falls open in a ring of horror, petrified that I've somehow guilted him into going this far. I sputter an apology and flip the edge of the blanket over my chest.

"Sorry. That came out wrong." He grabs my hand and crushes it into a fist, resting his chin on top to meet my gaze. "I want to, you know, do this, with you. I just don't want it to be here. Now. In this place. I don't want anything to happen that's worth remembering." He touches his free hand to the steel wall behind my head. "When we leave, we need to forget all of it. They don't get to keep any part of us here, even our memories."

23

IN THE MORNING, INSTEAD OF ROLLING OUT OF BED AND
throwing on a random mix of clothing, I spend an inordinate amount of time perfecting my appearance. I scrub my
callused feet in the shower and pick the dirt from beneath
my chipped fingernails. My legs are smooth from a fresh coat
of lotion when I slide Mom's dress over my body, buckling
the thin bronze belt around my waist. The sheer fabric is foreign to my skin, like wearing an oversize coral-colored doily.
I even manage to flat-iron my hair without singeing the tips
of my ears.

I hobble into the kitchen in a pair of beige peep-toe wedges.
Pain lances through my joints at the awkward angle, my lower
back cramping with the effort of remaining upright. Newborn
giraffes have more grace than this.

"You look like a girl," Katie observes.

"I am a girl."

She flops her hand in the air, bent at the wrist, and shakes her head both ways to toss out her hair. I smile as she continues her impression, prancing throughout the room and striking dramatic poses for invisible cameras. "A *girly* girl."

While her reaction to my clothes is a little over the top, I'm glad that I've done at least one thing right. I gobble a few handfuls of cereal from the box on top of the fridge and call it breakfast. "Hey, I need you to go to Mrs. Hepworth's house for a few hours. I'm going out with Roy."

"I don't want to," Katie says, pouting.

"Well . . ." I grab her before she can run away and march her to the front door. "Too bad."

She digs both of her bare heels against the baseplate. I hold her with one arm and toss her shoes onto the porch with the other. "Can't I come with you?" she whines.

"No. And you're not old enough to stay home alone while Mom's sleeping. Come on. Maybe Mrs. Hepworth will let you feed the goat."

"I said I don't want to!"

Nothing is ever easy with this girl. I toss her over my shoulder, almost dropping her on her head as I crouch to pick up her sneakers. My thighs quake and burn as I return to a standing position and carry her across the yard. Either she's getting heavier or I'm out of shape.

Katie is still punching my spine and screaming bloody murder as I ring the bell with my elbow. Mr. Hepworth opens the door wearing a set of flannel pajamas, his eyes crusted with sleep. "Delivery," I deadpan.

"Oh." He retreats into the living room. "Iris? Iris! George's kids are here!"

Mrs. Hepworth doesn't seem perturbed by the fact that I have a howling ten-year-old dangling from my body. She's used to it. "Katie! I haven't seen you in ages. Do you want to make pancakes?"

Smart woman. Lure the child with food. "Do you have chocolate chips?" Katie asks. "Can I feed some to the goat?"

Sensing the shift in her attitude, I deposit her on the carpet and set her shoes on the tile. I hug Mrs. Hepworth and pass Mr. Hepworth twenty bucks. He flattens the bill, nods, and disappears into the hallway. "I'm sorry I can't afford any more," I whisper to Mrs. Hepworth, staring at my upturned palms like they might suddenly fill with gold. "I'll hurry back as fast as I can."

She shakes her head, her horn-rimmed glasses swaying from a thin chain around her neck. "Take your time."

I glance at the gargantuan clock hanging beneath the vaulted ceiling of her living room. Time. I could use a little more of that.

▲ ▲ ▲

I scream when Roy opens the door to the shed.

His hair is gelled into rock-hard black icicles jutting around the sharp planes of his nose. The tips intersect with the beginnings of a mustache, which, upon closer examination, is colored in with copious amounts of eyeliner. "That bad?" he asks.

"Yes." I scowl at his all-black clothes, his shirt streaked with mud and speckled with orange bleach stains. The only source of color is a Tin Peas Trucking hat made of red-and-white mesh and the pair of wraparound sunglasses perched on its brim. "When we agreed to use disguises, I didn't realize you were dressing up as a hillbilly heavy-metal singer." I twirl in place, my skirt fanning into a wide circle. "What about me? How do I look?"

Roy smiles as his eyes dissect my outfit. "Bucket," he says, pointing at the white painting pail in the corner.

"I look like a bucket."

He crosses the room and picks it up, holding it below his chin. "Need a bucket for my drool. Caveman, remember?"

"I'll take that as a compliment," I say, finishing with a dramatic curtsy, almost breaking my ankle as I remember that I'm wearing wedges instead of sneakers. "Just don't whack me over the head with a club and drag me back to your cave by my hair."

"No promises," Roy says, jingling the keys to his dad's SUV. "I'll be right back."

I wait in the shade while he reverses into the blind spot created by the barn a few yards away. We load our supplies as fast as we can, emptying the built-in shelves of anything remotely valuable. I break into a fit of fake sneezes to conceal the sound of the hatch closing.

Roy stomps the gas and we lurch down the driveway, the tires squealing as we turn onto the open road. He fumbles through another shift and pats the dashboard in apology. "Sorry. I'm a little rusty. I haven't driven in a while."

"How'd you get the car?" I pull down the visor and adjust my sunglasses around the edges of the ridiculous, floppy sun hat I'm wearing.

"Um." He clamps his lips closed.

"Roy . . ."

"I might have told my parents that we're getting you sized for a wedding ring."

"What!" I punch him in the shoulder, hard, and the car jerks into the other lane, narrowly avoiding an unsuspecting pickup. The blare of the horn sends the birds screeching from their branches. "You did what!"

"I didn't almost get us hit head-on by a truck," he grumbles.

I recline my seat and pick at the sagging liner of the ceiling. "Statistically speaking, it has to be almost impossible for two members of the same family to get hit by two different trucks in such a short time period."

"Some guy in New York won the lottery two times on scratch-off tickets from the same store."

"How do you know this crap?"

"The Internet."

Unlike most of my fellow teenagers, I wouldn't mind a world without the Internet. When I checked my browsing history last night, it was full of conspiracy websites and links to sensational stories about children killed by ordinary household items. If Katie keeps reading that garbage, she's going to be afraid of socks and can openers.

For the remainder of the journey, I alternate between glowering at Roy and contemplating a future in which he could be my husband. I mentally list the traditional trappings of a desirable spouse: stable job, hot body, good sense of humor, hot body, nice personality, hot body.

My requirements are a little unorthodox by comparison. I sneak a look at Roy in my peripheral vision. Girls don't titter and faint when they see him, but they never danced with him to a love song or lit a fire together beneath the open stars. He will never shy from the scars of my past. Ours is a love forged in silence and measured in dreams.

"Rebecca Kang."

Roy misses the next gear and huffs with such force that matted pieces of his hair fan out in a crown of spikes. He lifts my hand and skims a kiss against it. "Maybe."

It sounds like an oath. "Maybe," I agree.

Neither of us speaks as we travel the remaining distance to the Tri-City Flea Market. It's peaceful not to fill the air with hollow words, to share in the tranquility we can never find at home. There, if it isn't lectures from our parents or the clamor of a scenario, it's the noise in our minds, the internal screams that last from our first waking moments until we anesthetize ourselves with sleep.

Eventually, a sign appears over the horizon, touting the wares of the vendors:

E-L-C-T-R-N-I-C-S,

F-U-R-N-T-U-R,

C-M-P-I-N-G

I nudge Roy. "While we're here, do you think we should pick up some FURRNNNTURRR?"

"Definitely need some ELCTRRRNNNICCS."

I shake my head. "It's like Scrabble and *Wheel of Fortune* had a baby."

"A baby that eats vowels."

Thanks to Ohio's endless rainstorms, the grass is more of a

swamp than a parking lot. The tires spin and search for purchase as Roy bangs his fist against the steering wheel, attempting to beat the car into submission.

Beyond the mud pit, rows of semipermanent tents reach skyward, supported by half-rotten beams and makeshift plastic splices. The entire place has the feel of a droopy traveling carnival. Roy wedges the SUV in between a pair of rust-eaten pickup trucks. My shoes sink two inches when I climb out. "Remind me to never wear wedges again."

Roy lifts the hatch and we crawl inside, divvying up our supplies according to where we intend to sell them. "Are you sure you want to split up?" he asks.

I nod, schooling my face into a blank slate to conceal the nervousness beneath. "We can finish this faster if we do it separately. I don't want to be here any longer than necessary. Some of these people might know our faces. I used to come here with my dad when I was younger."

He scowls and shoves a few waterproof notebooks into my duffel bag. "Me too."

With a sigh that isn't for the weather, we leave the parking lot and step into the aisles of the Tri-City Flea Market. The air is heavy with the stench of grease and food trucks, the smell somehow repulsive and inviting at the same time. Colorful signs advertise everything from deep-fried pickles to chicken cheesesteaks while patrons huddle around the windows with paper tickets in their hands. A stray cat weaves in between the benches of the seating area, its girth waddling as it darts after scraps.

"How much time do you think you'll need?"

"Ten minutes," Roy says as he shifts the weight of the boxes onto his belt. "You?"

"I'll work fast."

We knock our elbows together in lieu of a high five and set off in opposite directions.

My first stop is to an electronics salesman, his table littered with cell phone accessories and video-game cases. The expensive items are locked behind him in a glass case. He watches the passersby with hawkish eyes and runs an idle hand over the flat end of the baseball bat beside his chair.

"Hi. Do you accept trades?"

He dips his chin toward the massive sign that states TRADE-INS WELCOME. I can feel the blush burning across my cheeks like wildfire. At least my idiocy contributes to the hopeless-damsel routine.

"Whatcha got?" he prompts.

I hand over my old cell phone, naked without the bulk of its protective case. Without plastic clinging to the sides and the screen, the phone is immaculate and shining. There isn't any outward evidence that I threw it on the ground on a regular basis. I hold my breath.

"This is pretty old," he remarks, picking with his thumbnail at one of the buttons. It's only three years old, but that might as well be eons in the tech world. He powers it on, nodding as it displays a generic welcome message. "What else?"

I slide Roy's laptop onto the table and pray that it kept some charge on the ride over. The man clicks the mouse and scrolls through a series of screens. "Best I can do is eighty for both."

"Ninety." My voice cracks in between syllables. I was hoping for close to two hundred, enough to purchase two bus tickets to Pittsburgh and rent a room in a cheap motel for a few nights. "Please."

Maybe it's because I reek of desperation or maybe it's because my boobs are bulging out of this stupid dress, but after a moment's consideration, he sticks his hand in mine and says, "You've got a deal."

Sucker.

Next, I stop at one of the numerous survivalist booths, testaments to the fact that demand will always generate supply. These charlatans know nothing about our lifestyle, but they recognize that there's a buck to be made on discounted ammunition and military surplus, the sort of stuff that Dad was always too paranoid to buy online in bulk.

I flag down the attendant, a middle-aged woman with sunburned cheeks and a camouflage bandanna tied around her hair. She scowls at my headband and sandals, the frilly lace hemline on Mom's skimpy dress. "Can I help you, hon?"

I haul my duffel bag onto the table and unload my cache of miscellaneous supplies, most of which are unused Christmas gifts from the past five years. I set aside the base layers to sell to the athletics vendor and sort the remaining items into piles. I keep the flares that Roy gave me, tucking them under my arm for sentimental value. *On second thought, screw that.* I return them to the pile. *Sentimental* value doesn't buy squat.

The woman paws through my trauma bag and checks the glass on Roy's lensatic compass. "I'll give you eighty bucks for the lot," she says.

Eighty dollars seems to be a common theme in this flea

market. I chuckle and start packing up my gear without another word. I might be hurting for cash, but I'm not an idiot. The electronics guy might be interested in the solar-charging banks and maybe even the hand-crank radio. Some of the multitools are still in their original packaging. It could be easier to sell it all in piecemeal.

"Fine, fine," the woman concedes, hefting my most expensive flashlight. "How about a hundred?"

I purse my lips and hold up a jumbo package of lithium batteries that's worth at least twenty dollars by itself. "One hundred and fifty and I'll throw in the clothing. They're all brand-new with tags. Some of the shirts are merino wool." And hideously unstylish, restrictive, and at least one size too big. I jerk my head toward the end of the row where Bob, a contact of my dad's that I'm deliberately avoiding, is reclining in a collapsible chair. "I'm sure Bob would give me that much."

She cocks her hip and leans forward until I can smell fried onions and cheesesteak on her breath. "Hon, you strike an awful tough bargain for a first-time customer. Plus, what's a Cosmo girl like you doing with a bunch of rough-and-tough gear? You steal it?"

I throw down my driver's license and hold my index finger below my last name. Judging by the widening of her eyes, she recognizes her mistake, just as I'd hoped she would. So much for anonymity. "One hundred and fifty," I repeat.

She offers no further argument.

"I was never here," I say in my most dangerous tone as I flatten the empty duffel and snatch the bills from her nicotine-stained claws. "Understand?"

Her nods are so fervent that the bandanna on her head slips down and becomes a blindfold. I seize the moment to disappear into a throng of passing teenagers heading in the direction of my rendezvous point with Roy. A few men turn to leer as I pass, and despite the creeping chill climbing from the base of my spine, I'm happy to be just another pretty girl in a crowd.

Pretty.

The word calls to my inner self, the one who doesn't want to be frivolous and vain, but wants the option nonetheless. I want to be empty like the first page of a fresh notebook, the possibilities of my life uncharted and endless. It is a gift that I can share with Roy, my dearest friend who has lived too long as a mockery of himself, a charcoal rubbing suffocating beneath the paper that colors him gray.

I don't want to live in a black-and-white world anymore.

Roy is already waiting in the tent closest to the parking lot. I balance on tiptoe to peck a kiss against his cheek. "How much did you get?"

He produces his tattered leather wallet and flips through the bills inside. My apprehension grows at the sight of each five-dollar bill, then dissipates when I start to see twenties and fifties. "Three hundred. You?"

"A little over two hundred."

We walk back to the car in silence, calculating the price of our freedom. Even with the money tucked safely in my purse, I can't shake the crushing weight of uncertainty or stop computing the thousands of ways our venture could fail. I think back to Brian Wendland jumping over the fire, wondering if I possess the reckless courage to take such an impossible leap.

24

"ARE YOU HUNGRY?" ROY ASKS, EYEING THE CRUMPLED cash in the cup holder as we trundle along the street leading back to Tin Peas. "We could grab some lunch before we head back."

"Sure." The responsible thing to do is save the money, but I haven't been to a restaurant since Katie was in diapers, and the hospital cafeteria doesn't count. "What kind of food do you like?"

"No preference."

"Everyone has a preference," I insist. Now that I know Roy isn't just another mindless minion, there's so much I want to learn about him. "Do you realize that we don't know a single useful thing about each other? All we've ever talked about is doomsday doctrine."

He points to a diner on the next corner and raises his eyebrows. The neon signs out front are blinding even in the day-time. "There?"

I punch him lightly on the bicep. "Use your words like a big boy."

He sighs through his nose. "How about that diner? They probably serve a little bit of everything."

"Sounds good." I pick two twenties out of our stash and stuff them in my pocket. "And it's probably cheap."

Once we get inside, the diner isn't much more than a few booths and a lunch counter spanning the length of the narrow building. Two men perch on round stools watching the news, cutting off their commentary about the weather girl's physique whenever one of the waitresses darts past juggling order slips and dirty dishes. Rectangular windows line the wall behind us, giving the impression that we've stepped into a train car. In a small alcove across the room, there are paper plates on the black-and-white tile floor, painted to resemble a set of checkers.

The best part about this impromptu, out-of-town stop is that no one notices our presence, to the point that it takes Roy several attempts to attract the attention of the hostess. She seats us without a word, scurrying off to retrieve the teenage girl scrubbing silverware at a nearby table.

I flip through the laminated menu, my mouth watering at the choices. "When was the last time you went out to eat?"

Roy snorts and rolls his eyes to the left, as if consulting an internal calendar pasted on the inside of his skull. "I don't remember. Maybe that time our stove broke and Taco Bell was the only place open. That was ten years ago."

I decide on a cheeseburger and Roy chooses the pot roast

special. We sip at our pop, exchanging smiles over the untouched bread basket between us. I rip off a chunk and slather it with butter. "I've never seen you eat in public."

"It's good practice for starving to death at the end of the world," he jokes, though the humor doesn't quite match the flash of nervousness in his eyes. He reaches out and grabs my hand. "I'd rather starve to death with you than anyone else in the universe."

I snatch my hand free and clamp it over my mouth to avoid spitting bread in his face. "You're such a romantic. I love it when you talk doomsday to me." I sniff at a passing platter of fried chicken, my stomach rumbling. "What's your favorite food?"

"Doomsday food or real food?" he asks.

"Real food."

He nudges the menu. "Pot roast. What about you? What's the best last meal from whatever's in your bunker?"

I can't pretend that I haven't thought about it. Anything with vegetables is out of the question. "I'd crack open a few packages of chicken and dumplings. I don't remember if we have any cake down there. You?"

Roy leans back in the booth and shields his face with both hands. "My mom let me put a cup of noodles and a can of Coke in my footlocker as my two personal items. I had to shave down the top of the noodle cup to make it fit the height limit."

Last time I checked, noodle cups and pop were not approved for long-term storage. I bite into another roll and hold it up for examination. "This is food. Ramen is not food. Also, can you be more stereotypical?"

"Don't judge me. It beats eating canned octopus." He visibly shudders.

"There are just some things that don't belong in a can," I say, thinking of the many varieties of canned pork products I've tried over the years. "Would you rather run out of toilet paper or run out of ammunition?"

"Can't wipe your ass with bullets. Rather get dysentery or scurvy?"

Tough choice. "I'd go with scurvy, especially if I could only wipe my ass with bullets. Zombie apocalypse or nuclear holocaust?"

"Zombie apocalypse!" he says with a little too much enthusiasm. "It's a great excuse to bash some of our neighbors in the head with a shovel."

He has a point. I would spare Mrs. Hepworth, though, but only because she puts up with Katie. I'd build her a little zombie kennel in the backyard and throw dead rabbits over the fence. "I don't see why the zombie apocalypse is a prerequisite for wanting to bash them in the head with a shovel."

"It's not felony murder if they're zombies. Important distinction now that we're not minors anymore. Rather drown or get hit by a truck?" The color drains from Roy's face like there's a hole poked in the bottom of his chin. "Shit. Sorry. I didn't mean to make fun of—"

My hands clench into fists underneath the table. "It's okay." I take a deep breath, forcing the memory of Dad's accident from my mind. "Does it make me a bitch if I don't go see him before we leave?"

Roy pauses to contemplate the question instead of just telling me what I want to hear. I appreciate that kind of honesty. "Stone-cold."

Ow. I clap both hands over my mouth in exaggerated shock. "Not stone-cold! That's the worst kind of bitch!" The words aren't quite as funny as I thought they'd be. "It would be different if he knew I was there."

"There hasn't been a change in his condition?"

"If anything, it's only gotten worse. I don't think I can handle seeing him again. I want to hate him, but I can't. He's my dad."

Roy stares at the television above my shoulder, his eyes glazed and unseeing. "Have you ever thought about why anyone wanted to live in the community in the first place? I keep looking for answers, but I never find any good reason. At first, my parents just wanted to go camping a lot. Then it kept getting weirder until they told me we were moving to Tin Peas."

"I don't know about your family, but both of my parents are the kids of the two couples who started the community. I'm sure you've heard the whole history lesson. My mom was born in Bunker One. Our doomsday is genetic."

Roy wrinkles his nose. "I never knew the part about your mom being born in the bunker. That's—"

"Unhygienic and horrifying?" I suggest.

"Something like that."

I try to imagine Mom as a child, but all I can conjure is the mental image of a pint-size fanatic. "I almost feel bad for her sometimes."

"Do you think they'll still love us when we're gone?" Roy asks, the corners of his eyes crinkling with pain. "Our parents?"

I don't answer.

He nods. "You're right."

▲ ▲ ▲

Like two bandits, we sneak out in the middle of the night to bury the money. Twigs and undergrowth crackle beneath our feet as we enter the woods behind Roy's house, the full moon lighting our way. His steps are calculated and quiet as he climbs over the trees fallen across our path. While I wait for him to sidle between two hulking thorn bushes, I tilt my head to examine the depressions in the grass, the way the dirt is carved in a straight line. It's too wide to be a deer path.

I tuck my arms close to my chest as I follow after Roy, the thorns snagging against the fabric of my jacket. He signals for me to pause at the base of a steep hill. "Watch me first," he whispers.

He takes a running leap, both hands smacking closed against the nearest sapling. He hauls himself upright and twists around until the tree is at his back. Then he jumps again.

I mimic his movements, swearing at the mud as my heels slide, my shoulders screaming in pain. I hate hiking. Once I get to Carnegie Mellon, I'm not doing any physical activity for at least two years. The most strenuous thing I want to do is pick up a pencil.

When I reach the top of the hill, I stare at the mess of trees that we used as climbing poles. I'd rather hurl myself off this ledge than attempt a downhill trek. My nose aches at the thought of slamming my face into one of those saplings. "There had better be a good reason for this crap or I'm going to kick your ass all the way to Pittsburgh and save you the price of a bus ticket."

Roy holds up his palms in a placating gesture. At least he has the decency to be winded. "We're almost there," he gasps. "Promise."

We continue in silence for another few minutes until I no longer feel that my heart is on the verge of exploding. Roy slows his pace and clicks on a red lens flashlight, holding his fingers over it until only a tiny trickle of light filters through. I stifle a laugh. "We're far enough away to use white light, I think." I turn on my cell phone and scan the area. "Unless your parents have x-ray vision."

Roy tackles me to the ground, wrenching the cell phone from my grasp. My wrist throbs where it knocked against a stone. I cradle it to my chest and curl away from him, biting back a sob. "What the hell!"

"There are hunting cameras," he hisses, his eyes flaring with panic. He stabs his index finger into the soil. "Sends a picture straight to my dad's phone. I spent *forever* finding this blind spot." He punches the tree above my head and I flinch, picking pieces of bark from my hair. "White light! Damn it!"

"I'm sorry! If you had told me that your entire property was monitored, I wouldn't have done it!" Yet even as the words leave my mouth, I know that I'm to blame for being so reckless. I should have anticipated that there would some type of detection equipment, especially after the false alarm with the goat. I scrape the side of my boot against the soupy earth, trying to pinpoint how close we are to Bunker Two. It's been a long time since I've visited. It's not like we have sleepovers.

"'S'okay." He pinches the bridge of his nose as he stands, no doubt to avoid throttling me with his flashlight. Blood leaks along the ridges of his knuckles. "Do you see a brick around here anywhere?"

I flex my fingers against the dull ache in my arm and swipe at the dewy grass to reveal a moss-covered chunk of cinder block. "This thing?"

"That thing," he replies, already scrutinizing the nearby ground. He falls to one knee, clawing at the earth like an animal searching for a buried prize.

I drop the marker into the brush just as Roy extracts a waterproof radio box and presents it to me. I quirk a brow. "This looks suspiciously like the radio box that went missing two years ago from the communications locker." As a community, we spent weeks searching for it, interrogating each other even after the radios were found stuffed beneath the couch cushions in the meeting barn—the barn that sits on Roy's property. "You stole it. Why?"

He jerks his chin in a silent command to lift the lid. When I do, my jaw slackens, leaving me gaping. The box is filled with rolls of cash, each wrapped in a plastic bag to further fend off moisture. I squint in the darkness to discern the numbers printed on each corner. I'm holding at least a thousand dollars. "How did you get this?" I ask, both incredulous and wary. "You never mentioned that you had a stash."

"I didn't want to jinx it," he replies. "I tried to hide it as well as I could, but there was never any guarantee that someone else wouldn't find it. I only come out here every couple of months to add more."

His lack of a direct answer does little to quell my nervousness. Only criminals hide money like this. Fugitives. "Seriously, Roy, where did you get this cash?"

He eases back onto his elbows, his long legs straightening until we're sitting toe to toe. "Lunch money. I've saved it for almost four years."

I tackle *him* this time, my lips searching for his as my throat, my eyes, burn. I cry even as I kiss him, our tears mingling into two twin streams. He claws at my hair and wraps his legs around mine, molding me to his body as we speak in silent ways. I trace the contours of his chest, pressing my palm against his stomach, imagining the ache of hunger. "Four years," I repeat.

He smiles, his eyes shining with promises and moonlight. "Worth it."

I trail kisses along his collarbone, my chin trembling. "You had me so convinced that you were just like them."

"Never," he whispers, though nothing about the word is quiet. It is defiance. It is strength.

Together, we open the box and place our latest funds inside. We relocate several paces, choosing a new hiding spot concealed by roots and leaves. Roy insists upon waiting another half an hour to see if anyone arrives to investigate the light. No one does. We are invisible, as always.

Finally, we leave the box and its contents behind, like the seed of our future planted in the soil of the past.

25

I HEAR RAISED VOICES INSIDE THE HOUSE AS I RETURN from my excursion with Roy. I slip onto the porch and squat beneath the dining room window to listen. It sounds like Katie and Mom are having some kind of argument, but I can't discern the individual words. If both of them are awake, the possibilities are slim that they don't realize I'm gone.

I hear the scrape of the front door opening and launch myself toward the porch railing. I get my hands across the top and one shoe onto the bottom bar when Mom's head appears. "There you are. Get in here."

I follow her into the living room where Katie is already perched on the couch. Her new shoes are soaked in mud, the laces brown and frayed. There's a splatter pattern on her jeans from running through it.

"What's going on?" I ask.

Katie sucks in a deep breath. "I followed you and Roy and I saw that you have money and I told Mom because it's probably stolen and you're not being a team player because you're hiding it from everyone else."

I turn to Mom, folding my arms to stave off the sick feeling brewing in my stomach. I scrub the shock from my features and project confusion instead. "I have no idea what she's talking about. She's probably just making up nonsense. She has an active imagination."

"I'll show you," Katie offers, a determined edge to her tone. The worst part about it is that I think she can actually do it. Bunker Two is at the top of the ridgeline. You can be blindfolded and still find it if you know that it's there in the first place.

Mom sighs and leans on the wall to pull on her boots. "If you drag me out into the woods at this hour for no reason, I'm not going to be happy."

"I'm telling you that she's sneaking!" Katie insists.

"I am not," I snap, doing my best to sound offended. "In fact, I'll go out there with you and prove you wrong." And by "prove her wrong," I mean run interference until I can figure out how to misdirect her completely.

Mom throws on a windbreaker and grabs one of the flashlights from the hall closet. "No, you're staying here. You can't investigate yourself."

I wait for them to make it out the door before I call Roy, poking the screen twice with my sweaty fingers before it registers. There's no way that I'll be able to make it into the woods ahead of Mom and Katie without them seeing me. Roy is much closer, though. I bounce on my heels, chanting, "Pick up. Pick up."

I wince when I hear the robotic voicemail cue and send a text message instead. Go get the money right now! Katie followed us tonight and told my mom.

Roy?

ROY

ROY

ROY!!!!

I call six more times. Voicemail. He must have left it on vibrate or gone to sleep as soon as he got home.

I bop around the living room like a boxer before a match. Legs jumping. Arms shaking. My front teeth tapping together. Fight or flight.

More like fail or flight. I crumble onto the floor of the living room and pull Belle into my lap. Part of me wants to just pack a bag and leave now while I still can, but I won't get far without any money. And once Mom has her paws on it, she'll never let me have it back. It'll go to buying the defibrillators she wants or increasing our stockpile of non-genetically modified seeds.

I don't know how to tell Roy. After all these years of saving his lunch money and going hungry, I jeopardized the entire stash. I never thought Katie would be capable of this. Or maybe I just didn't want to accept it. I should have known that I was losing her the day she snitched on me about the permission slip. The old Katie, my sister, the girl who used to make her action figures zoom around on Belle's back . . . she's gone.

And when Roy finds out that the money is my fault, I'll lose him, too.

"Why aren't you consoling me?" I mumble against Belle's fur, feeling the warmth of my tears spread against her coat. "It's one of your dog duties."

She gives me a half-hearted lick on the cheek. *I'm off duty after midnight.*

I groan and slide down the wall until I'm flat on my back, looking at the bumps of the popcorn ceiling. It was naive to believe that I could ever outmaneuver so many people. I'm ready to just sink into this sun-bleached carpet and vanish. No one will miss me anyway.

I stand as Mom trudges into the living room with the communications box under her arm. She flips it open and peers at its contents. "I'm really interested in hearing why you and Roy were sneaking out in the middle of the night to bury money in the woods."

I mentally run through a list of plausible excuses, ranking them from most ridiculous to least likely to get me banished to the bunker for a month.

"I told you that she's a sneak," Katie says to Mom. "She thinks this place is stupid. She probably wanted to run away."

I almost just confess. In order to fight, I need something to fight for. The venom in Katie's voice is proof enough that she's beyond my grasp.

But if I implicate myself, then I drag Roy down with me. "We've been saving up our birthday money to buy wedding rings and I thought if you knew that we had it, you'd make us give it to you instead." It's a thin cover story. At a minimum, Mom is going to berate me for wanting to spend so much when a simple gold band is only a hundred bucks at the pawn shop.

I can see her mentally chewing on it, checking for substance.

"I wouldn't do that. Your wedding is the most important accomplishment of your life. You're expanding the gene pool for potential repopulation." Her tone sharpens from dreamy to suspicious. "But how do I know your sister isn't telling the truth about you wanting to run away?"

I keep my facial muscles completely slack while my heart flops around like a speedbag. "Uh, you could call Roy's parents. He told them that we were going to get our ring fingers sized today."

Mom narrows her eyes and pulls out her phone. One of Roy's parents answers on the first ring. I strain to hear the conversation, but all I can discern is a scratchy voice tinged with aggravation. Mom ends the call and shrugs. "You weren't lying after all."

Wasn't I, though?

Katie tugs on Mom's sleeve. "You didn't see them, Mom. They were sneaking around!"

I drop to one knee until we're eye level. It takes all of my willpower not to grab her by the ankle and start shaking her until the doomsday falls out. On the inside, I'm screaming, *YOU RUINED EVERYTHING!* On the outside, I say, "You'll understand when you're older, Katie Cat. I just hid the money because I wanted to make sure that Roy and I could get married as soon as we can. Like we're supposed to."

Mom smiles at me. Not a sneer, a grimace, a scowl. A smile. "You're setting a great example." She holds the communications box in the air. "I'll just lock this up in the safe until you're ready to buy your rings. We can go together. Plus, I don't think you need this much. The rest of it can go toward the supplies for this month."

Fantastic. Now I'm never going to be able to get the money back.

At most, Mom might give me a hundred dollars for a plain band, but only while she's standing over my shoulder at the jewelry store. "We were thinking about after graduation. That way we won't be distracted when we go to school to uh, start our new careers."

"You're a liar." Katie huffs at me and storms across the room toward the stairs. "And you don't have to talk to me like I'm an idiot!"

I listen to her stomping her way to her bedroom. She might think that I'm some horrible traitor, but the feeling is mutual.

My phone buzzes with a text from Roy. What happened? Can you meet me again?

I type a few responses and immediately erase them. There's no way to convey the magnitude of my error. We're back to square one. I've undone years of Roy's hard work and sacrifices by placing my trust in the wrong person.

I sit down on the couch and play through the potential ways he could respond to the news that I lost the money. Almost all of them end in him giving me the cold shoulder from now on or cutting me out of his plans entirely. Roy's an overall better, warmer, and more forgiving person than I am, but I can't see how he could ever look past this. No one is that angelic.

Another text pops up on the screen. Becca? Can you talk?

"I'm going to take the dog for a quick walk," I croak at Mom, the dread like a physical grip on my throat. I type a quick response to Roy. "She got all riled up when you left the house."

Belle isn't actually riled up, so I nudge her in the butt until she agrees to walk down the driveway. As soon as I'm out of sight of our house, I pick her up and tuck her into her customary spot under my arm. Her little legs dangle in the air as she rests her head against the curve of my hip. So trusting. She doesn't know that she lives in a house full of spies.

I linger in the street for a few minutes, my heartbeat slow and sluggish. I'm beyond panic. Instead, I just feel the beginnings of grief, like the prickles of an illness before it fully takes hold. I didn't want Roy when I thought he was another brainwashed fanatic, but I've grown used to his friendship, his unwavering support. It's only now, when I'm minutes away from losing him, that I realize I don't want to do this alone. It's selfish to be thinking like that when I still have my scholarship. I still have a chance.

Without that money, Roy has nothing.

I've doomed him.

Roy opens the shed door as soon as my foot connects with the ramp. He pokes his head out and scans the property for signs of eavesdroppers or tag-along sisters. The collar of his shirt is damp with sweat, his hair mussed in the front. "Hey. What's going on? What happened?"

"I'm sorry." I wrap my arms around him and memorize his smell, his touch, the feeling of being loved by someone. If Roy denounces me, I really have no one left at all. "I lost all of the money. I'm sorry. I'm the worst. I hate myself."

"Don't cry, Becca." He reaches into his pocket and presses a tissue into my hand. "Here. Wipe your nose."

I lift the tissue halfway to my face before I realize that it's a twenty-dollar bill.

Roy huffs a laugh under his breath. "I saw your text. I let your mom find the money because she was expecting to find *something*. But I made sure to pull out, oh, about seventeen hundred dollars first."

I smack Roy's chest hard enough that he almost trips over Belle as she snuffles around the floor searching for crumbs. "YOU START WITH THAT PART! I've been losing my mind about that money! Why didn't you text me back?"

He reaches over to the table to retrieve his cell phone and flicks through our conversation. "You said, and I quote, 'Go get the money right now.' I took that literally and started running. Plus, I didn't want to text you that I had the money in case anyone else saw it. I know you let your sister play games on your phone."

"Not anymore." I fall sideways across the couch and pull my knees to my chest. I'm dizzy with relief, sick with hope. "So you aren't mad at me?"

"It wasn't your fault." Roy scooches Belle out of the way to sit beside me. "But I don't know what to do with the money now. Should I keep it close or do you think we should bury it again?"

I groan and steeple my fingers over the top of my skull. "I don't like either of those options. This is like trying to decide whether our supersecret password should be one-two-three-four or one-one-one-one."

"I'll find another place that's easier to access and hidden enough that no one will find it by accident," Roy decides. "I have fewer people interested in what I'm doing all the time."

"That's a good idea. You should keep it. I'm obviously too stupid to protect us since I couldn't even tell that my own sister was about to stab me in the back."

"I'm sorry about Katie. Maybe she'll come around."

"She betrayed me once and she'll do it again. We're not on the same side anymore."

Roy doesn't argue, but I wish he would.

26

I LOUNGE BACK IN MY SEAT DURING HOMEROOM, DOODLING
with one hand and waiting for my turn to fall in line for graduation rehearsal. Most of our classes are canceled to accommodate
the schedule, much to the chagrin of the ruffled senior class, half
of whom are still hungover from partying all weekend. Thanks
to my drunken adventures in the woods with Sydney, I'm quite
familiar with the pallid faces and pained squints as we slog out
to the bleachers in the center of the football field.

The sky is cloudless and the sun shining high by the time we
finish assembling. Aiden and I are separate from the rest of our
peers, assigned to the front row along with the teachers. I fiddle
with my salutatorian's sash, wishing that I could find Roy in the
sea of strangers behind me.

It's the last week of school. We're almost there. Almost free.

Aiden groans and shuffles closer to avoid a long band of

sunlight. We stand for the school song and national anthem, then ease ourselves down onto the scorching metal bench.

"This is torture," Aiden mutters, swiping at his forehead. "We can't graduate if we die of dehydration."

"Oh, please. You can lose fifteen percent of the water in your body before it becomes life-threatening."

"Challenge accepted," he pants, but he's smiling, perhaps humbled by the fact that I seem impenetrable to the effects of the heat. Side perk of having a near-death experience every other Tuesday.

The rising volume of complaints is drowned out by the principal beginning his sound check. He clicks on the microphone and feedback squeals through the stadium speakers like the shriek of a wrathful hawk. The students lurch forward as a single entity, our fingers stuffed into our ears.

The principal recites a short portion of his opening statement and then summons Aiden for his valedictorian's speech. Aiden reads the first line, a quote from Frederick Douglass, and then waves me to the podium. I haven't prepared anything, so I seize the microphone and say, "Speech, speech, speech. Blah, blah, blah. You get the idea."

Next, the teachers practice introducing notable attendees from the community and recipients of academic awards. Monsieur Wheeler insists on reading his entire introduction for our keynote speaker, even though this rehearsal is only supposed to show the progression of events, not run through them in full detail.

Meanwhile, I have an escape plan to finish and it doesn't involve sitting in a cloud of Aiden's body odor. I nudge him with my elbow and whisper, "Maybe I should pretend to faint."

"Good idea," he replies, laughing.

He thinks I'm joking. Cute.

I feign a cry of pain as I tumble forward onto my knees, clutching at my stomach and curling into the fetal position. My skin prickles with goose bumps and chills race up my spine, evidence that this little drama exercise isn't entirely fake. The principal dashes over to check on me, his hands hovering over my rib cage like it's made of lava. "Rebecca, are you all right?"

"I'm just feeling a bit dizzy. It's so hot out here."

He twirls his finger in the air as a signal to wrap up the rehearsal. Aiden makes a show of taking my arm and escorting me off the makeshift stage, trailed by the hundreds of students in our senior class who file out in their assigned pairs. We reach the open doors of the gymnasium and the lukewarm air feels like an arctic blast on my scorched skin. "You're my hero," he whispers.

The sentiment is echoed by person after person as they pass us by, some patting my shoulders in gratitude. Roy catches up to me, his eyebrows knitted together in concern. "Are you okay or were you faking it?"

"Roy," I say with a chuckle. "You've watched me lick leaves to get enough water. I didn't really pass out from sitting in the sun for forty minutes. Give me some credit."

"Spoken like a true doomsday prepper."

I pummel him on the arm as we file into the cafeteria. He breaks away to save us seats with Sydney while I join the serpentine line snaking around the first row of tables. When it's my turn, I ask for larger helpings, earning an extra half scoop of potatoes, and guilt the register attendant into giving me a second milk carton by complaining that I fainted at rehearsal.

I ease onto the bench on the opposite side of Roy, shaking my tray to show my double helpings. I hand him a fork and nudge the tray in between us. He taps Y-A-Y against my shin in Morse code while he chugs the milk.

"You can have my cake if you want it," Sydney offers. Before she can speak again, Roy is already cramming it into his mouth. "Who the hell thought it was a good idea to make *carrot* cake? That's the worst kind of cake. Period."

Roy swallows a chunk and scrapes the frosting off the side of his thumb. It pains me to know that rather than caring about the palatability of his food, he's counting calorie intake. He wipes his hands on a napkin, looking a bit sheepish. "Doesn't matter to me. Thanks."

"Could be worse. I made my birthday cake out of vegetables this year." I don't mention that it was because Mom refused to spend any money on real food. Good thing we could afford those seismic-rated picture hooks, though. "The frosting was ranch dressing."

Sydney's eyes widen. "You poor, deprived soul."

"It could be worse," I add. "We have to eat this weird seaweed soup for Roy's birthday."

"It's a Korean thing," he mumbles, his cheeks reddening.

I laugh and nudge Sydney under the table until she sees the note in my hand. I debated keeping our escape a secret, but I can't live the rest of my life doubting the kindness of others. I've seen where that path leads. Sydney unfolds the paper and peeks down into her lap. *We're skipping town before graduation. Don't tell anyone.*

"By the way, thanks for getting us out of rehearsal," Sydney replies as she scribbles a response and hands the note back underneath the table. "I'm not looking forward to roasting on those bleachers again while everybody yammers about their feelings."

I unfold the crinkled paper and smile. Sydney's response is just what I expected: *Fight the Man.*

▲▲▲

Too much is still up in the air to know our exact departure date, so I decide to clean out my locker now. Most of my possessions are destined for the trash, even the Carnegie Mellon collage. One by one, I peel the pictures and pamphlets off the smooth metal, shuffling across the hallway to deposit them in the nearest bin.

I keep Scotty the Dog, placing him in the front pouch of my backpack next to the necklace from Roy. When we skip town, I won't have a lot of space for personal items, but I can manage to smuggle out these few mementos.

Once the locker is empty, I hang the lock on the latch, check my watch again, and set out for Ms. Garcia's classroom. I step inside, noting how empty it feels without her fish tanks and terrariums lining the counters. "Hello?"

I finally spot her in the corner, tottering on a stepladder as she dismantles her bulletin board. "Hi! Give me one second." She rips off a strip of border decoration and tosses it onto the floor before climbing down. "I'm taking advantage of the short periods to start cleaning up early. Don't tell anyone. They get cranky about stuff like that."

She sits on the edge of a stool and pulls one around across from her. "What's up?"

"Just checking in," I reply, trying to sound nonchalant.

"I already scheduled my home study if that's what you're worried about. Once I have documentation that my home is safe, it'll make it that much easier going before a judge for temporary custody."

I blow out a long breath. "Honestly, I've been freaking out about it, but I didn't want to constantly bother you."

"You're not bothering me. It's okay to be worried."

I alternate between putting my feet on the bottom rung and the middle one. I can't quite bring myself to look her in the eye. "I promise that I'll be back to get Katie as soon as I can. I just need to find a job and a place to live and then I'll file for custody."

Ms. Garcia gets up and retrieves the candy dish from her desk. She won't stop shoving it at me until I agree to take a Tootsie Roll. "The hardest part is going to be proving that your home is unsafe in the first place," she reminds me.

"It's not going to be that difficult. You really can't imagine what goes on there." Like being forced to reenact your father's near-death experience in some kind of bizarre tribute. "I don't even know if my mom will care about losing us. I feel so cheated. Family's supposed to have your back."

"What about your dad?" Ms. Garcia asks. "Are you going to visit before you go?"

My throat tightens to the width of a flower stem. Mom has been so vague about his progress that I've stopped asking. "I don't know. I might. My mom won't tell us anything about his condition. She acts like he's already dead."

"Just a piece of unsolicited advice from someone who couldn't wait to get out of her hometown," Ms. Garcia says, waiting for me to nod. The unspoken joke is that she's still here, a lifelong resident besides her brief stint at Carnegie Mellon. "Go visit. Say what you have to say. You need some kind of closure or you'll end up regretting it."

I laugh at the thought. I'd rather picnic in the Sahara than waste another second thinking about anyone in that community. Yet the thought of not knowing what happens to my father is like watching a series that's canceled halfway through. I'll never know the ending. And part of that ending is mine.

27

DESPITE MY RESERVATIONS, I FIND MYSELF HOVERING IN
the doorway of the hospital, the thick band of a dirt bike helmet
strangling my wrist. My feet refuse to move beyond the threshold. The electronic door opens and closes as I continue to linger.
"Is this stupid?" I ask Roy.

He breathes warm air into the gap between his gloves and his
hands. A red line of windburned skin adorns his forehead where
the wind seeped through his visor. "Not if it's what you want."

Strengthened by the lack of judgment in his voice, I sigh and
force myself to enter the lobby of the emergency room. Roy follows along with a stilted gait, unaccustomed to the process of
sneaking into intensive care units. I lead him to the service elevators and idle by the vending machine until the bell chimes.

"Once we get up there, try to cover your chest. It's the only
floor where you're supposed to check in with your visitor badge.

In case we get separated, my dad's in room 505."

Roy nods and pretends to act nonchalant, but his eyes dart between the walls as the elevator ascends. "Chill," I grumble. "They're not going to throw us in prison if they catch us. They'll just make us leave."

We step out by the main intersection near the nursing station. At this time of day, I'm hoping that some of the personnel have snuck away for a dinner break. I hover by the corner and point diagonally at Dad's door. Roy squeezes my shoulder in acknowledgment.

I walk out into the hallway and keep my back straight, my steps purposeful. Half of going unnoticed is pretending to belong. Roy and I are experts at that, though you wouldn't know it by his unnatural smile and constant squirming.

I slip inside room 505 and keep the handle depressed to soundlessly close the door behind us. I smack both hands on my thighs, smug with satisfaction that I've thwarted the system again. "I told you that sneaking in here isn't rocket science."

"Um . . . Becca?"

I turn around and press my eyebrows into a confused line. The room is cleaned out, devoid of any signs of occupancy. Without the steady hum and hiss of the various equipment, it feels almost eerie. "We must be in the wrong room."

I stick my head into the hallway and check the placard screwed into the wall. Room 505.

I flag down a passing nurse, no longer concerned with the absence of my visitor badge. He pauses just inside the room and squints to scrutinize my face. "Aren't you Karen's daughter?"

"Yeah."

"Did she forget something at home again?" he asks, shaking his head. "I mean, I think your mom is great, but she can be so scatterbrained."

I'm starting to wonder whether the long hours are getting to him, too. Clearly, he needs me to state the obvious. "No, I'm here for my dad."

"Oh, sweetheart," he whispers, setting down his clipboard and wrapping me in a tight hug. "Take all the time you need in here. I won't tell anyone. I'm sorry. I meant to send a card or flowers or something."

I blanch, staring at the empty bed, the crisp edges of the sterile white sheets. The blood in my ears pounds to a disjointed rhythm, coloring the edges of my vision a matching shade of white. "Where's my dad?"

The nurse recoils and whips his head between the two of us. His expression of complete bafflement is tinged with panic. "Honey, he died two weeks ago."

I watch his lips form another sentence, but the sudden ringing in my ears swells into a painful drone, drowning out any coherent sound. "No, no, that's wrong. You must be mixing him up with someone else. His name is George Aldaine. He's in a coma, but he's not dead."

A few seconds tick away, interrupted only by the nurse's shuffling feet. "I'm sorry for your loss, but I'm certain that he passed away."

I step closer to the bed, pulling open the drawers of the nightstand without knowing what I expect to find. I shred the pages of the Patient Care pamphlets, the notepad, the television guide. The pieces fall from my fingers like ashes scattered in the wind.

The sound of a phone dialing draws my focus back to reality. The nurse mutters into the receiver and keeps his eyes on the floor, a bead of sweat forming at his hairline. "I'm calling to see if a counselor's available for you."

"Time to go," Roy says, grabbing on to a corner of my sweatshirt.

"I'm not leaving without answers." I realize that tears are streaming from my eyes, though I don't feel the burn of their making or the cold sting of wetness on my cheeks. "Is he really dead?"

"He's dead. We have to go."

I dig in my heels and refuse to budge. Blindly, I reach out and set my palms against the doorway, pushing back against Roy's urgent shoves. "I'm not leaving until I know what happened!"

Roy pins my arms and waddles into the hallway, his toes pressing against my heels. As he steers us toward the elevator, he whispers into my ear. "Think about it from their point of view. A girl whose dad died two weeks ago just broke into a monitored hospital unit to see her dad's old room. Then she acted like she didn't understand that he was dead and started ripping up random papers looking for hidden information." When I don't respond, he adds, "If they formally document this, you'll have a hell of a time explaining it when you're trying to get custody of Katie."

"Okay. You're right." I snatch a handful of tissues from a sitting area and dab at my tears, tending to my sadness like an inconvenient leak. "Let's go."

The trip home is a twisted blur of emotions and silence, the weight of Roy's hand pressed against mine. A scream brews in the depths of my chest. I feel unplugged, like my heart and my brain and everything in between have retreated into separate compartments to grieve.

When the bike slows in front of my house, I keep my eyes on the ground, scanning for a piece of plastic, a bit of bumper. Evidence to prove that my father was ever here at all. Besides an angry scar slashed across a tree trunk, the world shows no sign of his life, or his convictions, or his malice. He's gone.

"Come on," Roy says, beckoning me inside. He enters without knocking and tenses when he notices my mother waiting in the kitchen, already bundled in her coat and clutching her purse.

"We were at the hospital," I say in a low voice, touching the puffs of inflamed skin below my eyes. "I know about Dad. Why didn't you tell us? We had a right to say goodbye."

Mom huffs and adjusts the fall of her hair around her collar. "You should have cut ties after the accident. I kept telling you not to count on a recovery."

"How can you just act like he didn't matter at all?"

"One day, when I was sixteen years old, my mother told me that I was going to marry the boy across the street. She made me promise that I would never, ever love anyone because love makes you reckless and stupid. Then she told me that no one would ever love me, either. And unlike you, I listened to my mother."

Roy sidles in between us as she leaves, probably to prevent me from giving her a facelift with the frying pan in the dish rack. I watch her climb into her car and choose a radio station with meticulous focus. I wonder if she wore the same uncaring expression while she picked out a casket or an urn or however she decided to dispose of Dad's remains. Maybe she left him in the morgue to be dealt with by the hospital as another employee perk.

I have to tell Katie before I completely unravel. I knock once on her door before pushing it open. She turns on her bedside lamp. "What?"

"I want you to know that I will always love you. You might not always understand everything I do, but I promise that there's a good reason."

"You woke me up to tell me that," she deadpans.

"No, I came in here to tell you something about Dad. I don't know how else to say it, but he's dead, Katie Cat. They couldn't make him better."

I sit down on the edge of her bed, my arms outstretched for a hug and my eyes scanning the room for a box of tissues. But she doesn't cry. She doesn't scream. She just pulls the blanket back over her shoulders and says, "I know already. Mom told me."

I stop breathing while I process what she just said. "What do you mean, you know already? Why wouldn't you say something to me?"

"Mom said we have to let go." She snaps the cable on the lamp, plunging her bedroom into darkness. "You never tell me the truth about anything, so why should I tell you?"

I wander across the hallway and try to ignore the memories of my father that hover in this house as surely as any ghost. Exhausted and alone, I fall into a fitful doze, waking every hour to clammy palms and aching joints. Even in my nightmares, I can't shake the feeling that I've lost something. I run through forests and dreamland mazes, searching. But I never find him.

28

I CAN'T FINISH MY SCIENCE FAIR PRESENTATION IF I HAVE A heart attack before it starts. My stress level heightens as I realize that my chest does hurt a bit, a dull ache beneath my ribs that refuses to be massaged away. Once more students start to fill the gymnasium, my anxiety threatens to develop into full-blown panic, but I'm too preoccupied with breathing and maintaining consciousness to spare any brain cells to fuel its rise.

I glance behind me toward the basketball court, where pale rays of orange sunlight trickle in through the row of windows above the collapsed bleachers. Ms. Garcia paces between the hoops, spinning on her heel at the boundary lines. She taps her watch and frowns. I shake my head. It's not ready yet.

I haven't told her about Dad, and I don't think I will. There's numbness in the place of grief, a divider that separates his death from this last bid for freedom. I can't afford to feel. Not today.

It's funny how, in trying to escape her, I've become my mother, if only for a moment.

Beside me, Roy fiddles with the photo slideshow that's supposed to be appearing on my laptop. He wiggles the flash drive in frustration. "Still not working." He unplugs it and plugs it in again for the fortieth time in a row. I hate technology.

Aiden saunters by and appraises my presentation, smirking. He straightens his Columbia-blue tie and shines the silver lion tacking it in place. "Have you considered that the port you're trying is dead?" he says to Roy. "There's another port right next to it."

Roy freezes and I can tell from the spasm in his neck that he's fighting back a wave of colorful profanity. He pops out the flash drive and inserts it into the second port. The laptop pings as our photographs successfully load. "Was going to try that next."

"Sure you were," Aiden replies, slapping him once on the back as he continues down the aisle. I hope his tie isn't a clip-on because I'm dying to strangle him with it.

With the computer issues sorted out, the only remaining task is to set up the model. I unpack it from its newspaper wrapping and arrange it in the trapezoid of space formed by the folds of the tri-paneled poster board. A miniature bicycle totters on its stand, created by Roy with a soldering gun, a pair of pliers, and some steel wire. Lines run to a pile of sugar cubes that serve as our battery bank. It even has a working drive belt, which is actually a black hair tie.

I step back to view the arrangement. It all appears to be in order. With a sigh, I trail after Ms. Garcia. We meet midway, facing off at center court.

"My presentation is ready if you want a sneak peek."

Ms. Garcia's face hardens into the unyielding expression of a battlefield commander. "Dazzle me."

"I didn't have a big budget," I warn. "I'm trying to win this based on the science. I didn't have time to worry about the glam."

She pouts as we walk over. "The glam is the best part."

"Thank you, by the way, for never asking about the doomsday stuff."

"It never mattered to me," she responds. "You aren't your home life. I've met great kids who came from horrible backgrounds and vice versa."

I know that I shouldn't ask, but I can't resist. My conversation with Dean Barton was too simple, too smooth. "Did anyone call you from Carnegie Mellon?"

Ms. Garcia's cheeks bulge with an overwrought smile that doesn't quite meet her eyes. "Hypothetically speaking, if a dean called to a discuss a student, I would never compromise that student's privacy."

"But if you did," I prompt, "what would you hypothetically say?"

"I don't know." She keeps her eyes trained on the distant stage recessed in the wall on the other side of the room. "I wouldn't, for example, tell him that I believe the student is highly capable of managing her own affairs and that it would cause extreme personal hardship if he denied her request to live off-campus."

"I don't know what to say. You're the reason I can leave, can have a life now."

Ms. Garcia clicks her manicured fingernail against the foam edge of the poster board. "The only reward I want is a science fair trophy to taunt the biology and chemistry teachers."

"I think I can manage that."

Upon reaching the table, Ms. Garcia examines my project with cold precision. The pain in my chest grows more pronounced as she flips through the materials and slides the model into a better location. Finally, she gives an almost imperceptible nod of approval. "I like it."

I hunch over with my hands on my knees, sucking in air like I've been standing in a vacuum for the past thirty seconds. "Oh, good."

"I don't really have a choice," she adds, the disapproval heavy in her voice. "You took so long setting up that the judges are almost here."

"What?" I bolt upright and scan the immediate area. A group of three individuals rounds the corner and pauses at the nearest display. They're within spitting distance.

"Don't worry. You'll be fabulous." Ms. Garcia pats my arm and bounds away. I want to throw myself on the ground and cling to her shins, but it's against the rules for mentoring teachers to be in the vicinity when the judges are conducting evaluations.

I lean over the table to confer with Roy. "Where are the reporters?" I suppress a groan. This plan was too ambitious; it has too many moving parts to succeed. "They need to be here, too. I invited, like, twenty of them."

Roy pivots on his stool to peek around the corner. "I see a couple of guys with cameras. That has to be them." He hesitates. "Are you sure this is a good idea?"

"I don't know any other way to make all our neighbors lose their shit in public. I'd try to film them the next time they're doing something horrible, but there's never any opportunity since it's usually happening to you and me. Otherwise, I've already had a social worker investigate our house when I was a kid. She didn't find anything wrong. It's all too easy to hide."

As the trio of judges approaches, I curl my fingers inward to grasp the tips of my sleeves, pulling them close to conceal the scabs from breaking the car window. I don't want them to think that I'm violent and deranged—my project is proof enough of that. Just for tonight, I want to be a scientist, my research nothing more than a quirky topic rather than an autobiography. But there's none of the usual pain at the motion, surprising me enough that I steal a glance at my hands. The scabs are gone. Only pinkish skin remains, new and tender.

My smile is genuine.

I recognize the female judge from assemblies and school functions, but I can't recall her name or what she teaches. She beholds me with awe, her gaze lingering on my braids as though she can unscrew my skull and scoop out the secrets like pumpkin pulp. "Hi," she squeaks. "Can you walk us through your research?"

"Sure." I sidle a few steps to the left to give them a clearer view of my poster board. I try to remember all of Ms. Garcia's feedback from last year, including the fact that I ramble when nervous. "My name is Rebecca Aldaine and I'm a doomsday prepper. My project is about emergency energy generation and how we utilize electricity in our underground bunker."

With Roy as my assistant, I explain the model and its purpose, contrasting the limited efficiency of the bicycle generator with the massive output of the hydroelectric. Next, I narrate the slideshow with labeled pictures of the real systems and the electronics they power within the bunker. The judges jostle closer for a better vantage point and scribble notes on their clipboards.

"While the bunker seems impenetrable, it relies heavily on external support systems like the hydroelectric generator to maintain habitability. In reality, anyone with a pair of wire cutters could do a lot of damage."

There's an ebb and flow to science fairs, a certain amount of time that all but guarantees a winning ribbon. With dozens of projects to evaluate, the judges can't afford to spend more than a minute or two examining each. I'm aiming for ten.

"These are some of my family's procedures," I say, distributing packets of handouts containing our strategies for maintenance, defense, and energy conservation. They're ruined now, of course. Secret plans are only as good as their keepers. "Is anyone here from the media?"

A woman at the edge of the growing crowd raises her hand and almost leaps in the air to attract my attention. "Over here! *Tinker Peaks Times!*"

"*Jackson County Journal!*"

Roy muscles through the parents and judges to hand-deliver our press packets. Aside from my personal testimony about children in danger and a picture of my bloody face after training, I made sure to include Elijah's drawing of the end of the world. If that isn't enough to sensationalize a story, I don't know what can. The real kicker is the invitation to stop by and see it for themselves.

"In a disaster, we can't worry about luxury items. We direct all of our electricity into essential survival equipment that helps us communicate, stay warm, and detect intruders." I point to the chart on the poster board that details the energy consumption of radios, light bulbs, and heaters. "As you can see, it takes quite a lot of effort to sustain life underground.

"Are there any questions?" I ask with forced casualness. The onlookers are too proper to ask anything inappropriate, but I can sense the nosiness swarming beneath their innocent smiles. I know from experience that most people tend to be curious about our bathroom arrangements or how we plan to repopulate the planet if we're the only survivors. Gross.

"Do you live underground full-time?" one of the judges asks.

Yes, I have this tan from sleeping under a heat lamp like an iguana. "We have a regular house, too. The bunker is only for emergencies and training."

"Why are you sharing this information with the public if it's supposed to be classified?"

I smile as the reporter snaps my picture. "I think you deserve to know who your neighbors are."

The rest of the questions are as insipid as I expected, but they distract the judges long enough that Ms. Garcia stops counting minutes and breaks out into a victory dance instead. I shake the judges' hands before they move on to the next project, some snore-fest about the chemicals used for dry cleaning.

I watch the reporters leave, wondering if I chose the right people to trust with the only life I value more than my own. In hushed voices, Roy and I discuss the rest of our strategy until the lights dim to signal the start of the awards ceremony. I squeeze his hand and follow my fellow presenters to the stage.

We assemble in a line at the front with our advisors hovering over our shoulders. I badger the girl next to me until she moves out of the way, leaving me standing next to Aiden. Even though I have an ulterior motive for being here, this is still a competition between supernerds. I want to see his face when he loses.

Ms. Garcia jitters a step behind me, her knees bowing with nerves against the taut confines of her pencil skirt. I flash her a confident smile as I recall the interest of the judges, their eyes gleaming with curiosity as they glimpsed the inner workings of my screwed-up life. She returns a wan grin and wipes her forehead to remove the sheen of sweat from the hostile glare of the stage lights. As the ceremony begins and the spotlight lowers to frame the principal, she mouths two words that swell my heart with pride: *prize pony*.

I don't hear any of the introductions or speeches besides the short statement announcing my name and that I'm a senior working with Ms. Garcia. I only tune in when my classmates lean forward in anticipation.

"Now, let's get to the good stuff," the principal says, earning a chuckle from the crowd. He reaches for the white ribbon. "Third place is awarded to Brian Wendland for his project on how caffeine affects the growth of household plants."

The principal affixes the ribbon to Brian's lapel and waits for the polite smattering of applause to subside. My palms are slick with sweat as the second judge reaches for the red ribbon. Aiden angles his torso to face me, licking his lips in preparation to offer his congratulations. "Second place goes to Aiden Pilecki for his research on exothermic reaction rates."

A woman in the crowd gapes at him, her mouth twisting into a snarl. Her delicate fingers steeple and then fold across her chest, her thumb snapping against her collarbone in a dissatisfied clap.

All the while, her blue-ribbon eyes never leave Aiden's face. I feel a surge of pity, noting the slight drooping of his head as he stands, straight-backed, to receive his award.

I resist the urge to reach over and squeeze his hand. My parents never cared about my academic prowess, but I can see how caring too much isn't any better. After a moment of contemplation, I shake my head, remembering his chronic boasting and insufferable arrogance. No, Aiden doesn't deserve any sympathy. There's no room for mercy when it comes to the science fair.

"Lastly," the final judge announces, "first place belongs to Rebecca Aldaine for her explanation of the physics behind doomsday survival."

I creep forward to retrieve my trophy, a resin monstrosity featuring a plastic medallion engraved with a factually incorrect atom. The principal reaches for the front of my blouse to pin the blue ribbon, then changes his mind and allows the female judge to do it. The tip of the safety pin pricks my skin. I notice that none of them offer to shake my hand. Maybe they're afraid that my community's craziness is contagious.

I say my goodbyes to Ms. Garcia on the edge of the stage. I can't guarantee that I'll be around for the last few days of school. There's no predicting what's coming next.

I let her keep the trophy. I don't need it to know that I have finally won.

29

WE DON'T SUBSCRIBE TO THE NEWSPAPER, SO THE FIRST indication that my plan is working is an unfamiliar vehicle drifting through the neighborhood. I text Roy an update since his line of sight to the road is partially blocked by the barn. They're here.

I pretend that this is a normal morning. I feed Belle and make eggs for Katie, even though I'm still devastated that she kept our father's death a secret. I roll all of that resentment and pain and fury into a tight knot and lock it away for later. If there's one skill I've perfected over the years, it's how to fake it.

Once my chores are completed, I check on my bags and make sure that I haven't forgotten anything. The important things, like my laptop and Dad's Father's Day rock, I check twice. As soon as I can convince Child Protective Services to take Katie, I'm leaving.

I just hope that my neighbors respond the way I think they will when they find out that I gave away all of our most protected secrets. I can just imagine the coverage of Mom screaming at a camera or someone brandishing a gun from their front porch. They're going to lose their minds. Proof is good; proof on the front page is better.

The sudden clang of the doorbell interrupts my plotting. I ignore it, hoping that Mom will wake up. It clangs again. And again.

Katie appears at my side, her eyes rolling toward the ceiling. "There's a stranger at the door and he won't go away."

I move as slowly as I can without seeming suspicious. Mom cuts me off in the hallway, tying the edges of her bathrobe against her body. "Who the hell is that?" she barks, mashing her hair flat. "I'm trying to get some sleep."

Katie and I follow behind as she lowers her eye to the peephole and opens the door a sliver. Faintly, I can hear the sound of a large vehicle idling in front of the house. I step to the left and whip out my phone to text Roy again. Holy crap. There's a real news van all the way from Cleveland!

"What do you have to say to allegations that you're endangering the lives of children?" the reporter asks, holding up a copy of the *Tinker Peaks Times*. "Is it true that you threw young girls into a frozen lake?"

Pond. Lake. Maybe I exaggerated a little bit.

"Who's making these so-called allegations?"

The reporter consults the article. "A member of your, uh, organization released a statement yesterday."

"That's absurd." Mom opens the door wider and stabs her finger at the road. "None of us would ever leak information to the public."

Katie tries to wriggle in front of me for a better vantage point. I drop to one knee and watch over her shoulder, making sure I'm positioned to grab her if she gets any stupid ideas.

"Does that mean you acknowledge that you're training children to survive the apocalypse? Doesn't that put them in danger?"

The cameraman swivels to get a shot of the security system on the porch. He seems particularly intrigued by the colored light bulbs, each of which represents a different emergency that will probably never happen. Blue for flooding. Red for intruders. Purple for epidemics.

Mom skips onto the porch and tries to block the camera. "That's sensitive equipment! You have no right to come on to my property and film my personal possessions! You're trespassing!"

The cameraman continues to film as they back down the driveway to their van and the safety of the public road. There are more cars parking along the curb, more people jotting down notes and taking pictures.

I scramble to get out of Mom's way as she stomps back inside with her nose buried in the paper. I watch her facial expressions flash from confused to murderous in the span of three seconds. When she lowers the paper, her eyes glow with ire, like staring into the face of a demon that contributed half of my genetic material.

"You stole our procedures," she whispers, her bare feet sliding across the floor as she advances on me. "You betrayed us."

I retreat into the kitchen and curse myself. I'll have to go right past her to get out of the house if this goes sour. I'm the idiot in the horror movie who runs down the dead-end alley.

With me cornered, there's no one to keep Katie from hanging her head outside, though she seems to have enough sense not to leave the house. Mom pauses to pull up the surveillance feeds and grab the portable radio from its charging dock. She types in the code for an intruder alert on the security system and the sirens start a few seconds later. "Everyone barricade your property and man your stations," she shouts into the radio. "There are trespassers on our land!"

I make a move toward the living room where our gear is stashed, but Mom cuts me off in the doorway. "Don't even think about going anywhere." She keys up the radio and finds a replacement who can watch my post by the river.

"Katie!" I shout, beckoning to her. "Get in here."

She ignores me, and for once, I can't really blame her for being curious. I open the cabinet under the sink and stand on the ledge to see out of the window. I've taken part in intruder drills before, but I've never had the opportunity to watch it play out. It's all so clean, so organized.

Within three minutes, my neighbors are crouched behind porch-mounted fighting positions with rifles trained on the crowd, their houses awash in scarlet emergency lighting. Tamara's once-pristine lawn is chewed and scarred, the aftermath of her rapid deployment of temporary barricades. The radio crackles every few seconds as various personnel check in with Mom.

Most of the reporters have backed toward the corner with

their hands raised, but a few holdouts are still in the main part of the street. One photographer is so entranced that he turns in a circle too many times and loses his balance. He almost falls onto the grass, which would have put him beyond the public property line.

There's relative peace as my neighbors monitor the remaining media, at least until the first police car turns the corner and parks next to the stop sign. The reporters congeal around it, their arms waving along to their conversations. An officer gets out of the vehicle as more patrol cars arrive. He shouts something at the remaining people and they follow their colleagues to the end of the street.

Ten minutes later, Katie pulls her head back inside and yells, "Mom, the police are here and they have all of this fancy stuff!"

I crane my neck to see what she's talking about. In the gaps between the crowd of reporters, I catch glimpses of black helmets bobbing their way to the front.

"Shut the door!" Mom yells at Katie. "If you want to watch, do it on camera."

Katie huffs. "That's not fair! Heather gets to be outside!"

I shuffle a few inches until I see her standing by our shared property line, half of her body concealed behind a tree. She shouldn't be out there either. She's too young.

"You need to tell everyone to stand down before someone gets hurt," I say, venturing out into the living room. Belle slips underneath the coffee table and cowers there, mewling in distress. "The police aren't messing around. They have a SWAT team out there."

When I staged my science fair project, I wanted to rile the

community, but not like this. I didn't expect for there to be actual violence or a police presence of this magnitude. In my head, I just imagined a bunch of reporters filming from the street while Mom ran around the front yard with a rifle.

"I can't stand down!" She swats a glass off the coffee table, shattering it without any concern for Belle's paws. "You gave away our defensive strategies! Our generating network! Anyone can attack us now and they'll know exactly how to do it!"

"They're not here to attack us, Mom. They're just reporters. You need to tell everyone else that they're not here to hurt anyone."

"They were trespassing on our land. How do I know if they're reporters or they're here to attack us? I can't take chances with our safety! They're intruders!"

"Are you even listening to yourself right now?" I shout. "You're not going to win against a SWAT team!"

"There wouldn't be a SWAT team or reporters if you didn't sell us out!" Mom's palm crashes across my cheek before I can even register the lift of her arm. I tilt my body to avoid the dog as I fall, my head banging into the edge of the coffee table. Belle bares her teeth and pounces, but Mom diverts her in midair with a swift kick to the ribs.

Katie squeals in horror and scrambles to pick up the dog, but Belle is far too evasive for that. Before I can stop either of them, they bolt in the opposite direction. Belle slithers through the opening between the front door and the jamb, closely pursued by Katie. I scramble to my feet, but I don't even reach the threshold when a gunshot rings out.

I stumble onto the porch, the breath leached from my lungs by shock. Katie is facedown on the lawn with her arms still reaching for the dog. Heather is standing twenty feet away, her parents gaping at her in horror. She raises her trigger finger and turns it in the light as though it can rewind the past.

I launch forward, throwing myself over Katie's body as the police swarm the neighborhood, their shots thunking off our barricades. I sob into Katie's hair as I feel for blood soaking into her clothes. "Katie Cat? Are you okay, baby? Say something. Please, please."

"It missed me," she wheezes, her voice trembling.

I lift her into a crouch, staying between her and the bulk of the conflict breaking out in the street until I find shelter behind the nearest tree. The ground is strewn with rubber police bullets and smoke canisters, the silence broken by shouts and the wet smack of fistfights. No one is stupid enough to fire on law enforcement, but that doesn't mean they're going down easy.

"I need to find Belle!" Katie cries, her nails dragging bloody lines across the backs of my hands. "She was running this way! She must be close!"

I renew my grip around Katie's stomach and bodily haul her to the side of Candace's house where I know there's at least a window. We have to take shelter until this madness is over. "There she is! There she is!"

When I see Belle, I forget about holding on for a split second, just long enough for Katie to wriggle free. I crawl the rest of the way to the bushes, my vision blurring as I register Belle's lack of movement. There's no dash for cover, no scrabbling of tiny paws against the dirt.

Only stillness.

"Belle, are you okay?" Katie moves a branch and reaches inside. There's a muddy footprint stamped across the side of Belle's snout and blood ringing the edges of her mouth. Someone must have trampled her when the police swarmed in.

"Let me see her." I want to assess the damage first in case the worst has happened. I don't know how much more Katie can take.

"She's crying." Katie pats Belle's head, smoothing back her ear. Each of her exhales is a faint whine. "Do something!"

I flatten myself onto my stomach and lift the dog as gently as I can. She snarls, but she doesn't have enough strength to actually bite. "I know you're in pain. It's okay, girl."

"We need to take her to the dog doctor right now," Katie pronounces with an urgency that breaks my heart. "We need a car. Do you have Mom's keys?"

"Just give me a second." I run my hands over Belle's body, checking her stomach and ribs for injuries. She doesn't growl again until I wedge a finger under her lip and inspect her mouth. One of her canines dangles from half of its roots, her inflamed gums nearly swollen over the gap. I half sigh, half laugh in relief when I see the puncture wound on her tongue oozing blood. "It isn't internal bleeding. She's going to be okay."

Katie tugs on my sleeve. "She still needs help!"

I flinch as someone starts screaming about retreat, the sound carrying easily now that the fighting is starting to wind down. I pick up a rubber bullet and pinch it between my fingers. "Katie, don't you see that you're too good to believe in this doomsday stuff? You love Belle, right?"

She nods, her forehead wrinkled in concern and confusion.

"If you follow the rules, you have to stop caring about Belle. She's not important. We'll just get another dog if she doesn't get better. That's why there's no dog food in the bunker. We're supposed to leave her behind."

"That's not true!" Katie sniffles as Belle's breathing grows more labored. "I love her. She's my best friend."

"It is true. Because everyone else thinks that surviving is more important than love. But I don't believe that and you didn't used to, either." I force Katie to meet my eyes for the most important question I will ever ask. "It's up to you now. Do you want to be a doomsday prepper or do you want to help your dog?"

"She's crying!" Katie kisses Belle's head and picks the stray leaves off of her coat. "I don't want her to cry. I want to take her to the dog doctor. Right now."

Good enough. I'll take what I can get.

I let Katie carry Belle while I lead her along the fence toward the street. Most of the community is in handcuffs and sitting on the curb, including Mom. The cops are hovering around them, talking into radios and asking questions. I recognize one of them as Buzz Cut. He listened to me after Dad's accident. He cared. "Hey!" I wave at him. "I need help!"

He jogs over with another officer, both of them wary. "What's going on over here?"

I'm crying so hard now that my eyes are nearly swollen shut. I lean my face closer to Katie's and kiss her cheek, trying to squeeze a lifetime of love into a fleeting farewell. "I'm sorry. I love you. I love you. I love you."

I shove my sister and Belle at Buzz Cut. "Take them," I sob at him. "Take them. Don't ever bring them back."

"What?" Katie yells, fighting against us both. "I'm not leaving you! Becca!"

When Buzz Cut doesn't move, I grab his shoulders and dig my nails into the fabric of his shirt. "THESE PEOPLE ARE DANGEROUS. THEY HURT CHILDREN. GET MY SISTER AND MY DOG OUT OF HERE AND NEVER BRING THEM BACK."

Buzz Cut shakes his head clear, slings his rifle over one shoulder, and pulls Katie into a reverse bear hug. She screams and thrashes, but he doesn't let go. I grab Belle before Katie can drop her. The poor thing has had enough trauma as it is. Like the rest of us.

"We've got the other kids over there already," his partner adds, turning toward Tamara's yard where the youngest members of the community are huddled together. "Child Protective Services is sending someone over."

"I can't take the dog," Buzz Cut grunts, heaving Katie off the ground entirely and waddling off in that direction. "Sorry."

"Wait!" I call after him, baffled. "What do I do with her?"

His partner scrutinizes my face, then the makeshift holding area they're using to contain the adults. "Show me your hands."

I hold out Belle, making as much of an effort as I can to comply without letting go of her. "Please. She needs a vet."

His gaze drops to her limp body, the steady stream of pinkish blood dribbling out of her mouth. He doesn't move except for a twitch of his eyebrows, a pull at his bottom lip. His hand lingers over a set of flex cuffs dangling from his vest, his finger hooked through one of the loops. "I can't let you go just yet."

"Can't you?" I plead, trying to make myself look as pathetic as possible. It doesn't take much. "Please. I didn't do anything. I just want to get some help for my dog."

He glances to his left and right, but no one is watching us. He sighs and fixes his gaze on a nearby tree. "Wow. That sure is an interesting tree. I think I'll look at it for the next ten seconds."

I take a step back, testing. Two steps. Three.

Before he can finish counting or change his mind, I tighten my grip on Belle and run.

30

I DIP INTO THE WOODS AT THE FIRST OPPORTUNITY, SINCE getting caught running away is unlikely to convince any other law enforcement of my innocence. I whisper encouragement to Belle in my happiest tone of voice, nestling her to my chest to minimize the jarring as I weave around the various security barricades.

I follow a secondary dirt trail along the northern edge of the trees, watching to ensure that I'm hidden from the bystanders and police concentrated at the roadblock in the distance. I dart across the street to a dead-end cul-de-sac, pausing to confirm that Belle is still alert. "Hang on, pretty girl. I've got you."

Most of the houses have fenced yards, but I manage to find a rancher with a straight route into the adjoining neighborhood. I'm so petrified of someone stopping me that I careen around a tree with too much speed, throwing out an arm to maintain my balance.

My throat is hoarse and raw from the effort as I sprint up Sydney's driveway, slamming the side of my fist against her front door hard enough to pop my knuckles. "Sydney!" I rasp as loudly as I can. "Help!"

A man in a Cleveland Browns jersey opens the door, his eyes wide with alarm. He sets his drink down on a table in the entryway. "Uh, is everything okay?"

"No," I sob, holding up Belle. I'm so exhausted and overwhelmed that I can't even articulate what I need. "Please. My dog. Sydney."

"Becca?" A voice calls from within the house. "Oh my God, Dad, would you freakin' move?" Sydney shoves her way into the doorway. "You're on the news! What's up with all the pol—"

"Someone trampled my dog," I explain before she can ask the question. "Will you take her to a vet? Please?" Only then do I realize how completely unhinged I must look, with blood speckling my filthy shirt and twigs poking out of my hair. "It won't be expensive. It's just her tooth and her tongue. I think. Please."

Sydney holds out her hands to take Belle, then pulls them back. "I'll drive you, but you should come too. It's your dog. She doesn't know me."

"I can't go with you. There was this whole fight and the cops are detaining people. I have to go check on my sister and Roy."

Sydney retrieves a set of keys and sticks the fob in her mouth while she shrugs on a jacket. She pulls the door closed, yelling, "Dad, I'm going to go spend a whole bunch of your money, okay?"

"Okay!" he shouts back. "Be careful!"

I stand dumbfounded as I process their exchange, the ease of their banter. It is literally unfathomable to me. Even in the most fantastical of my illusions and delusions, I never dared to dream that I could have a father like that.

"Let's see . . ." Sydney mumbles, scrolling through her phone as she searches for the nearest animal hospital. "Looks like there are a few nearby."

I point to the second listing. "That's her usual vet. He's really nice and they might still have my mom's credit card number."

Sydney waves away my concern. "It's cool. Don't worry about the money. I'm loaded from early graduation cards if my parents freak out about it."

"Thank you." I wrap her in a lopsided hug as I try to avoid jostling Belle. "I didn't know who else to ask."

"You can put her in here," Sydney says, fetching a cardboard box from the garage and setting it on the front seat of her father's truck. "It'll buckle in better." She pulls the seat belt around the edge and snaps it securely into place.

"One more thing." I hesitate, knowing that once I do this, it can't ever be undone. "When she's finished at the vet, will you take her to the pound? Tell them she's a stray. I'm leaving soon and I don't trust anyone else to take care of her."

Sydney offers her hand to Belle, earning a half-hearted sniff. "Even me?"

"You'd keep her?"

She scoffs. "Man, my parents were so stoked that I didn't fail Bio that they'd buy me a llama if I wanted one. I'm keeping her. She's cute. What's her name?"

"Belle."

Upon hearing her name, Belle groans low in her throat, as if to say, *Would you two idiots stop yakking and take me to a dentist already?*

I say goodbye to Belle, kissing the top of her head, then her paw. I bop her nose with my finger. "You're a good girl. Best girl." I scratch behind her ear in her favorite spot. "I love you. Be good."

Next, I pull Sydney into one more hug, thanking her for everything she's done, and everything she hasn't. She alone gave me a chance at true friendship, an opportunity to prove that I was more than the myth of my family. "I'll call you when I get where I'm going," I promise.

"You better," Sydney says, shaking her fist at me. "Or I'll break your eye socket."

▲ ▲ ▲

It takes some convincing before the officers manning the roadblock believe that I'm coming back after escaping their cordon. "I'm not a reporter," I repeat for the third time. "I just had to bring my dog to a friend's house because she got hurt. I live in the yellow house. My mom is . . ." I cup my hands into binoculars and scan the group sitting on the curb, boxed in by two cruisers. "Right there. Black shirt. Blond hair. Knockoff SWAT vest."

Buzz Cut's partner ends up vouching for me, escorting me to the holding area with the other adults. "By the way, thanks for uh, letting me go earlier," I whisper.

He stares at the tree in front of us. "I have no idea what you're talking about."

I take a seat next to Mom, leaving a slight gap between us in case she's still angry. She's wearing flex cuffs like the rest of my neighbors who thought fighting the police was a brilliant idea, but I don't put it past her to bite me. "Betrayed by my own daughter," she mumbles. "Ridiculous."

With all of the mayhem of the past hour, I completely lost track of Roy. I don't remember seeing him during the riot and he's definitely not here.

I catch a glimpse of Roy's mom at the edge of the group, but I don't want to seem too interested in his whereabouts. If they don't know he was involved in this whole scheme, I'd like to keep it that way.

I scan the faces of my neighbors, mentally running through an accountability list while Mom berates me under her breath. There are a few people, like Matt the Asshole, who are markedly absent. Roy must be with them. He wouldn't have run away without me, even if his cover was blown.

No way.

Maybe if he had no other choice.

Or he's going to come back for me.

Crap.

The only mildly reassuring part of this situation is that I doubt Roy's parents could resist publicly denouncing Roy if they caught him trying to orchestrate a doomsday coup d'état. At least, that's how my mother seems to be reacting.

"In case you care," I say, over her continued criticism of my moral character, "Katie is with Child Protective Services and I took Belle to a friend's house. She's going to keep her."

Mom fidgets, lashing out with her foot until a cop gives her a pointed stare. "You had no right to do that. You had no right to give away the dog."

I tip my head back and groan, holding my palms out to the sky. "Why are you still yelling at me? You don't care about the dog, or me, or Katie, or Dad. You don't care about any of us. We're all expendable, right?"

"How can you say that?" Mom hisses. "I gave up everything for you! All of this was to make sure you're safe."

"Maybe I didn't want to be safe. Maybe I just wanted to be happy."

"You're a fucking disgrace," she snaps at me. "Your father is turning over in his grave. And your grandparents. All four of them."

I ignore her, again, and go back to pretending that I'm having a telepathic conversation with the pebble in front of my boot. A patrol car rolls up, halting directly in front of us. Tin Peas is so short on vehicles that they apparently need to shuttle everyone to jail in batches.

An officer touches Mom's arm and leads her to the open door. I lost track of her after the gunshot, so I'm not sure if she's likely to be charged with anything. She turns her head at the last moment to glance back at me. She doesn't know it, but these will be her last words to me: "I always knew you were a rat."

I don't answer. If they didn't want a rat, they shouldn't have kept me in a cage.

I wonder whether she realizes that this is a second chance for her, too. With no husband and soon-to-be no kids, maybe she'll be able to start over. I might even be happy if she did.

In the end, the police haul away Mom, Ronald, Tamara, Mr. Hepworth, and Heather's entire family for various and interesting methods of assaulting a law enforcement officer. The rest of us didn't do anything illegal. Apparently it's perfectly acceptable to sit in a fort on your porch with a bunch of guns. My social studies teacher must have forgotten to mention that.

The rest of us are left standing in the street as the last of the police vehicles turn the corner and disappear from view. I need to find Roy as quickly as possible, but there are a thousand places he could have gone. Guarding the greenhouse, the bunkers, the generator.

In the mass confusion that remains, and the lack of a clear leader, there isn't a better time for us to leave. I jog into the house and retrieve my backpack from its hiding spot in the rear of my closet. I take a second to send Ms. Garcia a quick message telling her that my plan, as mad as it was, actually worked. The first half, anyway. Katie is safe. Ms. Garcia will go claim custody. Still, I won't call this a total victory until I'm sitting in Introductory Physics.

I spare a look at my abandoned belongings before I shut the door, closing this chapter of my life for good. I have my laptop, some leftover birthday money, and the painted rock that I gave Dad for Father's Day all those years ago. Everything else is replaceable.

Except my sister.

Except Belle.

I dial Roy as I cross the street, forcing myself to move in a slow, nonchalant way past my neighbors. But before I can take a single step onto Roy's property, a dozen hands are on my body, pulling at my hair, my limbs. My feet leave the ground as I fight to find the weakest point in the crowd.

Someone tears the backpack from my shoulders, tossing it

to the ground. I lunge for it, twisting and kicking with all of my might. "That's mine! That's mine!" I drop my cell phone, but I don't care. All I can think about is that little painted rock. *World's Best Dad.*

"You thought you could stab us in the back and get away with it," Mr. Kang snarls in my ear. "Don't worry. We'll get you right."

I make a dive for freedom when the people carrying me shift their balance, but it's hopeless. Roy could be anywhere by now. In the end, I forgot the most important rule of any strategy: Leave yourself a way out in case absolutely everything goes to shit.

31

THERE'S MISCALCULATING AND THEN THERE'S IM-IMPRIS-
oned-in-a-bunker miscalculating. They didn't even have the
decency to imprison me in my *own* bunker.

I cry over the loss of the rock until my eyes are almost swollen
shut and my nostrils are geysers of runny snot. Only then do I
admit that it isn't about the rock or Belle's tooth or the fact that
I am so, so hungry. It's because I'm lonely.

I want my mom. I want my dad.

I want them to be as I always imagined, before they were
transformed into the people I knew. I wonder if, given enough
time away from here, they could have reverted to their true
selves, like an actor who ceases to be the villain the moment the
curtain falls.

And more than that, I want Katie. My baby sister. Who knows
when I will see her again, whether she will forgive me for what

I've done. I squeeze my eyes shut, trying and failing to erase the look on her face when they took her away. Is she with Ms. Garcia now? Is she safe?

But there's no point in wondering and wishing for the impossible when I can't even meet my basic needs. I sigh and lick my lips again, desperate for the feeling of moisture after sitting in the hot sun waiting to be released. I should have asked the cops if I could go with them. Hell, I should have punched somebody. At least then I'd have rights.

I make another half-hearted attempt to reach the light switches, even though I know that they're several feet beyond my reach. The fact that they left me here in the dark with no food or bathroom bucket tells me that they won't be gone too long. I'll just have to hope that they're dumb enough to send Roy to check on me.

My ankle is chained to the post of the nearest bunk beds, but I don't have enough lead to take advantage of the bed. Instead, I ease back onto the cold floor and stare up in the blackness. It's interesting how I can still sense the span of the room without being able to see it.

One hour passes, then two.

If I weren't so dehydrated, I'd probably have peed my pants by now. They must be eating a late lunch before they come to check on me. No need to worry.

Another hour. And another. And another.

My chest starts to tighten with panic when I consider the possibility that they're going to leave me here indefinitely. I already said goodbye to Ms. Garcia and told her that I wouldn't be at graduation. Sydney thinks I'm running away.

Does Katie care enough to miss me and alert the authorities if I'm down here too long? I feel like we had a heart-to-heart moment earlier, but that doesn't change all that's happened before. She betrayed me so many times. I lied to her and kept secrets. If I can't escape from here, will she grow up and understand why I did the things I did? That all of this was for her?

I clap both hands over my mouth and drag my fingertips down to my jawbone. What if they're leaving me here to die? It's just like what I explained to Katie about Belle. Anything or anyone that isn't useful anymore is expendable.

But Roy would save me. He would figure out a plan to bust me out of here. Unless . . . unless they found out that he was helping me.

I pick up the chain and slam it on the ground in frustration, earning a new bruise against the side of my ankle bone. Every kidnapping exercise I've ever done involved being locked in the trunk of a car or tied to a chair. Pointless.

I tug on each individual link of the chain and inspect the thick bolts securing the bunk bed to the floor. Even if I had tools, I wouldn't be able to pry my way free. That leaves the locks holding the chain together on either end. I press one between my palms to get a sense of the dimensions. It's a standard padlock.

I know from my earlier explorations that I can't reach anything forward of the bed or stacked against the adjacent walls. Instead, I crawl backwards, straining to find out whether I can reach the nightstand. My fingers barely graze the handle of the drawer. I ease it out, gritting my teeth as my nails bend against the weight. The drawer falls to the ground with a metallic clatter.

"Of course it's empty," I seethe as I toss it off to my left. It collides with something that doesn't quite sound like a metal post.

I grab onto the end of the drawer and start fishing with it. I can feel the edge scraping along the mystery object, but there's nothing for it to catch on. I adjust the angle and try again, my ankle throbbing as the chain digs deeper into my skin.

When the drawer sticks, I drag it back toward me with all of my might. I set it down and grope in the darkness until my hand connects with the smooth plastic of an equipment case. "Please be tools," I chant as I haul it closer by the ridges on the lid. A second case stacked above it topples onto the floor. "Please be tools."

Now that I have a mental model of what I'm touching, I find the latches automatically and throw open the case. I stuff both hands inside. There's fabric. A shirt, maybe. Some socks. A glass figurine that's most likely a personal item. It's a footlocker. The possessions of whoever is assigned to this set of bunk beds.

I drop my forehead against the lip of the case in defeat. I can be pretty crafty when I need to be, but no one in the history of this planet has managed to escape from prison using a pair of socks. Maybe I could break the figurine and use it to cut my foot off.

I slide forward in the direction of the second case, waving the drawer around at random until it bumps against the side and pushes it farther away. I roll onto my side and consider how much I want this case. It's like one of those mystery game shows where you don't know the contents until after you've made your wager.

I pull the collar of my shirt in between my teeth, latch on to the vertical bar at the foot of the neighboring bed, and haul my body forward. I scream as a blinding pain shoots through my knee, but I don't let go of the bar. I flail my free arm in the direction of the case. My fingers sandwich around the lid as I let go and accordion back into my normal bodily dimensions.

I touch the tender spot throbbing beneath my kneecap and hiss. I don't think it's supposed to be squishy.

"This had better be worth it." I reach into the second case and sort the items into a pile on my right. "Shirt. Shirt. Comb. Oh, good, more socks." But then my thumb punches through a thin substance that feels remarkably like Styrofoam. I crunch it in a fist and rub the hard, brittle items inside. They break with such little force that I can't imagine their use.

"ROY'S RAMEN NOODLES!" I exclaim to the empty bunker.

I knock the case on its side and spread out the contents until my elbow nudges against a heavy cylinder. I pick up the can of Coke like it's a magical artifact and kiss it.

I chug the entire can as fast as I can without drowning. Once it's empty, I bite the side of it, waving my head like a shark. It mashes together more than it tears, so I grind the dents with my canines until there's a hole. Two minutes later, I have a tiny triangle of metal and a throbbing jaw.

As I shimmy the metal down toward the notch that keeps the padlock closed, I begrudgingly acknowledge that this particular doomsday skill actually came in handy. I jam the piece of can lower with one hand while I bop the top of the lock with the other. It pops open.

I take the lock and throw it away from me as though it might decide to close itself again. I force myself to also open the lock by my ankle instead of running away with four feet of chain rattling around behind me.

As much as I hate to admit it, that was the easy part. I flip a light switch on the control panel, squinting at the numbers displayed on the wall clock. It'll be dark in three hours. I turn the lights off, tuck myself into the corner by the ladder, and wait. With the exception of Roy, the first person who comes down that ladder is getting cracked in the head with a chain.

No one ever comes. Not to bring me water or take me to the bathroom.

I keep the chain wrapped around my chest as I climb the ladder in case I need a weapon. Once I open that hatch, there's a good chance that they're going to know I've escaped. They might have a guard posted outside or someone back at the house watching cameras.

I just need to find Roy and run like hell. I don't care about the money or the stuff or any of our preparations. We need to cut our losses while we still can.

With a shaky breath, I throw open the hatch and clamber out into the cool air. There's no one around, but it doesn't give me much comfort.

I move as fast as I can without making an inordinate amount of noise. The leaves are still mushy from the last rainfall, which helps to muffle my steps and the slight drag of compensating for my injured knee. I retrace the route that I took with Roy, hoping by some miracle that I've remembered the only unmonitored path through these woods.

I pause just inside the tree line to catch my breath and survey the sprawl of Roy's property. The lights are off in all of the outbuildings, which probably means that he's in his bedroom. The house is dark except for the flicker of a television in the living room. I just hope that they haven't set their alarm yet.

This would be much easier if I still had my cell phone.

I ease my shoes off in the shadows and creep forward in my socks. There are cameras dotting the perimeter of the house, waiting for me to make a misstep. I kneel in one of the blind spots and poke my head into the window well leading to the basement.

I press my palms against the glass and attempt to slide it, to no avail. The lock is a simple up-or-down mechanism, which is easily defeated by jiggling the window against the latch until it opens. I weigh my options. Opening this window is going to be loud, but it's also in the basement. I doubt I'll find an easier entry point anywhere else.

With a deep breath, I start pushing the window, wondering whether the scraping is audible from the ground floor of the house. If noise wasn't a concern, I could have this window open in less than a minute. Being careful, it takes five before the vibration forces the latch in the right direction.

I slide the window open and stuff the rest of my body into the well. I lower myself down with my stomach on the ledge and drop the remaining feet to the floor. I've never been in Roy's basement before, so I shut the window and start crawling. I'm less likely to knock anything over if I'm below the height of most surfaces.

I sit in the dark for another two hours. I've been doing a lot of that lately.

Eventually, whoever was in the living room patters into the foyer to set the alarm, then backtracks to the hallway where the bedrooms branch off. A door closes. That must be the bathroom. I wait for the toilet to flush, the sink to run, and another door to close.

I slither up the stairs on my belly to distribute my weight and avoid stressing the creaky wooden stairs. I press my ear to the door and hear only silence. The basement opens into the kitchen. If the hinges make a noise, I'm busted.

I turn the knob and shove the door open in a single quick motion. I exhale and give the door an appreciative nod before continuing down the hallway to Roy's room. Each of my footfalls is an earthquake. My breath is an air horn.

I ghost my fingers along the wall until I feel the molding around Roy's door. I reach for the knob, but it isn't there. I take a tentative step forward and bump into someone else. I jump back in alarm, gasping.

A shaking hand lands on my forearm. Somehow, I know it belongs to Roy. He tries to pull me into a hug, but I back away. We have our entire lives to hug. We need to get the hell out of here.

Roy picks something up off the floor and shuffles around me to lead us out to the foyer. The dim light of the alarm panel reflects in his eyes as he scrutinizes the various buttons.

I tap a Morse code message on his forearm with my index finger. K-N-O-W C-O-D-E-?

B-U-T-T-O-N B-E-E-P

H-O-W L-O-U-D-?

L-O-U-D

His last message spikes my adrenaline, washing away the fatigue, the aching pulse in my knee: R-U-N F-A-S-T

Roy types in the four-digit code, waits for it to process, and rips open the front door.

I literally run for my life. I run for my future.

Roy reaches the shed first and backs the dirt bike down the ramp as fast as he can. He tosses me the backpack and jams a helmet on his head. I throw the bag over my shoulder, grab a helmet, and vault onto the seat just as Roy's parents come sprinting out of the house.

Roy wrings the throttle and we lurch forward, the tires spinning in the grass. I swear that my heart and my stomach switch places until the bike finds traction and propels us across the lawn.

We're almost to our old bus stop when a car skids out of Roy's driveaway behind us. I map the town in my head, thinking of all the places that a car could outpace us. We have to use the bike to our advantage. "The railroad tracks!" I shout in Roy's ear, hoping he understands. "Turn around!"

Instead of slowing, Roy speeds toward the corner, increasing the distance between us and his parents. My head slams into his shoulder blade as he screeches to a stop and the rear of the bike slides sideways through the intersection. He spins around until we're racing in the opposite direction, dodging behind the trunk of his parents' car as they attempt to block our path.

We streak down the road ahead of them, our heads turning every few feet to assess the terrain on either side. Roy brakes as he recognizes the rise of the tracks and pops us onto the rails. I sit up straighter and keep watch over Roy's shoulder. I'm sure that nothing bad has ever happened from someone riding a dirt bike on train tracks.

Headlights cut the darkness behind us, but the beams don't pursue. We move from the light to the shadow until we can't see the light at all.

I feel each of those miles as surely as if I'd run them on foot. My heart alternates between a frenetic thudding and a slow, painful throb. As my panic subsides, the first thing to return is the physical sensations. I stretch my leg, opening my mouth in a silent scream as my knee flexes.

Next, it's fear.

Then sadness.

Rage.

And finally, after so long, joy.

I squeeze Roy's chest, careful not to disturb his hands as he rests them on the bars, his arms still locked straight and tense. I know he can't hear me over the whir of the bike, the rushing of the air, but I talk to him anyway. "I swear to you that for the rest of my life I will never, ever forget what you've done for me. I will love you with all of the love that my parents never wanted. We're going to find an apartment and go to college and have amazing lives together." I'm crying now, my chest heaving so hard I can barely force out the words. "I don't feel like I deserve you, but I will try every day to be what *you* deserve. I know exactly what that is, too. You deserve a lifetime of corny love songs and pot roast and dog snuggles and history books. I'm going to give all of those things to you, Roy. I promise. I love you. I love you."

I stay that way, my head nestled in between his shoulder blades, until we're so far away that we're running out of gas. I make Roy loop around the back of the convenience store to confirm that I don't recognize any of the cars before he goes inside to pay. I wonder how long it will take until that paranoia, that feeling of somebody watching, wears off.

Roy finishes refueling and rides the bike over to the curb. He cuts the engine and collapses onto the grass next to the dumpster.

"Hey," I whisper, sitting down beside him. "Cheer up. We made it."

He exhales longer than I would have thought possible. "Barely. I was so afraid about what was going to happen after we locked you down there. I didn't want to be a part of it, but I had to keep my cov—"

"You don't have to apologize. I understand why you did it."

"I saved this for you." Roy eases the backpack off my shoulders and reaches into the front compartment. He presses the Father's Day paperweight into my palm. "I heard you yelling about it."

I close my hand around it until I can feel the smooth edges digging into my skin. "Thank you. I don't know why I want it so much."

"It was your dad's," Roy says. "It's not like we can just stop caring. That would make us worse than they are."

"I guess you're right."

"I wasn't able to get the rest of your stuff. My dad confiscated it." He folds his arms across his knees and sighs. "I wonder if we'll ever have something that just goes our way the first time. I'm tired of improvising."

"Cheer up." I nudge him when he refuses to smile, to lift his head. "Roy. We made it. We'll figure out everything else later."

"It wasn't supposed to be like this. That bag only has the bare minimum. We're preppers. We have plans. Contingencies."

"We're not preppers anymore. We have the money, and that's enough for me." I laugh at the thought of interacting with the outside world again. "Plus, we have a cool story to tell people at parties. I bet no one else escaped from a bunch of deranged doomsday freaks after a high-speed car chase."

"It's not funny, Becca. I wasn't able to get your laptop or your physics notebooks. We don't have any clothes or snacks or toiletries. You don't even have *shoes*."

"You couldn't bring your toothbrush. Big deal." I curl my fingers beneath his chin and kiss away his protests. "It's not the end of the world."

Acknowledgments

I don't know how I will ever remember to thank all of the people who made this book possible.

To my agents, Jennifer Wills and Nicole Resciniti, and the entire Seymour Agency family—thank you for all of your support from the very beginning. Jennifer, I could write a second book about how amazing you are. If there was ever a single moment that defined my success as a writer, it's the day I signed with you.

I owe undying gratitude to my editor, Nicole Fiorica, for helping me realize my vision and make *Prepped* into the best possible book. Thank you for believing in Becca and Roy. And yes, Roy always wears hair gel.

None of this would have been possible without the incredible team at Simon & Schuster. My thanks to Rebecca Syracuse, Bridget Madsen, Irene Metaxatos, Tatyana Rosalia, Shivani

Annirood, and Brenna Franzitta, for all of your hard work in bringing *Prepped* to life.

Thank you to my family—my parents, Janice and Jeffrey Johnson, for always being my cheerleaders and for not murdering me when I was a snotty teenage girl; my brother, Andrew Johnson, who hates reading and is regretting his promise to read this book if it ever got published; my grandmother, Ingrid DiPonti, who wrote down my first stories; the Mangles (Howard, Dorothy, Andrew, Erin, Andie, Charlee) and Barnetts (Rob, Katie, Regan, JR), for your unwavering support; and all of the loved, missed, and cherished relatives who are no longer with us.

I can't forget about all of the people who encouraged me to keep writing when I wasn't sure of myself. Bethany Ruccolo, Colleen Frabotta, Megan Eyler, Alex O'Hearn, Craig Adelizzi, Mr. James Lapsley—I could not have done this without you. I would also be remiss if I didn't mention the members of my writing groups, Fullrequest Alchemists and The Real B Hive, for their continued support during this journey.

To my dog, Remi, who was content to sleep on the couch when I was too caught up in my writing to take him to the park. You are the best writing buddy in the world. I will always have dog food in our bunker.

And lastly, to my husband, James, who never complains, even when I'm writing notes on the kitchen floor in dry erase marker or ranting about plot holes at two o'clock in the morning.